P9-AFY-838

DEAD AIR

DEAD AIR

CHARLES JACO

BALLANTINE BOOKS • NEW YORK

A Ballantine Book
Published by The Ballantine Publishing Group

Published in the United States by The Ballantine Publishing Group, a division of Random House, Inc., New York, and simultaneously in Canada by Random House of Canada Limited, Toronto.

http://www.randomhouse.com

Library of Congress Cataloging-in-Publication Data
Jaco, Charles.
Dead air / Charles Jaco. —1st ed.
p. cm.
ISBN 0-345-42128-0 (alk. paper)
I. Title.
PS3560.A2475D4 1998
813'.54—dc21 97-51135

Designed by Ann Gold
Manufactured in the United States of America

First Edition: June 1998
10 9 8 7 6 5 4 3 2 1

TO MY MOTHER,
VIRGIE JACO

DEAD AIR

CHAPTER 1

JUNE 5, PORT-AU-PRINCE

Richard Marmelstein's voice had a gasping urgency to it, even over the scratchy Haitian phone line.

"I need to meet you now. The casino bar in the El Rancho. How fast can you get here?"

Peter Dees said he could make it in five minutes. In the three years he and Marmelstein had worked together as a reporter-producer team in network television—from being shot down in a Salvadoran army helicopter to talking their way past bandits in Afghanistan—his producer had never sounded panicked, until now.

"In the bar?" Dees asked. Marmelstein had been a legendary drunk in the press corps until a year ago, when he'd staggered to his room at the Managua Intercon with two hookers and passed out with them in the oversized bathtub. The overflowing water caused the ceiling in the room below to collapse, leaving Globe-Star Television—known universally as GTV—with a bill for ten thousand dollars.

Dees had spent the better part of a day explaining to corporate headquarters in Phoenix why Marmelstein had emerged from his room stark naked and tried to brain a Nicaraguan security guard with a champagne bottle.

Marmelstein had almost been fired. In the year since then, he had dried out, drank nothing stronger than club soda, and avoided bars like the plague.

"Yeah, in the bar," Marmelstein said to Dees now. "I'll feel safer there."

"Safer? Dick, what—" The line went dead.

Dees quickly pulled on his threadbare khaki sport coat, with its three hidden pockets inside, and raced out of his hotel room.

The sinking orange sun softened the vividly colored riot of soggy flowers and greenery, jet-black faces, and displays of primitive street paintings into a pastel haze. As Dees ground the gears of the Diahatsu, his throat tickled from the miasma of burning vegetation, rotting garbage, human feces, and diesel fumes that hung over Port-au-Prince like a damp wool blanket. He glanced in his rearview mirror. Three weeks in Haiti, and so far only his nose was suffering—both from the odors and from being moderately sunburned. He pulled into the casino parking lot, locked the car, then walked through the entrance into the bar.

Scanning the room for Marmelstein, he saw the dwarf. His name tag said EMILE PLUVIUS, but everyone called him Tigwo—in Creole, "Little Big." Dark as the mahogany tables, Tigwo was discreetly adjusting a nine-millimeter pistol inside his waistband; finished, he gave his white waiter's jacket a precise tug.

As the dwarf started to turn he caught sight of Dees and a lopsided smile cracked his face. "*Monsieur* Peter," he said, advancing.

"Tigwo." Dees nodded. "Seen *Monsieur* Richard?"

"No, *mon cher.* But I just came on duty."

"I see your brother and ten cousins are doing well." Dees nodded toward the gun and ten-shell clip in the bulging cummerbund.

Tigwo looked grave. "As Baby Doc used to say, 'Strong and firm as a monkey's tail.' "

Dees spotted Marmelstein at a table in the corner. His green shirt was soaked with sweat, and he stared at the ice in his club soda.

"Drink?" Tigwo asked.

"You still cutting the Barbancourt with formaldehyde?"

"Not me personally." Tigwo shrugged. "Some of our customers like the effect. But we do have a few bottles of *trois étoile* untouched."

Dees held three fingers together. "Straight. I'll be with *Monsieur* Richard over there."

As Dees walked to the table, Marmelstein looked up. His brown eyes were ringed with dark circles, and worry creases ran halfway up his almost bald skull. "Peter. You're here."

Dees sat. "Now that you've disposed of the obvious, are you okay?"

"No." Marmelstein shook his head. "No. Somebody's trying to kill me."

"What? When?"

"About half an hour ago. I'm in my room, the one with the red bathtub that looks like an Asbury Park whorehouse. I bend over to pick up some dirty socks, and *wham.*" He slapped his palm on the table, rattling the ice in the club soda. "Three bullets come busting through the window and blow the shit outta the mirror. I flatten. Nothing. I call you."

Dees's mind raced across the stories they had filed from Haiti—a profile on the post–Baby Doc president Ertha Troulott, two pieces on radical priest Jean-Bertrand Aristide and his chances in December's elections, a voodoo feature, and a piece questioning U.S. complicity with the pro-Duvalier thugs who ran commerce at the city's port. Those stories alone, he figured, had probably made them enough enemies to last a lifetime.

"So who? The *Macutes*? Stray shots?"

Marmelstein shook his head vigorously. "No. I got a phone call about half an hour before."

Puzzled, Dees ran his fingers over his brush-cut hair. "And . . ." he prompted.

Tigwo delivered Dees's drink and glanced at Marmelstein, who held his palm over the top of the club soda. As Dees handed the dwarf a filthy fifty-*gourde* note, he thought he saw the waiter shoot Marmelstein an acid glance, and decided he was getting paranoid.

Tigwo walked off. Marmelstein stared at Dees. "And I taped the call. It's not *Macutes*. It's—" He stopped, then abruptly said, "Look, the tape's in my room. You still carry that microcassette recorder?"

Dees nodded.

With his foot, Marmelstein shoved something against Dees's leg. "That's my laptop. Hold on to it until I get back. It's very important."

"Get back?"

"Yeah. I'm gonna get the tape for you. You listen. Tell me what you think."

Dees downed the rum. No embalming fluid. "I think I'd better go with you. If somebody's trying to shoot—"

"No. I figure I'm okay now that the place is jumping and there are people around. Just sit tight. And don't let that computer get out of your sight. There's something in my files you need to see." Marmelstein got up and loped off.

He had been protective of the laptop ever since he received it via air freight from Phoenix two weeks before. His old laptop had died in the Managua hotel flood, and he'd been requesting a replacement for months, without success.

That, Dees had reasoned, might have been because McKinley

Burke, pharmaceutical magnate turned global broadcast mogul, had frozen the GTV capital budget due to some unspecified difficulties in buying his very own satellite from the Indonesians.

Since receiving the computer, though, his producer had seemed distracted, Dees thought. Marmelstein would either vanish to his room for hours or sit by the direct phone line to the U.S. During the occasional call, Marmelstein would talk quietly and scribble furiously. Dees had asked if something was up, and was told only that it might be another story, a big one, that they could work on if they ever got out of this shithole.

Dees watched Marmelstein disappear into the now dark courtyard, headed for a facing building where the stairs ran up to his second-floor room.

Tigwo set his tray on a table and walked through a side door. As soon as he was outside he moved fast, scurrying around the far side of the casino. He saw Marmelstein standing by the courtyard fountain and realized the white man was pissing into it.

Marmelstein zipped up and walked toward the stairway. He had just placed his right hand on the handrail and begun to climb the steps when Tigwo ran to the shadowed stairs, pulled his pistol from his crimson cummerbund, and fired. The light *craacck* from the nine-millimeter disappeared amid the casino and traffic noise.

Marmelstein's hand slapped the back of his head as if swatting a giant mosquito. The slug had already burrowed through the cerebral cortex, heaving torn gray matter and blood vessels out of its way like a mole attacking a vegetable garden. It stopped just short of exiting, lodging behind the occipital bone on the right side of his forehead. Marmelstein landed on his back with a surprisingly soft plop.

Tigwo's crepe-soled shoes squeaked on the step. His victim was still breathing, but in ragged gasps. The dwarf stood over him, and Marmelstein twitched, as if trying to get out of the way.

Tigwo fired the pistol again, shooting out Marmelstein's left eye. Blood and viscera erupted from the socket like a tiny volcano. He picked up the two spent shell casings, jammed his hand into Marmelstein's right pocket, and took out his room key and a wad of bills, both U.S. and Haitian. He removed Marmelstein's chunky Tag Heuer watch, then sprinted up the stairs to room 209.

After opening the door with the key, he found the tape lying on the dresser, took it, and rushed back downstairs. Tigwo tugged on the body then, grunting as he dragged it from the steps to a deep and darkly recessed doorway that led from the courtyard to the outside. He paused, wiped the sweat from his forehead, took deep breaths, then managed to get the body through the door and across a walkway to the edge of a small gully that ran parallel to the hotel.

He gave it a heave. Marmelstein's body rolled three times before hanging up on a datura bush about ten feet down the slope.

Tigwo smiled.

It was ten minutes before the son of a Haitian army general, home from college in Montreal, decided he wanted head from a Dominican hooker who was willing to fellate, nothing more, for twenty dollars.

He pulled her by her arm toward the bushes at the top of the dark slope, where neither of them would have to waste too much time before getting back to business inside. She was hoping to turn a trick with one of the American *periodistas*, or relief workers, or at worst, one of the French diplomats. He wanted to return to the roulette table to recoup some of his three-hundred-dollar loss, but before that he wanted something to take the edge off the combination of a noseful of blow and three shots of preservative-laced rum.

He saw Marmelstein before the hooker did, and stopped cold, blinking his eyes and rocking unsteadily on the balls of his feet. She spotted the body then and screamed, then screamed again, and again, until he turned and hit her with the back of his hand. The blow caused her to howl even more, which finally brought two security guards at a run. When they saw the body, they stood rock still for a moment before gesticulating wildly and arguing loudly about whether to call the police or the army first.

Dees had been sitting in the bar, drumming his fingers, waiting, when he heard the screams. He looked straight ahead, at where the bar emptied into the casino, and saw three blue-uniformed police officers wearing olive-colored U.S. surplus helmets. They stormed past a roulette table, then through sliding plate-glass doors that opened onto the courtyard.

Standing up, Dees reached down and grabbed the faded blue, soft-sided computer case. He dashed after the police, elbowing his way through the gathering crowd of casino workers and customers. At the edge of the gully, his worst fear confirmed, he dropped the laptop and slid down the incline. Marmelstein's face was lit by pale yellow beams from the police flashlights. Dees shuddered and tried to speak, but could only gasp. His hand was shaking too hard to close the remaining eye.

As he climbed back up the rocky slope on all fours, he heard a distinctly American-accented voice. "*. . . avec l'embassade américain. Un américain mort, la juridiction américain, mon cher.*"

The American was imperially slim, dressed in a polo shirt and jeans, his black hair and eyebrows framing an aquiline nose.

Behind him were two other Americans, beefy, with sunburns and bristly military-style haircuts. The thin one was Dennis Kingen; the other two were identified as embassy guards.

Kingen aimed his flashlight down the gully at Marmelstein.

"Except for that mess over his eye, he looks almost natural."

Dees realized the shaking had spread from his hand to his entire body. He sat heavily on the ground and fished a Marlboro from his pocket. It took three tries before the brass Zippo stopped shaking enough to light the cigarette. He gulped in air and tobacco smoke.

"I met his mother last year," he said, glancing up at Kingen, then back down at the body. "We went to her place in Union City . . . in New Jersey. She told me she was glad he had a friend like me to help him stop drinking. . . . Oh shit."

Kingen pursed his lips. Two days before, driving an embassy car, he'd pulled Dees and Marmelstein from a crowd of a dozen dockside thugs who were unhappy with the GTV crew shooting them. That night, over drinks, Dees had thanked him and told him his title as trade attaché was as transparent as gin.

"I'm one of the duty officers tonight," Kingen said, not looking down at Dees. "We picked up the Haitian police radio traffic. What happened?"

Dees sketched his conversation with Marmelstein. Kingen raised his eyebrows when Dees mentioned the tape.

"Taped it? A little paranoid?"

Dees felt himself flush. "Look," he snapped, "I'd say he had a goddamned good reason for being paranoid. The phone call, whatever it was, scared the shit out of him. Dick didn't scare easily."

Kingen aimed his flashlight back down the gully. "Looks like maybe he should have."

He nodded at the other Americans, who began to scramble down the slope.

"Hold it!" Dees barked.

They turned and stared. Dees slid down the ravine on his butt. Ignoring the two embassy guards, he gently placed one arm under Marmelstein's knees, the other around his back. With a grunt, he forced his aching knees up, holding the 180-pound body in his throbbing arms. The body swung from side to side as he made his way up the slope, step by step. Dees was gasping for air when he finally stood eye-to-eye with Kingen. As he hugged the body close, Dees thought he could feel it starting to cool already.

"Where do you want to take him?" he asked.

"*Canape Vert.* We need to get the body away from here, out of the heat."

Without a word, Dees carried the body to the embassy's Chevy Suburban. The two burly Americans opened the door, and he placed the body inside.

Walking back to the casino, he saw Kingen pick up the laptop. "Whoa," Dees said, rushing over to grab the strap.

Kingen didn't release his grip. "Evidence in the murder of an American citizen."

Dees continued to clutch the strap. "Dick told me to keep an eye on it. If there's anything in it that helps, I'll call."

Kingen released the strap as Tigwo pushed to the front of the crowd. Kingen turned, seemed to study the dwarf briefly, looked out over the gathered heads and barked, "Back! Stand back!"

The crowd thinned. Kingen turned back to Dees. "Seems to me you'd better notify your people. Meet me at *Canape Vert* when you can."

Dees trudged inside, sat at the phone that provided a direct AT&T link to the U.S., and called Phoenix. He gave the international desk the details, and filed an ad-libbed telephone track. He was assured that it would not air until Marmelstein's family in New Jersey had been notified.

A voice on the other end said, "Peter, hang on. Mac wants to talk to you."

Dees suddenly felt exhausted, dulled. Mac? Oh shit. McKinley Burke. Broadcasting visionary, billionaire times two, mild psychotic, his boss. Oh shit.

"Hello? Peter Dees?" A rumbling, clipped western accent. "This is Mac Burke," he said needlessly. "I'm sending a charter jet to Haiti in two days. I want you and your crew and the body—what was his name?"

"Dick. Richard. Marmelstein. He was from Union City. New Jersey."

"Right, Marmelstein. All of you are to be here in Phoenix in two days. I've gotten clearance. Understand?"

"I need to be here for a while. I'm going to find out who killed—"

"Goddammit, I don't give a fuck about what you need!" Burke bellowed, clearing the line's static for an instant. "I sign your fucking paycheck! Get your ass here with the body or get fired! Got me?"

Dees stared at an ant struggling with a bread crumb on the mahogany reception desk. "Look, I need to find—"

The phone clicked dead. What the hell, he thought, he hated long good-byes anyway.

Dees skidded the dented Diahatsu four-wheel-drive to a stop in the courtyard of *Canape Vert* hospital. It was the only place where whites and embassy people came when they were sick, the only place with a refrigerated morgue. The embassy's Chevy Suburban was parked nearby.

He muscled his way past crowds of Haitians jamming the emergency room area. As he flashed his press ID and passport, he spotted Kingen talking to the pair of buzz-cut Americans who had driven the body to the morgue.

Kingen motioned to Dees, and opened the door of what was normally a doctor's office, blessedly cool, thanks to a grinding window air conditioner.

"What happened?" Dees asked flatly. He was too tired to yell.

Kingen eyed him for a moment, then took a plastic bag from his pocket and tossed it on the metal desk with a *thunk*. It contained a misshapen piece of metal, a little blood, three brown hairs, and flecks of ghastly gray material that looked like uncooked sausage.

Dees fought off a wave of nausea. He eyed the wastebasket in the corner, just in case.

Kingen leaned against the door, arms folded. "Nine-millimeter. Close range. Seems like a robbery."

He looked quizzically at Dees, who stared back.

"Robbery? Robbery, my ass," Dees said. "We've done a series of stories that've pissed off the bozos down at the docks, the Haitian military, the embassy, and Christ knows who else. That's a pretty good suspect list to start with."

"This slug was from the back, close range. His money and ID are gone. So it's robbery."

"Robbery? What about the left eye? You tell me, Sherlock, why somebody would do that."

Kingen shrugged. "Revenge? Voodoo?"

"And what about his call to me? And the tape. You find the tape?"

Kingen shook his head. "It may be political, but we won't know until we shake some of the trees around here. To keep things simple, we put it on paper as robbery."

Dees plopped into a metal office chair. "They don't kill white people in this country. There's no street crime, at least the kind we're used to. Voodoo means ceremonies of some sort, blood or entrails or feathers spread around. So that leaves politics, and the stories we've done. What happened? And who gave you permission to do an autopsy?"

"I gave permission. And I'm all the permission we need around here."

The two men glared at each other. The only noise was the bent fan blade inside the a/c clattering against something.

"And," Kingen finally said, "it's probably a robbery." He paused. "Anything in the computer that might help us?"

"You seem pretty concerned about a laptop. I haven't had a chance to look yet. I've got a couple of days to check it. I've been ordered—"

"I know. Get Marmelstein's stuff, I've given the okay, and when your boss's plane arrives, we'll help with the body, take it home. I'm heading back to Washington next week, for good, I hope. My parting gift was to clear the paperwork."

"How'd you know about the plane?"

A long pause. "I'm paid to know. Travel safely."

They shook hands, and Dees trudged to the Diahatsu, slapped it into gear, and ground his way up Avenue John Brown toward the hotel.

He glanced at the computer that Marmelstein had gotten by accident. The hotel fax had crashed, so Marmelstein had requested the home office to air freight a bundle of clips on voodoo and Haitian politics to him. When he opened the box, he discovered that he'd received a computer. A work slip on the case indicated it had been repaired and was destined for the GTV executive offices, no name attached.

Marmelstein had joked that some schmuck in the Phoenix executive suites was waiting for a computer and instead ended up with a bundle of magazine and newspaper articles on politics and voodoo in Haitian society. Too bad, he'd told Dees, but if those cheap assholes didn't want to buy field crews computers, he'd just keep this one and they could try to find it.

Traffic had stopped. Dees craned his neck to see what could be causing a midnight jam. Then he began to inch forward, and as he crawled past a large banyan tree by the roadside, he saw a crowd around a body, a black body. A very short Haitian, he thought. A woman was screaming and crying over it.

Great. Another dead Haitian. These poor bastards. The paramilitaries or the *Macutes* or the army or some voodoo was always killing them. He glanced again, and caught a glimpse of a familiar tiny jacket. He jerked to a stop on the shoulder and got out.

He saw the lifeless eyes of the Haitian staring up at the banyan, a splotch of red on his white waiter's jacket; Dees had heard that the little man always carefully washed and pressed the jacket each day when he got home from work. More red stained the face.

He'd been shot through the heart. A bloody, hollow socket where his left eye had been was already attracting flies. His mother wailed over the body. She was of normal size, but some genetic anomaly—or maybe the voodoo *loas* that floated through the countryside—had decreed that she would have only one child, and he would be a dwarf.

"Tigwo," she screamed, pressing her head to the matted blood on his chest. "Tigwo!"

The howl echoed off a stone wall across the road. It faded. Somewhere, a rooster crowed, several hours ahead of the sunrise.

CHAPTER 2

JUNE 6, PORT-AU-PRINCE

Dees scowled at the phone receiver. "So, you think two people with their eyes shot out is some sort of voodoo trademark? But probably just armed robbers? Is that what you're telling me?"

Dennis Kingen's voice came through the pop and buzz of Tele-Haiti's phone system. "Like I said, Marmelstein was robbed. The dwarf, too. In case you hadn't noticed, people are hungry around here. Maybe the eye thing is some sort of way to prevent the dead's spirit from coming after them. You know, in some cultures the left eye's considered the eye of God."

"No, I didn't know that and thank you, Margaret Mead. I was hoping for something a little more definite."

"Like what? Some great conspiracy? My money's still on one of those *Macute* hangers-on down at the docks. You and Dick ticked them off with a story on them getting payoffs from the U.S. government. Which was wrong, by the way."

The *Macutes* were the remnants of Papa Doc Duvalier's voodoo-based security forces. They had once been more than merely secret police. The very name *Tonton Macute*—Uncle Bogeyman—came from Haitian folklore. A *Macute* could appear as a man or woman, wolf or bird, wind or water, and was capable of casting spells to bring poverty, illness, death, or something far worse—zombification, the living death of a zombie.

Papa Doc had regularly consulted with voodoo *hougans*—priests—from around the country, and used them to help create *noirisme. Noirisme* meant "blackness," the triumph of Haiti's black majority over the country's mixed-race ruling classes. But it also meant the black arts, including using beefy secret policemen who wore Ray•Bans, even at night, both as enforcers and as emissaries from the dark side.

But Papa Doc died, and his heir, the flabby, effeminate Baby Doc, fled the country. Chaos ensued, and the *Macutes* went off on their own, loyal to whoever paid them. Dees and Marmelstein had reported that the U.S. embassy was paying some *Macutes* to terrorize supporters of the radical priest Jean-Bertrand Aristide.

"That story was wrong," Kingen repeated. "Anyway, this doesn't look like politics."

"So you say."

"So I said. Maybe one of them needed cash and figured some journalist had a lot of dollars or googoos. And everybody knew Tigwo had cash from his casino tips. So a political robbery, maybe, more robbery than political. But I'm checking."

"Me, too. With twenty-four hours before my boss says I leave or get fired, I'm short on time. I'll call you back in a few hours."

"We may not know more then."

"Yeah, well, it's all I've got."

Dees hung up, sighed, and took a sip of the acrid Creole coffee. The laptop sat open on the table next to his bed. He had spent the evening scanning the computer's files. He'd found six scripts and several pages of notes for the stories they'd done, and an incomplete Haiti phone list Marmelstein had been transcribing from his address book.

That, and a locked file, labeled XXXX. Whatever was in the laptop that had Marmelstein so spooked must be in there, Dees had reasoned. He'd tried to figure out the password until three A.M. He started with the obvious—hitting the return key. He tried the word "password," permutations of Marmelstein's first and last names, the dead producer's birthday, and the names of every pro and college team from New Jersey and New York.

He tried Marmelstein's middle name—Aaron—the names of every band he had ever liked from U2 to INXS, and every possible password that might have anything to do with Haiti, from Papadoc to voodoo. He tried Jersey, Newjersey, Phoenix, GTV, Unioncity, and Joisey. Dees tried his own name, the names of the various hotels they had stayed in, and the name of every country Marmelstein had traveled to.

Now, groggy from lack of sleep, he powered up the Toshiba and began fiddling again. What else? he wondered. Marmelstein had worked in television since he was eighteen, so Dees began idly trying various TV technical phrases.

Whitebalance. Liveshot. The screen blinked the familiar "access denied" at him. Hotswitch. Testtone. Ifb. Uplink. Downlink. Nothing.

He typed in "deadair" and hit the return key. Instead of the familiar blinking silence, the computer began to whir and hum.

The screen popped to life. Dees forced his eyes to focus. The first page looked like some sort of inventory and shipping list:

> Archgate: 20 bbl thiodiglycol, 10 bbl phosphorus oxychloride, 10 bbl phosphorus trichloride.
>
> Received Salman Pak 16/4/90. Payment Hong Kong received 21/4/90.
>
> Anthrax: 10 mml.

Dees sucked in his breath. Anthrax? He kept reading.

Anthrax 10 mml. Received M.O.D. 15/5/90. No payment received. Memo: check on delay.

What followed was a list of dates going back three years, some with asterisks beside them. Following each date was a figure—5M, 2M, 1M, and so on. M? Million?

He scrolled down to the next page. It looked like a chemistry flow chart. Archgate was underlined. A dotted line connected it to the words CAYMAN ISLANDS. Another dotted line connected it to the word EGYPT, and continued, ending in a question mark. Another line connected Archgate to the words BELGIUM? FRANCE? The line extended from there, and also ended in a question mark.

Scrolling down again, he found a series of notes.

TELL DEES? NEED MORE INFO.

THESIS—ILLEGAL EXPORTS OF CHEMICALS TO IRAQ. EVIDENCE—SHIPMENT RECORDS. ARCHGATE, CASCOR TRAILS RUN OUT. INTERLOCKING DIRECTORATES. FIND DETAILS OF LAW.

A page headed DUMMY SCRIPT followed:

AMERICAN AND EUROPEAN COMPANIES HAVE BEEN SUPPLYING SADDAM HUSSEIN'S DICTATORSHIP IN IRAQ WITH THE INGREDIENTS TO MAKE A NEW GENERATION OF CHEMICAL AND BIOLOGICAL WEAPONS.

SOME OF THE SHIPMENTS HAVE BEEN MADE LEGALLY UNDER COMMERCE DEPARTMENT EXPORT LICENSES. BUT OTHERS HAVE BEEN MADE ILLEGALLY, THEIR TRUE NATURE HIDDEN IN A MASS OF DUMMY CORPORATIONS, ALL OPERATING IN THE MIDDLE EAST.

IRAQ HAS USED POISON GAS BEFORE, DURING THE 1980 TANKER WAR WITH IRAN. AND MANY ANALYSTS FEAR THESE WEAPONS COULD NOT ONLY BE USED BY IRAQ, BUT ALSO BY VARIOUS TERRORIST ORGANIZATIONS SUPPORTED BY THE BAGHDAD DICTATORSHIP.

The next line read: BULLSHIT. GET MORE DETAILS. LINKS NOT FIRM.

There were two blank lines, then: NEED DEES SOONEST. COMPUTER FILE. WHO? CHECK IN MIDEAST ASAP. TRANSSHIPMENTS FROM CAIRO.

The final entry read: THREATS. THEY KNOW. CHECK FLIGHTS TO CAIRO. BAGHDAD?

Dees scrolled back. Marmelstein always wrote in all caps, a force of habit from his years of writing scripts. The entire file was in capital letters except for the companies, chemicals, and anthrax on the first page.

Meaning what? Meaning the first page wasn't written by Marmelstein, meaning it was in the computer when Marmelstein got it.

Tight-lipped, Dees locked the door to his room and took the computer to a table off the empty hotel lobby, to the direct U.S. phone link. He plugged the modem into the phone line. It took ten tries before he was able to connect his modem to the GTV mainframe in Phoenix and access the environment and science unit's data base.

Thiodiglycol, he read. Not too useful on its own. One of a class of chemicals called precursors. Mixed with other chemicals to produce mustard gas.

Dees lit a Marlboro and continued searching, hurrying before the notoriously bad Haitian phone lines crashed. Looking under phosphorus oxychloride and phosphorus trichloride, he also found the precursor notation. The end product was something called sarin. Looking under sarin, he found it listed as a nerve agent.

Causes nausea, vomiting, probable death if inhaled, instant death if touched.

Dees's heart began to flutter like the computer screen.

PHOENIX

It was like every other computer room, filled with glowing green screens and technicians in short-sleeved white shirts. Some screens ran constant diagnostics on the system. Others retrieved specific information.

A pair of hands stroked the keys of one terminal. It prompted: *Query?*

The hands danced across the keyboard, typing: *Unit 166.*

The screen went blank for a half second, then flashed *Marmelsteinlog. Unit 166.*

Typed on the next line: *Query: 166log.*

Another half second of blank screen followed, then a list came up of dates and times the unit had logged into the company mainframe. The top entry glowed *Jun6/03:45–* That meant the unit was logged into the system. Right now.

A finger ran down the screen. Three dozen system log-ins since May 15.

The finger flicked the screen with a fingernail. It made a soft, glassy clink.

PORT-AU-PRINCE

The laptop made a vaguely groaning noise. C'mon baby, Dees thought. A second later the description of sarin disappeared, leaving him staring at a blank gray screen.

He shut down the computer, restarted, and attempted to dial in again. It got as far as making contact with the Phoenix mainframe when the screen wiggled and went blank. Five subsequent tries produced the same result.

It was what, four A.M. in Phoenix? He dialed a number, and a voice on the other end said, "International desk. Volga."

It figured, Dees thought, that the anal little prick in charge of the internat desk would be in this early. "Timothy, it's Dees—"

Before he could say another word, Volga said, "Hold."

The line clicked and hummed. Dees was muttering "You arrogant little asshole" when the line was picked up.

"Excuse me? Asshole isn't the best way to start a conversation."

It was a lilting female voice. Dees cleared his throat. "Sorry. I was talking to somebody here."

A laugh that seemed to tinkle through the static came out of the phone line. "You sure you weren't talking to Timothy?"

"I see my reputation precedes me."

Another laugh. "Let's just say there are a lot of people here who'd like to call him what you did."

The El Salvador thing again, Dees thought. He changed the subject. "You're new."

"Just to this shift. Melinda Adams here. And everybody knows who you are, cowboy."

Dees found himself delighted at the way she said "cowboy." "So who'd you piss off to work the graveyard?"

"Remember, it's always prime time someplace. I'm here to work with the Middle East. They found out I speak fluent Arabic."

"You major in it?"

"Near Eastern civ, actually. It helped that my old man was in the oil business. We lived in Saudi five years, so I learned. So, what about you?"

"What about me?"

He heard the laugh again. "You must have a history, besides watching the mold grow in Haiti. Some people here think you're just slightly insane, you know."

"Only slightly? Nice to know my stock's rising at headquarters."

"Can you blame them?" she asked with what seemed to be amusement. "You start out at the company traveling inside Nicaragua with the Contras. You convince the desk there's a nifty little war in Angola with South Africans and Cubans fighting each other, and you vanish for three weeks before we hear from you. You disappear for another month in Afghanistan. You run around in Panama City with an eight-millimeter camera while the Army Rangers are fighting house-to-house. And then there's what you called Timothy in Salvador."

"He deserved it," Dees said tiredly. "He wanted a minor script change. I told him if we tried to drive to the uplink to feed after dark we'd have trouble. 'You're paid for trouble,' he said. So he delayed us an hour tinkering with a perfectly fine script. Sure enough, by the time we're driving back from the uplink, the guerillas ambush the car. I get a grenade fragment in the shoulder. My cameraman gets shot in the arm."

"Umm," she said. "And what about the company car in Puerto Rico?"

"It was a hurricane. They wanted video before the uplink shut down. We got it. I didn't arrange for a corrugated tin roof to take out the front end of the car on purpose. Besides," he added, "it wasn't a car. It was a four-by-four. An Isuzu Trooper. Or what was left of one. And it probably cost about the same as one of Mac Burke's suits."

"Umm" came again through the phone line. "So you're from where? Iowa? Nebraska?"

It was Dees's turn to laugh. "Arkansas. Seven years in Chicago flattens the vowels."

"College?"

"University of Chicago, plus three years free-lancing. You?"

"Radcliffe. Some grad school in Paris."

"Nice," Dees said. "If you've got a minute, I need—"

"Married?" she interrupted.

"Divorced."

He wondered if she was flirting or just fishing. He decided to let it drop. "I need a favor," he continued. "If you have a couple of minutes, I'm working on something here. I need to get some info from the business unit's data base."

"What's up? Your computer not working?"

Dees paused a half beat. "I don't have one."

Silence from the other end. "Umm. Okay. What'd you need?"

"Anything on a company called Archgate. A as in apple, R as in Robert, C Charlie, H like in Henry. Gate. G, A, T like in Tom, E. I only have the name."

More silence. "Why? I'm kinda busy."

"Look, I don't want to be rude, but I'm sitting here with a dead man. . . ."

"Yeah, I heard. I'm sorry. You all right?"

Dees took a deep breath. "Fine. But I have some loose ends to tie up before we leave, and I need this now, okay?"

The laugh again. "I live to serve. Hang on. This may take a while."

Dees occupied himself watching the ceiling fan turn lazily. A CBS reporter came through the hall, saw him on the phone and mouthed the silent words, You okay?

Dees nodded. An ABC producer walked up and kissed him on the forehead. Her body smelled of soap. She whispered in his ear, "If there's anything we can do for Dick's family, or you, let us know."

Dees nodded again. Being a friend of a dead man did wonders

for his popularity. A fat green fly waddled across the telephone table. Dees swatted at it and missed.

The phone line clicked back to life. "Sorry," Melinda Adams said. "Nothing. It must be private. No listing on the NYSE or any other exchange. Nothing on Nexis data base, either."

Dees scratched his nose. "Thanks. I might as well pack up my bag and head home."

"Cold, aren't you?"

"Laughing beats pounding my head into a wall about now."

"Where do you go from here?"

He thought her voice sounded concerned, almost tender. "Dunno. I've got an audience in Phoenix tomorrow. I may need to take some time off to do a little digging around."

"You ever consider Cairo?"

Dees almost let the phone slip out of his hand. "Why?"

"Well, the scuttlebutt is we're about to have an opening there. Just a thought."

Dees pursed his lips. "Thanks for the heads up. So, do I get to meet you when I'm in Phoenix?"

"Sorry. I start vacation tonight. I'm taking some horseback riding R and R. Maybe some other time, cowboy."

Maybe you bet, Dees thought. He thanked her, hung up, and went to his room. He borrowed two computer disks from the ABC producer, and after two hours of trial and error, duped the contents of the Dead Air file. He put one copy in a pocket of his photographer's vest.

Dees stripped to his T-shirt, then slipped on his bulletproof vest, and made sure it was hidden beneath a loose long-sleeved rugby shirt. He slipped on the photographer's vest, went to the front desk, put the computer and second disk into a large safe deposit box, and removed four hundred dollars in ones and fives. It was going to be a long night.

During the day, he drove across Port-au-Prince, spreading dollars at military and police headquarters. "Of course we'd love to help," he was told numerous times, "but we know nothing, *mon cher.* Not even rumors."

He visited two fixers he had used in the past in Petionville. More dollars. More promises to keep their ears open, but no hard information. They were not shocked by Tigwo's murder, since the dwarf had threatened people in the past with his pistol, and the fact that he was allowed to carry one at all meant a probable connection either to the police or the *Macutes*. But they were genuinely stunned by the murder of a white man. It just did not happen there.

"Unless, *mon cher,*" one of the fixers told Dees, "your friend had some very powerful enemies."

The sun was starting to set when he reached the U.S. embassy. Kingen was almost curt, saying they had nothing new. He gave Dees a card with his private number in Washington and promised to continue working the case, even from D.C. Then Kingen asked if he'd found anything on the computer.

"Not a thing," Dees said, before making a quick exit to drive to *Chez Pierre*, a Petionville restaurant with exceptional food, impeccable service, and a clientele that orbited around whatever center of power existed in Haiti at any given moment.

The Pierre of *Chez Pierre* was French-Canadian, a burly man with a larynx so damaged by tobacco that his voice sounded like a gargle.

"No, *mon cher,*" Pierre gurgled, "these people do not kill white men. I am a racist, of course, but also a realist. Which is why I have married two black women in my time here and have six dark brown children and four totally black grandchildren. But I will check more now."

Dees handed him fifty dollars and saw Pierre quietly palm the money to a series of waiters and bartenders, whispering to each one. The restaurateur then circulated to the tables where members of the lighter-skinned Haitian ruling class were having dinner.

Within fifteen minutes he came back to Dees's table. "Nothing, *mon cher,*" he growled as he sat. "Not even a whisper, except of course that it was an American and nothing of that sort has ever happened here, ever. You will try the crab claws?"

Dees did. Later he drove downtown. The garish lights of the Normandie Bar were the only thing that lit the littered and pockmarked street that ran beside *le chateau blanc*, the white house, residence of Papa Doc and Baby Doc and now the revolving door of presidential pretenders.

Dees entered, immediately feeling like a grain of salt in a pepper shaker. A series of red lightbulbs gave the bar and domino tables the look of some cheesy version of hell in a carnival haunted house. Every head in the place turned, every pair of eyes stared.

The Normandie was where the street thugs and dock workers hung out, men whose muscle was for hire by the hour or day for everything from offloading bicycles stolen in Miami to pounding in the skulls of political dissidents. A heavily muscled man at the bar's far end glared at Dees with red-rimmed eyes.

Dees was hoping no one was still too upset over his stories on the links between the dockside thugs and the U.S. government, when the man roared "GTV!" the G sounding like "zhee." The man got up so suddenly, he shoved over his bar stool.

In the miserable light, Dees saw him clawing at his waistband, his eyes bulging. The man staggered backward, bellowed something unintelligible, and grabbed again at the pistol grip protruding from inside his pants.

As he staggered again, Dees walked to the bar, said, *"Un Prestige, s'il vous plaît,"* and before the surprised bartender could react, grabbed an unopened bottle of the Haitian beer from a case on the counter. Without pausing, he took four loping strides to the back of the bar.

The man with the gun had just started to focus and was grabbing the pistol handle when Dees smashed the bottle across his forehead. He stared at Dees, and with a *whuummpf*, pitched forward. Dees rolled him over, careful to avoid the blood streaming from his forehead, grabbed the pistol, and stuffed it in his own belt.

He stared back at the half-dozen men at the bar. *"Pardonez-moi,"* he shouted. *"Je suis un journaliste américain. Ne parle-pas français ou Creole. Parlez-vous anglais?"*

"Yeah," a young man in a torn short-sleeved shirt said. "You better come over here before one of these boys forgets you're a crazy *blanc* and kills your ass."

"Like they killed another *blanc*?" Dees asked as he sat. The barflies turned their attention to their drinks, ignoring the body on the floor.

"Oh that," the young man said, chuckling. Dees noticed he had a scar that started beneath his right ear and disappeared under his shirt. "Haitians die like flies, no problem. A white man dies, they send in the Marines like they did in 1916."

Dees glanced at the body. "Think he's dead?"

"Nah, Jean-Baptiste, he got a head thick as a log. But he's gonna be plenty fucking mad."

"Maybe I should shoot him, then, so we can talk quietly."

The young man looked Dees up and down, once. "White man comes in here, comes in here at night, he's crazy enough to do it. And you got the gun in your pocket."

"Gun in my pocket? I'm just glad to see you," Dees said. The Haitian didn't get it.

Dees fished in his pocket and pulled out a small cylinder of bills secured with a rubber band. "Two hundred U.S." Six months pay in Haiti, on average. "I need information. You have any?"

The Haitian looked languidly at the bills. "What you need to know?"

"The word on the street. Who killed the American?"

The Haitian glanced hungrily at the money. "I might tell you, but I might be lying."

"It's Haiti. What else is new? Besides, like you said, I have the gun."

"Okay." His voice dropped to a hoarse whisper. "That little shit Tigwo. Little faggot with a big gun. And more guns at home. He has four, five. I hear the only reason he gets to carry the thing is because he gives blow jobs to the chief of police."

"Not anymore."

The Haitian grunted, nodding his head. "Yeah. So I hear Tigwo was told the white man had something worth *beaucoup gourdes*. I mean lots of money."

"Enough money for him to kill a foreigner, an American, no less?"

"Oh, yeah. I hear two thousand U.S. I hear three thousand. I hear seven, maybe nine years' pay. Oh, yeah, plenty, I hear."

"From who?"

"The talk down at the dock doesn't say. Tigwo was into lots of things. The police. The army. The light-skinned fucks in Petion-ville. Your embassy."

Dees tilted his head. The Haitian laughed. "Yeah, your embassy, they want to know who pulls strings at the docks or on the street, they pay lots of people to find out. Tigwo they pay. Maybe even me they pay."

"So?"

"So the talk is Tigwo did it for money. I don't know for who, just for money, that's the talk."

"And who killed Tigwo?"

"Who gives a fuck? Tigwo had enough enemies to fill one of those fucking rafts going to Miami."

Dees glanced at his watch. Three A.M. He sighed. "Anything else?"

The Haitian shrugged. "Just that whatever the American had worth so much money must be a big fucking whatever."

Dees shoved the cylinder of bills across the table. "Buy yourself a new shirt."

The Haitian balled and unballed his fists. "You better get the fuck out of here before I forget my manners. Maybe the *Macutes* wanted something, or maybe your fucking embassy, or maybe the army. Maybe I don't give a fuck."

Dees got up, pulled the revolver from his pants, opened the cylinder, and unloaded the shells into his hand. He tossed the gun toward the rotund body, which seemed to be snoring, and walked out.

As the Diahatsu approached the hotel, Dees tossed the bullets into the fecund vegetation by the roadside. Climbing the courtyard stairs to his room, he heard a soft rumble and saw the winking lights of a corporate jet heading into the airport in the plains below. He glanced down the hill, toward the barely visible lights of *Canape Vert*.

"Dick," he said softly. "Our ride's here."

CHAPTER 3

JUNE 7, PHOENIX

"No, Mr. Chairman," the gray-haired man with long western sideburns said into the phone, "I do not encourage my people to act that way. It is certainly not company policy. I would like to apologize for all of us."

Yasir Arafat's English was decent, better than decent even, but not good enough for him to take in a full telephone conversation from half a world away. So as Arafat sat in Tunis, staring at a speakerphone, waiting for an aide to translate the words, including nuances of retribution against the GTV employee who had offended the chairman, McKinley Burke absently ran his hand along the lapel of his light charcoal suit, a double-breasted number made by one of London's dwindling number of custom tailors.

The suit cost three thousand dollars. Burke figured that counting watch, shoes, shirt, tie, and belt, he was five grand worth of haberdashery on the hoof, worth several times more than the custom-made olive-drab ensemble worn by that man on the other end of the phone.

The line crackled with the voice of the translator. Burke nodded, once.

"Yes, Mr. Chairman, I quite agree. I personally guarantee you nothing like this will ever happen again. You may consider the problem solved."

Wanda Thrower, a GTV producer sent to Tunis with a camera crew to shoot the human side of Arafat for a half-hour profile, had asked a question about intelligence reports that Arafat was a homosexual and a pedophile. She had expected a denunciation of the CIA and other agencies spreading such lies. Instead, she was met with a stony silence, and Arafat stalked out of the interview. It was the worst mistake of her young professional life.

Burke nodded again, said good-bye, and clicked the phone back into its cradle. Then he pushed the speakerphone button, punched four numbers, and waited.

"Volga." Timothy Volga, a thin, jug-eared man of thirty-three with as little humor as his boss, possibly because of a family name that caused employees to hum "Volga Boatman" under their breath when he walked through the cavernous GTV newsroom, was GTV's overseas executive producer.

"Mac. Problem in Tunis?"

"Haven't seen the tape," Volga said. "I know what Wanda claims. She says Arafat's people were told in advance she would ask—"

"I don't give a shit what she says she told anybody!" Burke shouted. He swung his chair forward so even Volga could hear it creak. "She's through! More than through! This little cunt's screwed us with Arafat, and I'm supposed to be on-camera with him in two weeks!"

Volga paused, then said, "Understood."

"I don't just mean she's through with us." Burke's voice was dead calm. "She's not working in the Middle East again. I want you to wake up . . . what's his name, the producer in Cairo? The Egyptian?"

"Saed," Volga said.

"Wake him up. I want the locks changed on the bureau now. Tonight. I want the Egyptians to revoke her work permit."

"Understood."

Burke punched the speaker button off. He smiled. *Fortune* magazine had described his management style as based on the Marilyn Monroe theory: Screw the president and you die.

His intercom light glowed a soft green. "Yeah," he barked.

"Mr. Burke, Peter Dees's plane has landed. He'll be here in twenty minutes. He called from the airport."

"Who the—" he began, and, remembering, stopped himself. "Bring him here the second he arrives."

Peter Dees. About six years with the company. Wounded once by shrapnel in El Salvador. Salary, $55,000.

Almost fired twice. Once for calling Timothy Volga a ferret. Once for destroying a vehicle owned by the company.

The company. It was Burke's name for his globe-girdling conglomerate made up of broadcasting, nursing homes, fertilizer plants, phosphate mining, pharmaceuticals, and pharmacies.

It had been started by Dr. Samuel Burke, Doc Burke, his father, who founded a drugstore in Colorado Springs so he could fill all of his own patients' prescriptions. It had expanded into a regional chain of ten pharmacies—Burke's—in three states.

One snowy day as Mac was preparing to leave on Christmas break from the University of Colorado, Doc Burke showed up at his son's dormitory in a brand-new Buick. Mac barely noticed that the old man was slurring his words slightly, but was hit in the face with the smell of bourbon as he got into the car.

The leather seat made a crinkling noise in the cold as Doc slid behind the wheel. He started the engine, put the heater on full blast, and reached into an inside pocket of his camel hair overcoat. Then he pulled out his old silver pint flask, unscrewed the top, and took a long pull. He replaced the top without offering it to his son, set it on the seat between them, and skidded from the dormitory drive.

As he weaved along the snow-packed roads, he told Mac that he had just bought two drugstores in Pueblo, and expected his son to oversee their operation during the next summer break. Mac stared out the window at rows of spindly birches sagging under the wet snow before replying that he planned to attend summer school and take more courses in international finance.

The old man said nothing, merely picking up the flask, unscrewing the top again, and taking another long drink.

"Listen," he finally said, the flask in his right hand while he drove unsteadily with his left, "I'm not one of the most powerful men in these parts for nothing. Do it, or I'll cut off your fucking tuition money. Do it, and we can buy your own fucking international management school."

He was laughing, driving, and taking another drink from the flask all at once when he slid around a corner and saw the eighteen-wheeler stopped in front of them. All he could do was sputter and jerk the wheel hard to the right toward a snowbank on the shoulder.

The impact with the rear deck of the truck almost sheared the Buick in half lengthwise. It had thrown Mac against the windshield as the high rear bumper of the truck tore through the car, severing Doc's head cleanly between the second and third vertebrae. Mac, dazed but uninjured, had sat there, breathing through his mouth, watching the blood gurgle from his father's neck and roll down the overcoat. The old man was still clutching the flask in his right hand when the truck driver forced open Mac's door and pulled him out.

JULY 12, CAIRO

"Welcome in Egypt," the dirty-faced boy chirped, his striped djellaba bouncing as he hopped from foot to foot, always keeping a few paces in front of Dees. "I get you papyrus. Papeerus for you in Egypt."

Dees scowled. *"Emshee."*

The boy did not go away as ordered, but kept up his mercantile dance a few steps in front of Dees's stride. "Papeerus for you. Cheap. Good stuff. Made by artists. Looks old."

Dees stopped, crouched over and crooked his index finger, motioning the boy closer. The boy came forward. Dees looked straight into his liquid brown eyes and growled, *"Hamawitik!"*

The boy looked shocked, and stepped backward. Dees stomped one foot and repeated, *"Hamawitik."* The boy turned and darted away, quickly ducking into one of the shaded streets on Zamalek bordering the Nile.

In Cairo almost a month, Dees had been wondering how long it would take him to use the phrase "I will kill you" in ordinary conversation.

Dees walked in the direction the boy had taken. Last night's *hamseen* had coated everything—roads, bridges, cars, plants—with fine sand the consistency of talcum powder. The sky was still streaked pinkish-red from the airborne sand motes hauled from the Sahara and sent into low orbit over Cairo. Dodging fuming old Fiats in the roadway, Dees moved onto the bridge linking Zamalek island with the Corniche on the eastern shore. The concrete of the pedestrian walkway had long since disappeared in spots, leaving gaping holes some three feet across in the sidewalk, affording a clear view of the roiling brown Nile below.

Dees zigged through traffic, crossed onto the Corniche, finally reaching the GTV office building. He greeted the turbaned *boab* with a straw broom at the building's entrance and climbed the worn stairs to the second floor.

Saed smiled as Dees entered the office. In four weeks Dees

had covered exactly one Arab league meeting about obscure Iraqi claims to islands off Kuwait, and one story on the latest excavations at Giza.

Saed smiled again. Dees sighed. "Where is the crew?"

"Abdullah and Nasir are in the back room," Saed said, pointing at a closed door.

"You ready to go?"

Saed smiled, spreading his palms open. "Ah, I am not sure of the wisdom of asking these questions you are always asking. It could cause difficulties."

Dees had spent a month asking embassy officials, business people, and the Egyptian trade ministry if they'd ever heard of a company called Archgate—and about it shipping goods from the U.S. to Iraq through Egypt. No one had heard anything. But over drinks during the evening sandstorm, a TWA pilot he'd met at the Marriott bar told him that the airport's freight office kept records of transshipments. They were in Arabic, on paper, in piles of files, but a little *baksheesh* might get access, maybe.

Watching Saed alternately shrug and smile, Dees asked, "And what is your problem?"

Saed smiled again. "I do not think we should be asking questions at the airport without a permit."

Dees sighed. "We don't need a permit if we're going without a camera."

"Ah, but asking officials questions always requires a permit. And I do not wish to go without one."

Dees knew Saed had two uncles and a cousin at the television department of the Ministry of Information. He suspected the producer told them everything.

"All right," Dees said. "Forget it. Abdullah and I will go to Video Cairo to see about the repairs on the camera." The bureau's tube camera was constantly in the shop.

Saed nodded. "Then I will stay here and see about permits."

Abdullah was angular, with a scruffy black fringe beard and pictures of his children in his wallet. He was an indifferent soundman and an excellent father.

As he and Dees climbed into the bureau's rusting Fiat, Dees said, "I need you to translate for me and help me out on a project. Since this is extra work, well . . ." He pressed a hundred-dollar bill into Abdullah's palm.

The cameraman grinned.

"We're going to the airport. I need to find the office where they keep records of cargo that comes from the United States and then is shipped someplace else. No permits, no officials. Just tell whoever we talk to what I tell you and spread some *baksheesh*. Okay?"

"Okay," Abdullah said, and gunned the Fiat as they started the drive through the twisted dust-covered Cairene streets that would take them through the downtown towers, a mishmash of new construction and colonial remnants, and past the Necropolis, the mammoth aboveground cemetery where the dead had been displaced by the living in a desperate scramble for space. The tomb homes even had mail delivery.

They parked in a lot of the giant airport and walked toward the freight area. Dees handed Abdullah five twenty-dollar bills. "Use these, greet your friends, and get us into wherever they have the records of cargo for the past few years."

Abdullah grinned again, and greeted a soldier near the door with a kiss. They talked, the soldier pointed, and Abdullah hugged him, slipping a bill into his tunic pocket. The process was repeated with a soldier at the entrance to the freight area, a small man at a battered desk inside the freight area, and a *boab* sweeping the floor in front of a cubicle in a far corner of the cavernous freight hangar. The last twenty went to a soldier who came over to ask what they were doing.

Inside a dusty room, Dees and Abdullah found themselves face-to-face with piles of dirty ledgers and account books stacked on all sides around a rickety desk. Dees pulled a reporter's notebook from his vest.

"We need to look for a company named Archgate, doing business from April of this year, February and August last year, March, June, and November the year before. Maybe more than that. But with all these books, where do we start?"

Abdullah looked very serious. "I would suppose we start with the first book we find with the correct dates."

It took over an hour to find the ledgers from the right months and years. Abdullah opened April of 1990 and began scanning the Arabic entries. There were thousands of them, scrawled in various shades of ink.

"Ah," Abdullah said after half an hour, tapping his finger on the page. "Here. This Archgate shipped a very large shipment, twenty, no, thirty, how you say, drums? Barrels? In early April, they arrived, and left the same day. Transferred from Orbit Air Freight of Rome to, ah here, to Iraqi Air."

Dees's fingers tingled.

"To the Iraqi Ministry of Science," Abdullah continued. "From this Archgate. But from here in Egypt?"

Dees craned his neck at the unintelligible scrawls. "From here?"

"Yes, it says, from Archgate in Saint Louise, Misr."

Misr was Egyptian Arabic for "Egypt."

"Saint Louise? Is there anything like that here, maybe left over from Napoleon?"

Abdullah shook his head. "And I do not understand why after 'Misr' they have written 'USA.' "

Dees thought. Saint Louise? Misr? USA? Archgate? Arch . . .

gate. Gate . . . arch. The Gateway Arch? St. Louis? Not Misr! Missouri! USA!

Another two hours and they had found five more shipments from Archgate dating to 1988. A different air freight company in a different European city was used each time, but Iraqi Air was always the receiving carrier. From: Archgate, St. Louis, Missouri, USA. To: Ministry of Science, Ministry of Agriculture, even Ministry of Tourism, Iraq.

The *boab* knocked on the door. "We need to go," Abdullah said.

As they walked back through the terminal, Dees saw a familiar figure and elbowed his way into a crowd of tourists, pulling Abdullah with him. Saed was maybe fifty feet away, his back turned, talking to a pair of soldiers.

JULY 13, PHOENIX

Today, Armani: a black, light wool number with no vents, a Countess Mara tie, taupe flecked with black, and a dark blue shirt. The amphetamine he washed down with his mouthwash was coursing through his system, so by six A.M., Mac Burke appeared supremely energetic and almost beatific.

"Salaam aleicham," he said into the speakerphone.

"Aleicham salaam," came the reply from the other end, hissing and slightly clipped over several thousand miles of phone lines and satellite circuits.

"I trust you and your family are all well," Burke said. He was careful never to ask about the wife, which would have been bad form.

"Very well, and I trust you and your wife are well also."

Burke's jaw muscles tensed. It was a slap, small, but still stinging. His caller breached his own rules of protocol for a roundabout reference to tabloid headlines ten months before: MEDIA MAGNATE'S MYSTERY MISSUS, BURKE MARRIED IN SECRET, BILLIONAIRE CRADLE ROBBER? RUMORS FLY.

The tabloids had hounded him for years, ever since he'd become "Lord McKinley, Master of Megahertz," as one headline had put it. He had been especially galled when one found out about his fishing trip off the Baja peninsula in the Sea of Cortez in Mexico, five years before.

He had failed to land anything for hours, and tossed two rod and reel sets worth several thousand dollars overboard in a rage. Suddenly, the boat's pilot had yelled, *"Las ballenas!"* and pointed excitedly to a pod of gray whales, sounding less than a mile to starboard.

"Head toward 'em!" Burke had roared. The boat pitched through the azure water to within a few hundred yards of the whales when the dozen or so guests aboard the chartered yacht looked in surprise and saw Burke standing on the bridge with a .30-06 rifle. Burke had brought it on the trip even though the Mexican guide at the Baja resort said it was far too powerful to hunt doves or anything else that might be found in the province of Baja del Sur.

Before the pilot could stop him, Burke had fired off one, two, three rounds, each almost deafening the startled Mexican. The concussions echoed off the water and seemed to travel all the way to the peninsular mountains, barely visible in the distance beyond the stern.

While the guests stood with their mouths open on the deck below, the pilot yelled "No, no, *señor*! The whales are protected! You must stop!"

After the third shot, the pilot finally gathered his courage and rushed the larger man, surprising him as he grabbed the rifle by its barrel with both hands and gave it a yank. It slipped from Burke's hands, but the momentum carried it out of the pilot's hands, too. It spiraled, along with the custom-made burled maple stock and three-thousand-dollar telescopic sight, through the air and into the ocean, where it bobbed for a second and then sank in seven hundred feet of water.

Burke appeared not to notice. He gripped the railing on the open flying bridge and glared toward the disappearing whales, who hadn't seemed even to notice the shots that had splashed harmlessly several yards from them.

"Ahab!" Burke had screamed. "Ahab! Ahab! Fuck you! This is all mine! I have the power! Get out of my fucking ocean! I am the power! Ahab!"

Without even looking at the pilot, he'd stomped down the aluminum stairs and gone below, not moving from his cabin until they pulled into the port, met by several cars full of federal police who had been radioed by the pilot. Burke had come on deck calmly and talked quietly to the officers, one of whom translated. After some smiles and a few handshakes, he'd ridden in the front seat of one of the cars, next to the captain in charge.

After a conference inside a municipal building that lasted for an hour, Burke had emerged smiling. The pilot, who had shown up to give his version of events, was walking up the steps as Burke was descending. Without breaking stride, and with a smile still on his face, Burke slapped the pilot, hard in the face, as he passed. The pilot turned, his fists balled, but a policeman walking with Burke turned and shook his head, no.

Two weeks later the tabloids printed the entire story, including the fact that the local police command suddenly had two new police cars, the captain had somehow purchased a just-constructed villa overlooking the ocean, and the pilot had his fishing and guide licenses revoked. BURKE = POWER, one headline read.

Burke focused again on the speakerphone and the insult. He

smiled. "My wife is well. Working on several projects for me right now. But she seems moody much of the time, which may be because it is her time of the month. Kiss your wife for me, would you?"

In one statement, he had responded to the discourtesy with one of his own, had added the insult of referring to a kiss, and had gravely offended the Arab's sense of decorum by mentioning his wife's menstrual period. Burke smiled at the speakerphone.

"But then, as the saying goes," he continued. "Women. You can't live with 'em. You can't kill 'em. Unless you live in your part of the world."

"I see," finally came from the other end of the phone.

"I hope you can also see my problem here, since I have yet to have any records of the transfer."

"There were slight, ah, transportation problems," the voice said. "But it has been done. I suggest you look east."

Burke's left hand zipped the computer mouse across the pad, closing a subfile, then the main file, then exiting, reentering another program, opening two sets of windows and pausing, all within seconds. Hong Kong. Banks open. Deposit made three hours ago.

"I have looked east," Burke said, "and it is a beautiful day."

"Yes, a beautiful day here also. The gift of your voice makes it more so."

A gift on a beautiful day. Everything had arrived just fine.

"July is always hot here," the voice continued.

Burke's nostrils flared. His voice was calm as he checked the day and time on the computer. Six-seventeen A.M., July thirteenth.

"When does it get the hottest there?" he asked.

"The forecasts hint the end of July and the first of August will be especially hot."

Burke made an effort to stop clenching his jaw muscles. "One never knows when hot weather will start."

"True," the voice said, "but the forecasters seem to agree that the very hot weather this year will start the first of August."

Making the same sort of sucking sound he'd make at dinner if a piece of celery were stuck in his teeth, Burke asked, "We will speak again next week?"

"Insh Allah," the voice said.

Burke clicked off the phone, clicked it on again, and punched in four digits.

It barely had time to ring once when it was answered.

"Volga."

"Mac. My office. Now. And bring forms for export of a portable uplink, plus passport information for everyone we have between London and New Delhi. Road trip. My eyes only."

There was a pause on the other end. "Understood." The line clicked dead.

Burke flushed suddenly, his heart pounding violently. He opened a desk drawer with a trembling hand, withdrew a vial of pills, and fumbled with the cap.

He swallowed one of the blue pills without water and sat back in his chair, squinting at the label. Quaalude.

CHAPTER 4

JULY 13, CAIRO

As he sat at his desk, looking at Saed, Dees thought about the Kipling story where everyone was "most excruciatingly polite." Saed, on the telephone, would look up, smile and nod. Dees would smile and nod back.

Finally, Saed hung up and said, "We can go now. I have secured the permits."

"Go? Go where?"

"Go to the airport. I have secured the permits."

"As you've said. But we don't need to go to the airport anymore."

Saed looked puzzled. "But I have secured—"

"The permits. I know."

Saed managed to look offended. "But after I have the permits, we must go and shoot at the airport. Otherwise, why would the Ministry of Information give us the permits?"

"You know, Saed, if I didn't know better I'd think you were the product of a Jesuit education. In logic, they call it a tautology. We have to shoot because we have the permits. And we have the permits, therefore we have to shoot."

Saed nodded emphatically.

Dees sighed. "Okay. Take Nasir and Abdullah. Get all the

B-roll you can, especially of cargo planes. Also any shots of Iraqi Air jets."

Saed wrinkled his brow.

"Trade," Dees said. "For an Egyptian trade piece."

Saed nodded again. As he, Nasir, and Abdullah gathered the camera equipment and went out the door, Abdullah put his index finger to his lips, winked, and smiled.

Dees waited until they left before he unlocked the bottom drawer of his desk and pulled out the computer. He had gotten a metal desk, figuring it would be harder to break into than a wooden one. He entered the information from the airport in the Marmelstein file, then duped updated versions on the two disks. After he resecured the computer in the large bottom drawer, he locked the desk and put both disks into his pants pocket.

Dees looked out the window at the clear day that was starting to fade slowly. On an impulse, he dialed the GTV desk and asked for Melinda Adams. To his surprise and delight, he reached her.

"Well, cowboy, how's life in the sandbox?"

"Not bad. I was thinking about going riding. And you?"

Her voice brightened. "You ride, too?"

"When I can. It's cheap out by the pyramids. What kind of horse do you have?"

"Actually, it's Daddy's." He loved the way she said "Daddy." "Arabian gelding, fifteen and a half hands. Named Hamduallah."

"Praise God."

"And I do," came the voice with a laugh from eleven time zones away, "every time I'm out on him."

"I rent these hard-headed Arabians out by Giza who stop all at once and try to throw me over the handlebars."

"You must like them," she said. "You said 'who.' "

"Huh?"

"Who. You said 'who stop all at once,' not 'that stop all at once.' Personal, not impersonal, like a human. You must like horses."

I'm starting to like you, Dees thought. You know the personal from the impersonal. "So what do you look like?"

She laughed again. "I'm five-foot-five, blond, green eyes, fairly nice body, and I hate horny correspondents."

Dees chuckled. "Horniness is a state of nature here. As constant as the moon over the pyramids."

"Oh brother," she said. "A horny cornball. Say, you ever find out what you needed? About those companies?"

"Not much. Middle East traders. It may be a good story."

During the pause that followed, Dees heard the angry bleat of a Fiat horn below on the Corniche.

"Sorry," she said a moment later, "somebody here wanted something. A good story you said?"

It was Dees's turn to pause. He needed to share this with somebody he trusted, but not over an international circuit to GTV. "Maybe I'll fill you in sometime. If we ever meet."

"That could be sooner than you think."

"You're kidding."

"Nope. Rumor here is there's going to be a big move into the Middle East. I can't figure out why, since it's quiet over there."

"Comatose is more like it."

"Exactly. But all of a sudden it looks like we're scrambling people and equipment for some reason. To Iraq, of all places."

Dees swallowed. "Iraq? Why Iraq?"

"Beats the shit out of me. Somebody thinks something's worth covering. I'm going. I hear you're being shipped out, too."

Iraq, Dees thought. For somebody who'd told him to leave Dick's murder alone, Burke was making it easy for him not to. "Then," he said into the static-clipped phone line, "I guess I'd better use what horseback time I've got left here."

"I hear you can ride up to the base of the pyramids."

"Dodging all the archaeological excavations and repair work, but yeah, right up to them."

"So why not go? Relax."

Dees nodded at the phone. "Yeah, I think I'll do just that."

"I hear traffic in Cairo's a nightmare. How long's it take you to get there?"

"Hour, maybe, from leaving here."

"Listen, I gotta actually do some work here. Have fun."

Dees intended to do just that. He left the office, walked to his apartment on Zamalek island, and changed into jeans and riding boots. He kept one copy of the computer disk and stashed the other inside the refrigerator, wrapped in aluminum foil and labeled "Lamb Patties."

At the stable in Giza he mounted Pharaoh, the Arabian he usually rode, and trotted off across the dunes, Cheops and its two smaller brother pyramids to his right, streaks of pink light drifting above their apexes as the sinking sun refracted light off windborne sand.

During the flood season millennia before, the Nile flowed near the base of where Cheops now stood. The Aswan Dam and flood control had fixed that, but in the era of the Pharaohs, it gave the royal engineers one chance a year to move massive cut stones by barge from the quarry that still existed east of present-day downtown to the site of the rising monolith.

Near where the Sphinx now slowly disintegrated under the pressure of air pollution and weathering, there had been a workers' village recently discovered, where the artisans and engineers and laborers had lived. Several newly dug pits were scattered around the area, haphazardly marked by poorly built barricades made from scrap lumber.

It was growing dark quickly now, and Dees swore under his

breath for waiting so long to come out. A warm breeze from the west ruffled his hair and caused Pharaoh to shake his mane.

Dees rode to a dune rising just south of the pyramids. He reached in his pocket, felt the computer disk, wondered why he'd brought it along, and kept digging. He pulled out a wrinkled, bent joint. Uncas, he thought, the last of the Mohicans.

He clicked the disposable lighter and took a deep drag. Smuggling the occasional joint into far-flung corners of the earth was one of the things that had ended his marriage. Irresponsible, his wife had called it. Immature, she had called him. A vicious bitch who deserved the insurance agent geek she married, he thought, hacking as the smoke rolled out his nose.

It wasn't much of a doob, so three hits and it vanished in the air, mixing with the ancient incense, Roman campfires, Napoleonic tobacco, and modern pollution, all haze drifting above what he would have thought was the oldest place in the world if he hadn't once smoked a joint at the Olduvai Gorge and thought the same thing there.

Pharaoh tossed his mane again. Dees figured the horse wanted to get back to the stables, now that it was almost completely dark. He had tapped the Arabian lightly with the crop and begun trotting slowly toward the mud and timber barn when he heard the thumping in the sand behind him.

Dees turned and could barely make out another rider, coming fast. Ahab the A-rab out for a night ride? he wondered fuzzily. He watched as the galloping horse drew closer. The man riding it was dressed in dark pants and shirt. A cloth was draped over his shoulders and face, leaving only his eyes exposed, the standard getup for someone riding in a sandstorm who wanted to keep the sand out of his nose.

When the other rider was about ten yards away, he reached into his pants and drew something out. Dees strained his eyes. Shit.

Hugging Pharaoh's neck, Dees bent over and dug his boots into both flanks just as the rider's gun went off. Small caliber, Dees thought with some wonder at his ability to think anything at all at this moment. The bullet made a soft *crraccking* sound. He pulled Pharaoh hard to the left, and galloped west. The horse tried repeatedly to turn toward home, but Dees kept the reins pulled toward the crepuscular glow from the vanished sun.

Head still low on the horse's neck, he glanced over his shoulder. The other rider had wheeled his horse and was following. Dees used the crop now, and Pharaoh leapt over the sand, pounding up a slight incline to another dune top. Dees pulled the animal hard to the right and almost flew down the dune side toward the pyramids.

He heard another light *crraacck*, a noise he wouldn't even have noticed if it hadn't been someone shooting at him. Glancing over his shoulder again, he saw the figure still behind him. He thought his heart was about to explode, since pot always increased his heart rate anyway. Great. I'm Ichabod fucking Crane being chased by the headless horseman. Or a headless horse. That was it. He'd kill the guy, and put his horse's head on his bed. Godfather six, Cardinals four, bottom of the seventh.

Dees wasn't a bad rider, even stoned and free-associating. He tugged the right rein and turned the horse again, galloping parallel to the pyramids, south of the Sphinx, toward the stables.

He looked behind again in time to see the wink of the pistol flash. He braced himself but nothing happened. The other rider was a shitty shot, he decided. The wind whistled past his ears as Pharaoh lunged forward, driven by the desire to get to the barn.

Dees could barely make out a jury-rigged guardrail about twenty yards ahead. He waited, waited, waited . . . then jerked the left rein and slapped the crop as hard as he could. The horse abruptly turned left with almost enough force to throw him off the saddle.

As Pharaoh began to pound ahead again, Dees heard a crash, followed by the sound of a ton of horse slamming to the bottom of a thirty-foot pit excavated where workmen had dumped their trash three thousand years ago.

He pulled up the reins. Stopped, all he could hear was his own heart and the gurgling, labored breathing of a fatally injured animal. Quickly, then, he urged Pharaoh into a gallop. They were back at the stables within ten minutes. Another ten minutes of arguing with reluctant stable hands, and another ten-minute ride, put Dees and three Egyptians back at the excavation.

Two flashlight beams penetrated the hole's darkness. The horse was silent, but wild-eyed with pain.

"We must get it out," one Egyptian said.

"No," another said, "we must shoot it."

The third Egyptian didn't say a word. Dees looked into the pit. The rider was gone.

It took three hours for the police to finish their questions and fill out the paperwork. The U.S. embassy was notified, but never sent anyone. After the authorities were satisfied that Dees's work permit was in order, that he was a *sahafi* working in Cairo, and that he was not drunk, he was allowed to go.

Finally, after trudging up the three flights to his flat, Dees wasn't terribly surprised to see the lock jimmied. He went inside to what looked like a scene in the aftermath of a tornado. His mattress was upended, bookshelves emptied, food from the shelves scattered on the floor, contents of the refrigerator piled and splattered on the linoleum.

The fridge had been pulled from the wall. The foil-wrapped "Lamb Patties" package was gone.

He expected to find the same scene at the office. When he got there a half hour later, he wasn't disappointed. His desk drawer had been twisted by a crowbar. The lock lay five feet away. The laptop was gone, along with a fax machine and two TV monitors.

Dees swore under his breath. A perfectly good pot buzz wasted.

JULY 14, WASHINGTON, D.C.

The only sound in the room was a hiss, an antiseptic sigh, like air being let out of a tire, as one still image after another appeared on the screen. Dennis Kingen nodded at the young technician who had been testing the system. It worked.

Suits from State and the SecDef's office, from the Company and the DIA and NSC, were spread out in the dark in chairs around the conference table. Kingen stood at a small podium in front and off to one side.

The room was in the basement of a nondescript Capitol Hill brownstone. It was code-named the DMZ, as in demilitarized zone, as in neutral ground, since it wasn't at Langley or the Pentagon or the White House or State. The walls were filled with three feet of soundproofing, laced with mesh-fine wires with just enough current of various frequencies pulsing through them to frustrate any listening devices. The walls were painted a mossy green, and had all the charm, Kingen believed, of a dentist's office.

"This is the Hammurabi Division," he said. "The tanks are circled, positioned for defense, turrets pointing out. The same is true for the other two divisions. We figure roughly one hundred thousand men in all, and around fifteen hundred tanks. It seems to be their entire arsenal of T-72s, about a thousand of them."

He paused. The satellite images were snapshot quality, crisp edges, plainly visible individual turrets. All the armor and men were arrayed a dozen miles north of the border with Kuwait.

A voice came from the Joint Chiefs' seat. "Maneuvers?"

Kingen said, "Probably not. It would be unusual to commit three elite divisions and their most modern armor just for maneuvers, especially in light of their dispute with Kuwait over debt forgiveness. The Kuwaitis want the cash they loaned Iraq during the Tanker War, and they want it now. The Iraqis are furious. They're also accusing Kuwait of slant-drilling across the border into Iraqi oil fields."

A voice drifted from State's chair. "All that involved diplomacy, which is out of your ballpark."

Kingen waited for a rebuttal from his boss, nestled in the chair reserved for the DIA. None came. He could barely make out the silhouette of the body in the State chair. Tall, on the thin side, with the kind of George Bush receding hairline that hinted of patrician connections stretching from the Ivy League to Foggy Bottom. Kingen's fieldwork over two and a half decades admitted him to the circle, even though his curriculum vitae showed nothing more distinguished than Ole Miss.

After clearing his throat, Kingen said, "Diplomacy certainly is out of my ballpark, sir, but analyzing the motives behind this deployment is my job. Saddam is a predictable poker player. He never bluffs. He's been reminding his people for weeks that Kuwait used to be Iraq's nineteenth province. He's short of cash. He's angry with Kuwait. He wants their oil, which would give him twenty percent of the world's total."

"Actually, nineteen point seven percent." It was State again. "But that is not the issue. The issue is what we do about an inter-Arab dispute."

Silence. Kingen prepared to speak, but State beat him to it. "We have already instructed Ambassador Glaspie to treat this as such. She has been told to tell Saddam his quarrels with a neighbor are of no concern to the United States."

Another voice came out of the darkness from the CIA chair. "A potential invasion of one of the world's most oil-rich states is not the concern of the United States? Bullshit."

Kingen rocked softly on his heels. The latest picture, covering a large area, showed the three Iraqi divisions coiled like three neat lines on a ship's deck. The angle was wide enough to show the Kuwaiti border, twelve or so miles to the south.

State's leather chair squeaked. "Saddam is our counterweight to Iran," the man said, as if explaining addition to a difficult child. "He needs this kind of latitude to flex his muscles. He won't attack. Number one, he owes us for the satellite photos and every other asset we funneled to him during the war with Iran. Number two, he knows we reflagged those Kuwaiti tankers two years ago to get oil past the Ayatollah's missiles. Both he and the emir are clients, of a sort. This is a purely Arab conflict—lots of noise, no fight."

More silence. Finally, a voice from the SecDef chair. "Dennis?"

"What you see is what we have," he said. "My analysis? Uncertain. But if Saddam's doing this to make noise, he could make a racket all the way to Riyadh."

JULY 14, CAIRO

"It is a great shame," Nasir the cameraman said, clucking his tongue as he watched Dees phone Phoenix with the theft report.

"It is an awful thing," Abdullah the sound man said.

Dees nodded absently. Volga was on the other end of the phone. Dees was just about finished. "And a fax machine, Panasonic."

"Anything else?" Volga asked.

"I think that's it."

"Any computer equipment?"

"Nope," Dees said flatly.

Silence. "So," Volga finally said, "editing gear, a TV set, a VCR, and the fax machine. Nothing else is missing?"

Dees's jaw clenched. "Everything else is here."

Silence again. "I see," eventually came from the receiver. "It seems the bureau's out of business for now."

"We can still shoot," Dees said. "I can go to Video Cairo and rent some more equipment."

"Don't bother. Just take your passport to the Iraqi embassy soonest. There's a visa there for you."

"Why?"

"Because you're going to Baghdad."

"Where?"

"Iraq. Baghdad. It's the capital."

"Funny," Dees said.

"Get there soonest. I mean it." Volga hung up.

Dees cradled the receiver and turned to the Egyptians. "We cannot work without equipment. You might as well go home. I will call you when you need to come back in."

Nasir and Abdullah tried to look mournful but didn't quite succeed. "It is a shame," the cameraman said.

"As you've said." Dees nodded. "Enjoy the time with your families. By the way," he added as Nasir's hand reached for the doorknob, "where is Saed?"

Nasir looked at Abdullah. Abdullah stared back. Dees bet himself a Stella Export after work that Nasir would speak first.

It was Abdullah who said, "Saed called me. He is ill. It seems like the flu. He is having trouble breathing."

"I'll call you both when we can work again," he said. "Good-bye."

They left. Dees waited ten minutes, then walked to the U.S. embassy. He presented his passport and half an hour later went into the press attaché's office.

"Peter," George Dobson said, "you okay?"

Dobson was the press attaché, in charge of liaison work with U.S. journalists and of handing out press releases detailing the latest in billions of U.S. aid every year to Egypt. A former wire service reporter, Dobson was honest, helpful, and totally out of place at a United States embassy.

"I'm fine," Dees said, "except for a murder attempt and a robbery. Just fine."

Dobson smiled.

Dees said, "I need a favor."

"Who doesn't?"

"I need a secure phone line to Washington."

Dobson looked quizzical.

"Don't worry," Dees said, "I only need to handle some things that I can't at the office since the theft. It'll take maybe a half hour."

Dobson pointed to a phone in the corner. "That one's mine," he said. "Direct, courtesy of Uncle Sugar. Bypasses the 'Gypto operators."

Dees looked at him. Thinning black hair going gray, tobacco-stained fingers. Himself in a few years? "You're decent for a government asshole," he said.

"I know." Dobson grinned. "But don't take too long. I have a cocktail reception downstairs now. It'll take about twenty or thirty minutes. Since I'm not supposed to leave you here, I'll lock the door. Just be finished when I get back, and I'll take that Stella you were about to offer."

He left and locked the door from the outside.

Dees picked up the phone's receiver and punched in the overseas code for the United States, followed by Washington, D.C., followed by a number he had committed to memory, in case he ever needed it.

Two rings. "Kingen."

"Dees."

"Well," said the voice on the other end, *"savah akirr."*

"Savah anool," Dees replied, using the greeting that Egyptians alone in the Arabic world used. "How did you—"

"My business to know," Kingen said. "You've been there about a month, and if the visa goes through, you'll be in Baghdad in a few days."

"Busy, aren't we? Since you know so much, who'll win the Super Bowl this year? I need the cash."

"Giants," Kingen said. "Over either the Bills or Dolphins. Now that you know your uncle can fix football games, what else do you want?"

Dees paused. "How secure is this line?"

"Depends on where you're calling from, and what you want to say."

"From the embassy, and plenty. More than plenty."

"From there, I doubt our friends in Cairo could intercept it. Can't promise much on this end."

Dees lit a cigarette, found a crushed Coke can in a wastebasket, and used it as an ashtray. "I'll chance it. I have some information. I need more."

"Quid pro quo," Kingen said. "He gives as good as he gets."

In three minutes Dees sketched the barest details that were on the disk, the break-ins at both the office and his apartment, and the shooting incident.

For moments there was only the phone line's hiss to entertain Dees as he lit another cigarette. The office door's lock rattled, and Dobson came in, saw Dees smoking, and raised both his palms. Dees put his thumb and index finger together, the Arabic gesture for "just a minute."

Finally Kingen spoke. "Whose office are you in?"

"The PAO's. He just came in."

"Put him on."

Dees motioned Dobson over and handed him the phone. The public affairs officer didn't have a chance to say a word. He only listened, his brow occasionally furrowing. After a few minutes he hung up. He did not look pleased.

"I don't know what's going on," Dobson said, "but it seems I have my orders. Follow me."

They walked down three floors, along a corridor, past a Marine sentry, and entered a room Dobson accessed by swiping his ID card through a slot and rapidly punching a series of numbers into a wall-mounted keypad. The room contained three telephones, a table, and three chairs.

"Sit," Dobson said. "I'll be back. You leave this room, and that bad-ass Ozark jarhead outside shoots you through the head. You have a phone call."

One of the phones beeped, twice. Dobson picked it up, listened, handed the receiver to Dees, then left the room.

Kingen's voice sounded squeaky, almost like he'd inhaled helium. "Don't talk. Listen. Until whatever grease your boss has gets you into Baghdad, you have a problem. Until then, you also have a house guest. His name's Salah. Your friend the PAO is upset because he just got the hint that Salah works for us, not State.

"This pretty well blows his cover, but he was scheduled to transfer anyway. He sticks to you like glue until you're safely out of country. He'll do anything you want except leave you alone."

"Hold it," Dees said. He felt a little dizzy. "What about—"

"I said listen. All I can say is you may have something."

There was another long pause. Dees ground out his cigarette in a big square ashtray near the phone and lit another.

The line hissed to life again. "Sit on it," Kingen said. "You told me a couple of things I didn't know. I'll return the favor soon enough when I find out a few things myself. But I think you're going to be very busy, for the next few weeks anyway."

"So you know more than you told me in Haiti. Well, remember, this is only another robbery, Dennis."

Kingen said, very quietly, "You could be dead in a week. Maybe less. And I know more now than I did then. But believe me this is much bigger than Marmelstein."

"But who—"

"I don't know. It's a pretty big who, is all I'm sure of."

The line went dead, and almost simultaneously the door opened. Dobson came in, followed by an Egyptian roughly the size of a linebacker, dressed in jeans, a polo shirt, and a sport coat.

Dobson frowned. "You're a nice guy," he said to Dees, "but this is it for us. You're in the hands of a higher authority now. Meet Salah Gheta."

Into the deepening dusk, Dees stalked down the sidewalk, Salah beside him. "It looks like we're roommates," Dees said.

"It means only we will both be leaving Egypt soon."

Dees stared at him quizzically.

"Dual national," the Egyptian said. "My home's in Bethesda."

As they walked toward Zamalek, they passed the GTV bureau. It was dark now, and when Dees looked up, he saw the bureau's lights were on.

He started to go up the steps, stopped, and turned to Salah. "If I ask you to do something, are you supposed to do it?"

"Within reason."

"What's reasonable?"

"I'll know it when I see it," Salah said.

They walked up the three flights of stairs. Dees put his key in the lock, turned it, and started to go in when Salah put a hand on his chest and strode in first.

Dees followed. Saed, seated at Dees's desk, looked up in surprise. His face was swollen so that his right eye was almost shut. His left arm hung uselessly at his side in a splint. Under his shirt Dees could see what looked like a giant bandage wrapped around him.

"Ah, Mister Peter," Saed said thickly. Dees could see two of his front teeth were chipped. "I was sitting here because this chair is more comfortable than mine. Larger."

Dees stared at Saed, looked at Salah, then back at Saed. "What happened? Abdullah said you had the flu. You get mugged by a virus?"

"I did not tell Abdullah I had the flu," Saed said, as indignantly as he could through chipped teeth. "I said I had a fall."

Dees and Salah stood over the desk. "From where?"

"From the roof of my house. My wife wanted me to put up a television antenna. I fell."

"You know what I think?" Dees said. "I think you fell off a horse. I think you fell a long way off a horse."

"A horse?" Saed said, mustering a look of injured innocence. "I have not ridden a horse—"

"For a couple of days," Dees said. He turned to Salah. "Would you mind taking out your gun and putting the barrel between this gentleman's eyes?"

Salah thought a moment, then said, "Sounds reasonable."

In a fluid movement he pulled a .45 automatic from a holster in the back of his pants and pressed the barrel into Saed's forehead, just above his nose.

"Saed," Dees said, "this fine specimen of Egypto-American manhood will blow your brains out and will get away with it unless you answer some questions."

Saed's eyes crossed as he tried to look at the gun's barrel. "This is an outrage. You cannot do this. Why?"

"Salah," Dees said, "if this piece of camel turd says one more word, I would be most grateful if you would kill him."

"Sounds reasonable," Salah said, and thumbed the hammer of the .45 back with a soft click.

"Now then," Dees said, lighting a cigarette, "if you say anything except the answers I want, you will be dead, *hamdulallah.* It was you who shot at me, yes?"

Saed looked at the gun barrel again, then at Dees. "Yes." His voice quavered.

"Why?"

No answer. Salah pressed the barrel harder into his forehead. He barked at Saed in Egyptian. Saed's eyes grew wide.

"I told him," Salah said, "that my arm is growing tired, and I would rather shoot him now so I can rest it."

Dees shrugged. "Oh hell, just kill him."

"No!" Saed said. "I was paid. Five thousand dollars U.S. Cash."

Dees stared. So did Salah. "Well?" Dees asked.

Saed smiled slightly. At least Dees thought it was a smile. Through the bruises and scrapes it could have been a grimace. "It is something you do not wish to know," Saed lisped through his damaged teeth.

"That's it," Dees said, turning his back. "I can't stand the sight of blood."

"Keeping me alive is worth more to you than killing me," Saed said. "I may be able to help—"

"*Mafeesh!*" Dees said as he turned on his heel. "Zero! The end! Tell me the answer to every question I ask you or I swear to God this guy will shoot you."

Salah nodded his head slightly.

Saed stared at the pistol again. "I need to show you something," he said, "in my desk." He indicated his desk by the French doors.

"I'll get it," Dees said.

"I would prefer," Saed said. "Let me get it, and this one"—indicating Salah—"can stand over me. I can barely move. And he can shoot me if I do something."

Salah raised his eyebrows. Dees said, "Salah, guide him to his desk. If he so much as sneezes, be reasonable with him."

Saed rose slowly and hobbled to the desk, sitting next to the open French doors letting out onto the balcony which overlooked the street that ran beside the rotting Nile.

Saed bent over, fiddled with the lock, and reached inside the drawer. Salah stood almost on top of him, the pistol pressed to the man's bruised temple.

Saed withdrew his hand from the drawer suddenly. Dees heard a soft *plink* at the same time Salah muttered, "Motherfucker."

In his left hand, Saed was holding something.

"A fucking grenade," Salah said in amazement, still holding his pistol aimed straight at Saed's head.

"A grenade with the pin pulled," Saed corrected.

"With the pin pulled," Salah agreed.

Saed was wearing his grimace-smile again. "The pin is in the drawer. So we all walk out when you put your gun down or I drop this and we all die."

Salah said, "Not all. Just you," and pulled the trigger. Saed's body spun violently to the right and spiraled onto the balcony. The grenade clattered to the floor.

Salah picked it up, stuffed it in Saed's pants, heaved the body over the balcony and toward the deserted sidewalk. With a *crrrumpp*, the grenade ignited. Saed seemed to bounce, a bloody entrail following him like the tail of a kite. He bounced up almost level with the second floor before landing back on the sidewalk with a plop.

Dees was bug-eyed and trying to stop hyperventilating. He started to speak, but only a dry croak came out.

"This guy was scared of someone more than he was scared of me," Salah said, going for the telephone. He spoke rapid-fire Arabic for almost five minutes, never raising his voice. Finally, he turned to Dees. "Egyptian internal security. Told them a fundamentalist tried to blow us up. Says they'll keep it as quiet as they can."

Dees tried to speak again, but still sounded like a frog.

CHAPTER 5

JULY 26, WASHINGTON, D.C.

The aroma of cigarette-smoke-impregnated clothes hung in the room. Dennis Kingen adjusted his notes. With a *hmmmm* and a hiss, an image appeared on the screen.

"There are eight Iraqi divisions in place now," he said. "The three elite units have been joined by five others. Supplies keep pouring in. They're preparing to move."

The CIA chair growled from a larnyx thickened by tobacco. "Our assessment exactly. Probable invasion of our skittish Kuwaiti friends, who wouldn't ask for help in any case for fear of offending Iraq."

State snorted. "In around two hours our ambassador meets with Saddam. Her orders are clear. This is an inter-Arab dispute, and the United States will not interfere."

CIA sighed. "Insane."

With a squeak, the State chair turned ever so slightly. "Really," he commented acidly. "Brave words from the people who supplied him with raw intel for eight years."

"Here it is," Dennis continued, "our assessment is Baghdad won't do much. They may take Kuwait's northern oil fields and islands, at the very most. We supported Saddam against Iran. We winked at his adventures. We were low-key when he gassed his own people. Iran is the issue, gentlemen. We're in for a penny with Saddam. We're in with a pound."

There wasn't a sound in the room except for the hum of the electronics and Kingen's cough when the CIA chair lit another cigarette.

"That does it for now," the DIA chair said, the only words he'd spoken all day. Kingen shuffled his papers as the others left.

"Dennis. Stay." The DIA chair creaked.

An aide moved to turn on the lights.

"Leave 'em off," DIA growled. The room remained in darkness.

Kingen spoke. "Any more from our friends the Italian financiers?"

DIA grunted. "Their Atlanta branch continues to funnel loans to Saddam. Nothing new there."

"For fertilizer manufacturing equipment, road building machinery, and general agriculture?"

DIA laughed. "Too cynical too young, Dennis. Fertilizers. Roads. Farms. Which means new jet turbines, ammunition, and a nifty poison gas plant in the Baghdad suburbs. Also R and D on a new generation of biologicals."

Kingen's right hand went slowly toward his throat, a small, elegant gesture as he adjusted the half Windsor on his black and red rep tie. "Anthrax?"

DIA nodded. "Last shipment to them in early 'eighty-nine from some Maryland outfit that specializes in viruses. Some others that don't seem as legal as that. The Maryland company shipped research samples with a full export license from Commerce."

DIA rose to leave. Kingen asked, "Does any of this bother you?"

"It does not bother the administration."

The room was still dark. Kingen leaned against the door, contemplating the shorter, wizened, older man. He said, " 'Say you that I have been of some service to the state, and how, in Aleppo once, I took the circumcised dog by the neck, and slew him, thus.' "

DIA nodded. "Othello. Right before he kills himself." He looked at Kingen, walked out, and closed the door. It latched with a click.

AUGUST 1–2, BAGHDAD

"To the nineteenth province of Iraq!" The heavyset man with the dark, bushy mustache weaved as he pushed the chair away from the plank table to make his toast. On the platter in front of him the crucified fish—a local dish served, literally, nailed to a wooden plank—had been reduced to a pile of oily bones. Dees, an attractive blonde, and a sallow man with large ears watched uncertainly as the Iraqi hoisted the shot glass filled with amber *irak*, a sweet, burning anise liquor.

The Americans waved their glasses in front of them and drank. The blonde poured herself another shot of the fiery liquor, and stood. "To a great American, Alferd Packer."

Biting his lip, Dees stood and clinked glasses with the blonde. "Packer. The famous American chef, who would have been delighted at this delicious meal our hosts have provided."

Smiles all around, clinking of glasses, sharp intake of breath as the *irak* was fired back. Outside, the great gray greasy Euphrates gurgled, sloshing past the wooden patio precariously attached to one of several riverfront restaurants, oozing down the shallow valley that had spawned Abraham and Nebuchadnezzar.

"This Alferd person, Miss Melinda," Jaffir, the heavyset man, said. "He is famous in America because he is a cook? That is work for women."

The Iraqi Ministry of Information contingent, headed by Jaffir, chuckled at the deft cut.

"Jaffir," the blonde said, filling her shot glass again, "Alferd Packer is famous for what he ate, not how he prepared it. Alferd Packer was trapped in the snows of Colorado on a hunting trip with other men. The snows got worse. There was no game, no animals to hunt." She paused, and drained half the shot glass. "So Alferd Packer killed his companions and ate them."

Jaffir began to speak, but Melinda Adams held up her hand. "When he went on trial, he was sentenced to hang. And the judge at the trial said, 'Alferd Packer, I'm not hanging you because you killed four good men. I'm hanging you because there are only five registered Democrats in this county and you, you voracious son of a bitch, you ate four of them.' "

Volga's prominent ears began to glow pink.

Jaffir said, "What is the point of this story?"

Dees turned and said, "I think what the lady's saying is that if you eat your friends, always beware of their friends."

"So," Jaffir said, studying his glass and Dees, ignoring Melinda, "the friend of my enemy is my enemy."

Melinda started to speak. Dees, with surprisingly gentle pressure on her arm, pushed her back into her chair while maintaining eye contact with Jaffir.

"Or as you so often say here," Dees continued, "the enemy of my enemy is my friend."

Volga had had enough. "Gentlemen and ladies," he said, pushing his chair back, "we appreciate your hospitality. But we have an early morning and many interviews."

"Of course," Jaffir said smoothly. "And as a token of our appreciation at being here, I would like you to have this."

He reached into his valise on the floor and brought out a thick paperback book with a slick cover. As he handed it to Volga, Dees saw the title: *Speeches of Saddam Hussein, Volume I.*

After many thanks, the Americans and their driver piled into the hired Mercedes and were driven toward the Baghdad Sheraton, past town houses and date palms that reminded Dees of Los Angeles.

Dees had arrived two days before. Egypt Air, Cairo to Amman, Iraqi Air, Amman to Baghdad. He got there because the phone call from Salah, the bodyguard, to the U.S. embassy in Cairo led to a call to Washington, which led to a call to the Egyptian Interior and Defense ministries, which led to the conclusion that Saed had been a member of the Islamic Brotherhood and had blown himself up with a grenade that had somehow been stolen from the army. Saed's two cousins at the Egyptian Ministry of Information—one of whom actually was a supporter of the Brotherhood and who actually had given Saed the grenade, months before as a souvenir from a Brotherhood theft at an army depot—were detained and questioned. One was released. The other confessed his Brotherhood activities after electric shocks were judiciously applied in the basement of a Cairo police station, and died in custody within a day.

When Dees arrived in Baghdad, he was dismayed to find Volga and a dozen other GTV producers, technicians, cameramen, and reporters, and delighted to find that one of them was Melinda Adams.

Several times Dees asked Volga why GTV was in Iraq, of all places, with so many people. Several times Volga replied with terse epigrams about producing live television that "would put GTV on the map" by "exploring the inside of Iraq."

They drove past a thirty-foot-tall mural of Saddam in a topcoat and fur hat, his hand extended in a cross between a sieg heil and a wave, Saddam as Stalin reviewing the troops in snowy Red Square. Down the street was another mural of Saddam smiling, wearing a guayabera, Saddam as Fidel. Saddam's Ba'ath party employed four intelligence services, Dees knew. Three spied on the military, the government, and the general population. The fourth spied on the other three. And all of them had their hooks into the GTV contingent. Word was, for days before the visas were approved the Interior and Defense ministries had been fighting over who would actually keep tabs on the foreign *sahafis*.

Volga led the other two into the GTV work space on the fifth floor. It was deserted. He slapped a CD into the portable player and blasted Stevie Ray Vaughn's *Greatest Hits* through the Fostex speakers.

Volga motioned Dees and Melinda to come close. "Listen," he hissed, "the only reason I don't send both of you home now is that it took too much leverage to get you here in the first place. But for now . . ."

He paused as the CD ended one song and held a finger to his lips. A wailing blues note soared from the speakers and hurtled out the window, echoing off the walls of a city that had been ancient when the first pyramid block had been laid in place on the banks of the Nile. Then Volga continued softly.

"For now, no melodrama. No games. You say one thing that offends this government, and I guarantee that the very best thing that happens is that you'll be behind a basement desk in Phoenix forever."

He looked from one to the other and strode out of the room. Melinda wrinkled her nose. "No style," she sniffed.

She turned and glared at Dees as he walked to the door, closed it, and dropped the dead bolt.

"And you, cowboy," she said as he walked back, "don't ever lay hands on me like that, don't ever try to shut me up, don't—"

"You're drunk," Dees said, clutching her elbow and steering her onto the balcony. "Besides, you were just trying to piss them off."

"So were you," she said, gripping the balcony railing. "Trying to piss them off, I mean." She thought for a moment and nodded. "And drunk, too."

"But drunk with a good deal more style," he said, bending over, removing a plastic sack from his boot, taking out one of two joints, and replacing the small sack while Melinda stared, "than a pissant twenty-six-year-old with just enough Arabic to honk off every minder they give us. You're smart. You're beautiful. You speak their lingo. They hate that, and you went out of your way to make them even madder, so I decided to take the fall and have them mad at me instead, which they already are."

He stoked the marijuana with his lighter, sucking in a lungful, then releasing it to mix with drifting smells of cardamom, lamb, diesel fumes, sweat, and dust, all floating free above the streets where every man and woman was locked in fear. They lived under surveillance from the intelligence agencies, Ba'ath party members, and sometimes, it seemed, from the posters of Saddam himself.

"I'll tell you why they were already mad at me," Dees said. "Because when I arrived at the airport, Khalid, the skinny one, asked me, 'Are you an American spy?' with that greasy smile of his, and I did my Elmer Fudd. 'Shh, be vewy, vewy quiet. I'm hunting Iwaqis. Hahahahahaha.' "

Melinda didn't want to laugh, and managed only to make a sputtering sound between her lips. Dees looked at her, smiled, sucked up the remaining half of the joint in one toke, held it, exhaled, and popped the still glowing roach in his mouth.

"You are an astonishing asshole," she observed. "They'll cut your balls off and stuff them in your mouth for that here, and toss the rest of us out."

"That won't happen," Dees said, "because they want us here for some reason. And we've been told to softball them all the way."

Melinda nodded. "And in two weeks here we've done—"

"Squat."

"Except I've noticed between the dipshit features, you've asked a lot of questions about trade. I mean, who gives a shit about trade with Europe and the States and Egypt, for chrissakes?"

She was drunk and beautiful. He closed one eye. "Can you keep a secret?"

She stared at him. "Undying lust?"

"Better," he replied, and moved closer so he could speak softly.

In five minutes he sketched the disk's contents, filling her in about Dick, Tigwo, his almost fatal horseback ride, Saed, and his phone conversation with Kingen.

The CD ended. Dees opened the sliding glass door, recued the music, and let the white boy's blues wail from the speakers. He left the door open when he stepped back outside.

"Confuses any listening devices they might aim at us up here," he said.

"So," he whispered, leaning so close he could smell a scent both sharp and musky, and wondering how much of it was her and how much was cologne, "we're locked-down here, sucking up to this government, and I'm looking for anything that would confirm any of this. I need help. Just information. We . . ."

He paused for half a second. We? Where the hell did that come from? "We," he continued, "couldn't do anything until we're well out of here. Volga knows something, I think. He knows the computer was stolen, I'm pretty sure, even though I never mentioned it. He's cagey. Burke's office had a pile of Haitian voodoo clips, maybe the ones for Dick. So is Burke involved with what was in the computer? Now Kingen tells me this involves more than one dead man. So far, I count three.

"The secret's here someplace, I figure. Dick wanted to get to the Middle East. He mentioned Baghdad and Cairo. Maybe if we find out what's going on, we find out why he died."

He looked toward the horizon, and leaned next to her against the railing. "Besides, they have to be stopped from selling this shit."

She glanced sideways again. "Who's they?"

He shrugged, and looked at his watch. Half past midnight. He stretched. "C'mon," he said, "time to rack. Just think about it. Tomorrow's probably a busy day doing more meaningful stories about Iraq's place in the modern world. Tomorrow? I mean today," he corrected himself. "It's August second already."

AUGUST 2, NORTHEAST KUWAIT

Rasheed al-Sabah was a third cousin of Kuwait's ruler, but an al-Sabah nevertheless, so he would end up a staff officer, a colonel at least, for being blood-related to the band of Bedouin traders who originally signed the deal with British petroleum companies back in the days known in the West as the roaring twenties, back in the days when Kuwait had to import even the oil that tribesmen used in their lamps.

But first he would have to put in his time commanding this British-made tank facing the pathetic seacoast town of Uum Qasr, not two kilometers over the border inside Iraq.

Rasheed regarded the Iraqis as poor cousins, much like the old American television show of which he had collected almost every videotaped episode. The Iraqis were like the Beverly Hillbillies—crude bumpkins.

The noise on the tank's radio crackled through the chilly night air. Even in August the desert is cold at night. "Breakthrough! Breakthrough!"

There was a hiss of static, and the signal went dead at the same moment Rasheed saw a flash, maybe a thousand meters away, followed by the thump and concussion of an explosion. He could hear people yelling, faintly. He thought he heard a distant scream, but it could have been noise in his headset.

Five hundred meters up the blacktopped road, a car exploded, a fireball that shot into the air like a breath of flame exhaled by a circus fire eater, pulsating until it disappeared, casting a brief, hot light over a line of tanks that shimmered in the reflected blast, grinding straight for Rasheed's position.

Rasheed keyed the intercom. "Full power! Ninety degrees right turn now! Turret transverse one-eight-zero! Now!"

The tank, which had been idling, erupted in a blast of diesel smoke as it pulled from the sandy shoulder and headed south, away from the incoming tanks. The turret smoothly rotated until the Chieftain's 120mm gun faced the flames at the tank's rear.

Rasheed thought about firing a round at the Iraqis while he was trying to get away. Maybe he knew firing a round would illuminate his position. Maybe he thought he should fire anyway. Maybe he didn't know what he thought as he saw two muzzle flashes and felt the concussion from a shell that landed about twenty meters away and to his right. Then he felt a rush of scorching heat as the second armor-piercing 125mm shell tore through the Chieftain's inadequate rear armor and detonated.

Rasheed's torso was incinerated and tossed free from the tank. His legs burned like two logs inside the turret, which was catapulted fifteen meters by the force of the blast. An Iraqi T-72 gunned its twelve-cylinder diesel engine and shoved the remaining wreckage aside. It ground along at the head of an armored column toward the Al Muttwa ridge, where the four-lane highway temporarily shrank down to two lanes before opening up again and becoming four lanes of cement and hard-packed macadam, a superhighway running straight into Saudi Arabia.

WASHINGTON, D.C.

Dennis Kingen motioned toward the five-foot-high monitor at the rear of the room that smelled of people roused from sleep. No soap. No aftershave. Just a stale aroma of interrupted dreams and unbrushed teeth. "This is real-time, or as close as possible. These images were recorded fifteen minutes ago."

The coils of the Iraqi tank divisions had unwound. "They've taken Kuwait City. Some fires along the northern border, but mostly they've walked in. Advance units are already within fifteen klicks of the Saudi border. The emir has fled. Kuwait Air pilots managed to fly out four 747s from the Kuwait City airport. Three are heading to Cairo. One's landed in Dhahran.

"They've taken Bubiyan Island. They're using massive force, tank battalions from the north, amphibious landing supported by several squadrons of attack helicopters.

"The embassies are surrounded, but no effort has been made to move inside them. Radio traffic indicates an almost flawless operation. Only token resistance from the Kuwaitis."

He paused as a light flashed on a phone console mounted on the side of the podium. He picked up the receiver, nodded, listened, and put it down.

"We have a report that a squadron of Kuwaiti Tornadoes has landed in Dhahran. No confirmation yet."

No one spoke for a full minute.

CHAPTER 6

AUGUST 24, BAGHDAD

Machmoud Shafir, B.A. Northwestern, MBA Wharton, dribbled the basketball, shifting it from one hand to the other, getting pleasure from the *thunk* it made on the blacktopped court—all the while staring at the American guarding him.

"Ah, Mister Peter," he said, deliberately using the form of address common in the Middle East, but one he never used now that he'd lived in the States for a decade, the last of which he'd spent in the banking centers of Chicago's LaSalle Street. "Mister Peter, I am going to show you why a slam dunk is worth three points in this country."

Dees, sweating, tired, and giving up a good six inches to the lanky Iraqi, spoke while keeping his gaze intently on the ball. "Camel boy, you jam on me and I'll buy you dinner in Kuwait City once you get me there."

Dees and Shafir had met a week before, when Shafir was assigned to GTV as a driver. The young man had been visiting his parents in Al Hillah, sixty miles south of Baghdad, just as the invasion came. The authorities refused to let him go back to Chicago and take his new job in international accounts at Harris Bank. Instead, because of his excellent English, he was hustled off to Baghdad to work with and keep an eye on the foreign *sahafis*.

Staggering home with Dees one night from the usual crucified fish and *irak*, Shafir had first been shocked, then delighted, when Dees took him to the GTV work space, locked the door, stuffed a towel between the door and floor, and produced his last joint from the sock pouch. He and Dees had been inseparable ever since; when his own minder from the intelligence services told him he was spending too much time with the Americans, Shafir smoothly replied that it was the only way to gather information, and he proceeded to pass on innocuous tidbits every day.

"Mister Peter," Shafir said mockingly, "fuck you." He faked left, drove right, and leapt, extending himself full-length, reaching over the shorter American and preparing to stuff the ball, barely, over the rim, when he felt the air leave his lungs with a *whoof*. He twisted in midair, landing on his side, the ball bouncing off the rim and back onto the blacktop.

Dees stood over him. "Shit. I think I may have fouled you. Let me see."

He picked up Shafir's arm, examined it, looked at his head and said, "Nope. No blood, no foul."

"That's illegal." Shafir glared.

"Yeah, and so's invading your neighbor. Just remember, pal, youth and energy are no match for age and treachery."

Shafir winced. "And a knee to the balls."

"Moi?" Dees looked incredulous. "No way. It was an elbow."

Shafir got up, and both men trudged toward the car Shafir used to ferry the GTV crew around town, and for which the Iraqi government charged other news organizations five hundred U.S. a day, but which GTV received free. Dees had tried to figure that out, but Volga muttered something about "GTV's global reach," and "planetary access for the Iraqis," then told him to mind his own business.

Shafir started the car, rolled up the windows, turned on the air-conditioning, and turned the radio up, loud. He figured, correctly, that being in a sealed, noisy, moving car was the one sure way to avoid any eavesdropping. Plus Dees had had a pair of GTV satellite technicians, under the guise of admiring the mechanics and handiwork of the Egyptian-made Ford, go over the thing from headlights to trunk. They were fairly sure no bugs were planted in it, unless they were buried in the seat cushions. Tuning to Baghdad's English-language rock station at full volume was the insurance policy against that possibility.

They drove past the al-Rasheed Hotel, used now as a clearinghouse for Western hostages—or "special guests," as the Iraqis called them. Various American, Canadian, British, and French nationals—all men—who worked for various enterprises doing business in Iraq were held there before being shipped out to various chemical, electrical generating, or steel plants. The human shields were supposed to deter any air attack by the hundreds of planes that were rolling into Saudi Arabia from a dozen countries, but mostly from the United States. Add that to the thousands of troops, and the biggest movement of people and matériel since Vietnam was under way.

"So," Dees said, staring at the al-Rasheed, "any word on us getting to interview the guests?"

"My cousin at Project 9230 says because we are GTV, we may have a chance," Shafir replied.

Project 9230 was the once-secret code name for a chemical facility at Al Fallujah, forty miles west of Baghdad. Dees wondered why Arabs all seemed to have a cousin somewhere, doing something, with some government.

"But," Shafir added quickly, "I want out of here before I end up in the army."

Dees studied the younger man. He was clean-shaven, unlike most Iraqi men old enough to shave, who sported bushy mustaches, much like Saddam's. The unspoken fear ran so deep in Iraq that grown men were terrified of standing out, so they all imitated the maximum ruler. Dees wanted to sell razors in this country if Saddam ever decided to shave.

He sighed. "And I'm supposed to do what? Smuggle you out on a ten-hour drive to Jordan? The best chance you've got is with us. You're valuable to GTV. And we're valuable to Saddam. So stick with us, and Volga can probably keep you out of uniform."

They drove in silence. Shafir looked sideways at Dees, started to speak but didn't, and kept driving. Dees felt tired. He still had the disk, hidden inside the mattress in his room, a corner near a seam slit with a pair of scissors and the disk inserted.

Great. And it was doing him exactly how much good? He hadn't heard from Kingen in the weeks since he'd arrived in Iraq. He had been filing two stories a day, plus dozens of live shots, on unfolding events. He still had no idea how he would fill in the holes to use the thing. His brain felt packed in cotton.

They arrived at the Sheraton, where another minder with another bushy mustache was waiting in the lobby.

"Mister Peter," he said, "we are to leave now. We are to go to Al Fallujah. The ministry has decided you may speak to our guests."

Peter grinned. So did Shafir. Dees slapped Shafir a high five, and was immediately sorry he'd done it. The lobby minder glared, and other journalists lounging in the area looked sour.

A woman from Agence France-Presse stormed over. She had dark hair, blazing dark eyes, and hairy armpits, and needed a shower. But what the hell, Dees thought, everybody was stinking at the moment.

"This is most unfair," she said in the lobby minder's face. "The rest of us have asked for days to see the guests. You cannot do this."

The minder stared at her blandly. "The ministry says this is only for the GTV."

She pivoted and faced Dees. "The GTV," she sneered, "the great GTV, without one reporter who can even speak Arabic, the GTV that gets interviews we cannot get, that gets everything because of its great American connections."

"Charm," Dees said. "You forgot charm."

She pushed her face within three inches of his. "How much do you pay these people," she spit, "to get this? Your GTV apologizes for them, makes excuses for them, gets the interviews no one else gets. Why do you not just call yourselves Saddam television?"

Dees stared into her liquid eyes, smelled her acrid breath, and felt itchy all over. She gouged her index finger into his chest. Before she could open her mouth to speak, Dees grabbed the finger and twisted it. She tried to jerk her hand away, and he gave the finger one hard twist, not hard enough to dislocate the knuckle, but hard enough so that it would swell a bit the next day.

He shoved it away and said flatly, his face still close to hers, "Next time I break it."

Dees stomped upstairs to the office, found a sound technician and cameraman, grabbed a notebook, and led them out, past Volga, who sat at a computer and merely glanced sideways as the team left.

They drove fast through the ochre and tan landscape that, Dees thought with astonishment, probably had been familiar to Abraham. Within two hours the three-vehicle convoy of the GTV car and two Iraqi sedans holding three security agents arrived at Al Fallujah and were waved through the gates. The installation was surrounded by three concentric circles of ten-foot chain-link fence spaced thirty meters apart. Each was topped with razor wire. Dees noticed lumps in the sand between the fences and caught the eye of Shafir, who nodded slightly. Land mines. Dees glanced around quickly. Three buildings the size of football fields made up the complex; sunlight glinted off the muzzles of antiaircraft artillery on the flat roofs of the warehouse-type buildings.

The lead car drew up to the first building, and within seconds they were ushered inside the cool, dim interior. Trailers were parked with their sides against one long wall, and evidently provided office space and sleeping quarters. Inside one of the trailers, they found three men sitting at a table, playing cards. Hearts.

The three glared at the Iraqis who jammed themselves into the trailer ahead of the GTV crew. Dees squeezed in.

"How're you guys doing?" he asked. Silence.

"I'm Peter Dees with GlobeStar Television. We—"

"We know who you are, Mr. Dees," a heavyset man said grimly. He appeared to be in his mid-fifties and was clean-shaven, with a round, florid face topped by snow-white hair cut in a flat top. He wore a short-sleeved white shirt that seemed to be freshly pressed. There were nicotine stains between the index and middle fingers of his left hand, and he wore a wedding ring. The man glared at Dees with ice-blue eyes. "We're allowed to watch GTV every day. You do a fine job presenting the Iraqi point of view."

Dees turned to Shafir. "Get them out of here," he said, nodding toward the Iraqi security agents. "We have to put lights in here, and six people's a tight fit. Nine won't do. So take them outside. Tell them they can watch and listen through the windows if they want, but there's no room in here."

Shafir spoke in American-accented Arabic, indicating the tripod and light kit with his hands. The guards whispered between themselves, nodded, and left, Shafir trailing behind them.

"Look," Dees said, leaning over the table and staring at the heavyset American, ignoring the cameraman and sound tech, as well as the two other hostages, "you can tell us what's going on, and let us take video so your families know you're okay, or you can be a tough guy and leave them hanging, because if you want to turn this into a pissing match about GTV sucking up to the Iraqis, the Iraqi censors and my bosses will make sure not one frame of this video ever gets seen."

The American thought about it while the tripod was being unfolded and the lights arranged. He stuck out his hand. "Ben Miller from Pensacola, Florida. My colleagues, Jacques Malval from Belgium and Brian MacAdam, a Canadian. The boys in R and D used to call us the three M cartel."

"That who you work for, 3M?"

"Nope. Outfit called Archgate. Out of St. Louis."

Dees felt his heart skip a beat. He took a deep breath. "So what happened?"

Miller looked ruefully at his companions. "We were visiting the facility here on a scheduled trip when they invaded. The next thing we know, they're telling us we can't leave. Treated well enough so far. But I don't want to be here if a B-52 runs an arc light mission."

"Why should it?"

"Because this man is capable of anything," Miller said, waving his hand in a short arc, indicating the rest of the building, the rest of the country, the air itself, all personified with one motion as Saddam Hussein. "Whatever he says he'll do, he'll do.

"He used his . . . unusual military assets"—again, the entire plant was indicated, this time with a roll of Miller's eyes—"to control insurgents here and as part of the order of battle with Iran. He says he'll use them again. I believe him, and if something happens between Iraqi and Saudi or Brit or American troops, and he keeps his word, then the question 'Why should a B-52 arc light this plant?' becomes pretty absurd."

Poison gas and chemical weapons, Dees knew, had been used to kill thousands in the region around one village inside Iraq when

Saddam decided to act against Kurdish separatists. When Iranian troops were slogging across the marshes of the Shatt-al-Arab south of Basra, Iraqi artillery would pound them with a round of antipersonnel shrapnel, followed by a barrage of chemical weapons. While the panicked conscripts were trying to struggle into whatever rudimentary chemical protection had been supplied them, more antipersonnel rounds would burst overhead or just above ground level, flaying, maiming, and killing the holy warriors who hoped to use human wave attacks to bring jihad to Iraq.

Dees bent over the table, close enough to smell Miller's iron-hard cigarette breath, which, Dees reflected, was probably as unpleasant as his own.

"Look," he rasped, his face four inches from Miller's, "we have, maybe, ten minutes. The minders are outside, so if you have anything you want to say, say it now. All I can tell you is that I'm trying to expose where this shit comes from in order to stop it. I can have my guys slow down their preps, blow a bulb or something, but that's about all. I don't know when I'll be back, but we can try to get you out of here, moved if not released. But you either tell me now, and fast, or don't tell me at all."

Miller nodded, barely. Dees turned to his cameraman, and while pretending to look through the viewfinder to approve the shot's framing, whispered to the shooter to stall, fog a lens, blow out a bulb, something, but make it last ten minutes. The shooter, Pedro Marco, a burly six-foot-four, former high school wrestler from Miami, bobbed his head, then adjusted the bulb on the camera's light head, plugged it into a wall socket, and smiled when the bulb exploded with a muffled pop.

While Marco and the soundman fiddled with the bulb and made shrugging gestures toward the Iraqi security men and Shafir, waiting outside, Dees plopped into an empty chair at the table, lit a cigarette, looked at Miller, and said softly, "Now or never."

"Growth medium," Miller muttered, as the sound tech made a purposeful racket with one of his light stands. "We export it. That and some virus samples. Four years ago we start coming to Baghdad. We work with the Ministry of Health, we go to research hospitals. They're trying to fight anthrax in the sheep herds up north, and we're exporting growth media for them to culture in, plus some anthrax. Just a little. All legal, okayed by Commerce.

"Last year, Phoenix calls—"

"Phoenix?" Dees asked.

"Yeah," Miller said.

"So that's headquarters?"

Miller snorted. "I work out of my home. We all do. We get paid from St. Louis, but the return address is a P.O. box. I've never even been to St. Louis. We always get phone instructions from Phoenix."

He looked up. The guards and Shafir were fidgeting restlessly. Marco was still rattling around in his run bag, pretending to look for a new lightbulb. Miller spoke even more softly, the words coming out in a torrent.

"Not much time. Was told I'd be going to Iraq, to Salman Pak this time, straight south of Baghdad. No hospital. Big research office park. They're figuring out how to mount canisters of anthrax, and cholera, and botulism, plus some chemicals I'd never heard of, so they can be dispersed as an aerosol. Seeing how strong they can make the canisters so they'll survive an explosion, like an artillery shell or missile warhead.

"I'm shook. Even more shook when I run into my colleagues in the first class lounge in Amsterdam. I'm coming out, they're going in, and they're heading to Salman Pak, too. Turns out Archgate's shipped them all the other goodies besides anthrax through Europe.

"So I call my man in Phoenix. He sounds pissed at the Iraqis, says this is supposed to be medical only. I come back this time, pitching a new growth medium, and end up going from the Ministry of Health to here in three days. Timing sucks."

The guards outside were gesticulating. Dees glanced at Marco, who made tiny circles with his index finger, the sign to speed it up.

"So," Dees said flatly, "Iraq is making chemical and biological weapons with companies in the United States providing what they need."

Miller sighed and nodded. "But you didn't hear it—"

"From me," Dees said, "and I was never here, we never talked, and I could tell you, but I'd have to kill myself."

Miller smiled thinly. "This place. Look outside at the drums near the door where you came in. Phosphorus trichloride. That ain't for fertilizer."

Miller pulled a sweat-stained business card from his pocket. "Gimme," he said, gesturing toward Dees's pen. He wrote on the card.

"That's Phoenix. Ask for Arnie Johnson. Tell him to call my wife in Pensacola."

"Your wife'll see you on the tube within twelve hours," Dees said. The guards clattered in, and Dees glared. They stood, impassive.

"Okay, Pedro," he said, "B-roll."

"What's that?" Miller asked.

"Term left over from the film days," Dees explained as Marco shot. "A-roll was sound bites. The B-roll was just pictures. You'd edit them together. So pictures are B-roll."

Marco shot three unshaven men who said they missed their families. As they shook hands to leave, Dees whispered to Marco. The bulky cameraman, carrying his Sony nonchalantly by its carrying handle as he walked out of the plant, got six seconds of perfectly focused video of the phosphorus trichloride barrels.

Dees wrote the script on the drive back to Baghdad, spent an hour crashing an edit, and before heading to the Iraqi uplink had Shafir take him to the U.S. embassy.

Only a skeleton staff remained, but it had opened up the USIS office to journalists to phone home. The wait was relatively short, and after half an hour Dees was dictating a script over the secure line.

The Iraqis often censored pieces by fast-forwarding or freezing the video. Dees patiently explained there would be a flash frame—one frame of video, 1/32 of a second—of the chemical drums right before the countdown. They should insert it as a still over whatever the Iraqis censored. They should put any sound bites that were censored on the screen, verbatim, and use his voice phone track in case the Iraqis censored the video and his satellite audio track.

Unfolding the laptop, Dees counted to ten for a level, made sure Phoenix was rolling tape, and read instructions into the phone.

"Open with desert beauty shot. Then, medium shot plant. Then wide shot hostages. Then slo-mo the video of the chemical drums. File B-roll of the Iran-Iraq war. File video of bodies from the gas attack in Iraq two years ago. Medium shot, hostages. Sound bite, Miller, incue 'We just want . . .' outcue 'peacefully.'

"Sound bite, MacAdam, incue 'We've been treated . . .' outcue 'my wife.' File B-roll. Saddam. Dees stand-up. Medium shot plant. Repeat slo-mo of chemical drums. B-roll Allied troops in Saudi. Beauty shot, desert. Cool? Okay, script coming in three, two, one . . ."

He paused, and read from the screen:

"ABRAHAM MAY HAVE LED THE ORIGINAL EXODUS FROM BABYLON TO ISRAEL ACROSS THIS

DESERT. BUT THESE SANDS ARE HOME TO SOMETHING FAR MORE MODERN . . . A CHEMICAL PLANT OPERATED BY SADDAM HUSSEIN'S GOVERNMENT. THE IRAQIS CLAIM IT PRODUCES FERTILIZER.

"INSIDE, THREE OF WHAT IRAQ CALLS SPECIAL GUESTS. THEY ARE HUMAN SHIELDS AGAINST ANY AIR ATTACK. WHY SHOULD THE ALLIES BOMB A FERTILIZER PLANT? THE ANSWER IS INSIDE THESE DRUMS. THEY CONTAIN PHOSPHORUS TRICHLORIDE. THAT CHEMICAL IS NOT USED FOR FERTILIZER. IT IS USED TO MAKE SARIN . . . ONE OF THE DEADLIEST NERVE GAS AGENTS KNOWN.

"IRAQ HAS USED NERVE GAS AND CHEMICAL WEAPONS IN THE PAST . . . AGAINST INVADING TROOPS FROM IRAN . . . AND AGAINST ITS OWN PEOPLE. AN IRAQI VILLAGE OF KURDS WAS WIPED OUT IN 1988 BY AN IRAQI CHEMICAL ATTACK.

"THESE MEN HAVE BECOME PAWNS IN IRAQ'S GAME TO PROTECT A FACILITY THAT APPARENTLY MANUFACTURES THOSE SAME KINDS OF CHEMICALS."

Dees paused. "Insert sound bite of Miller, butted up against sound bite of MacAdam. Script resumes in three, two, one.

"SADDAM HUSSEIN HAS PROMISED TO UNLEASH THE MOTHER OF ALL WEAPONS AGAINST ALLIED TROOPS.

"Insert Dees stand-up here."

The script for the stand-up, the third take, a walking shot

that had Dees walk ten steps across the desert and stop, while the camera slowly zoomed over his shoulder toward the barely visible plant in the distance, read "THE DESERT IN IRAQ WAS SUPPOSED TO BLOOM WITH THE PRODUCTION OF FERTILIZERS BY SADDAM'S GOVERNMENT. BUT ALL THAT'S BLOOMED IN THIS REMOTE STRETCH OF ROCK AND SAND IS A FACILITY THAT MAY BE USED NOT TO MAKE LIFE BETTER, BUT TO END LIFE ALTOGETHER FOR ANYONE WHO GETS IN THE REGIME'S WAY."

Dees paused. "Back to track, three, two, one:

"CHEMICALS LIKE PHOSPHORUS TRICHLORIDE ARE HARMLESS ENOUGH BY THEMSELVES. THEY'RE CALLED PRECURSOR CHEMICALS. IN THIS CASE, THE PRECURSOR OF ONE OF THE DEADLIEST NERVE AGENTS KNOWN TO MAN.

"THE ALLIES BELIEVE PLANTS LIKE THIS . . . POSSIBLY MAKING THE SAME TYPES OF WEAPONS . . . ARE SCATTERED AROUND THIS COUNTRY. THEY KNOW IF THE WORST HAPPENS, AND WAR ERUPTS, THE ALLIED TROOPS GATHERING IN SAUDI ARABIA COULD BE TARGETS OF NERVE AND CHEMICAL WEAPONS.

"THEY MIGHT NOT RULE OUT AIR RAIDS AGAINST THESE PLANTS. AND USING HOSTAGES IS ONE WAY THE IRAQI REGIME CAN MAKE SURE THOSE RAIDS ARE NEVER LAUNCHED, AND THAT WHAT SADDAM HUSSEIN HAS PLANTED IN THIS DESERT CONTINUES TO GROW. PETER DEES, GTV NEWS, NEAR BAGHDAD."

Shafir drove Dees back to the hotel. They picked up Marco, the tape, and a portable Sony model 35 beta tape player. Iraqi TV still used 3/4-inch tapes, so anyone who wanted to feed the smaller, more modern, and almost universally used beta tapes had to bring their own feed machine.

At the first mention of the phosphorus trichloride drums, an Iraqi censor's finger hit the pause button on the 35, as expected. He shuttled the tape forward to the hostages, listened to their sound bites, re-wound the tape, and let the B-roll of their captivity and their innocuous bites feed. Dees's stand-up was stopped a third of the way through. The end of the piece was not allowed to feed.

While the censor screamed at Shafir, who smiled, stammered, sweated, and repeated the high-volume objections to Dees in English, the producer supervising incoming feeds at GTV in Phoenix saw what had happened, and reassembled the story, using Dees's telephone voice track, file B-roll of Saddam and Allied troops, and the flash frame over what the Iraqis had censored about the chemical drums.

The piece, along with the tape of the interrupted feed, went to the supervising producer, who decided to run them both. A writer scripted copy for the anchor, who told the audience they were about to see two tapes. GTV ran the original feed, showing Iraqi censorship. They then ran the story as it would have appeared if it had been allowed to feed.

It all took place in the hour Dees, Shafir, and Marco were being yelled at by Iraqi censors and officials from the Ministry of Information. So by the time the tape was confiscated and the crew returned to the Sheraton, the story had just finished airing on GTV.

—

Volga saw it at the GTV work space, which, along with the hotel and all Iraqi ministries, was now equipped with a dish to downlink the network.

Volga had been scribbling in his journal. It was actually more of a screenplay, titled "Live from Iraq." He had already written the section detailing his own genius at coordinating all of GTV's coverage from, as he put it, "behind the lines of a misunderstood enemy," and was now backfilling with details of his meteoric rise inside the company.

He had started with his radio news directorship in Laredo, leading to a TV producing job in Tulsa, and how he'd applied for a writer's job at GTV at age twenty-eight.

"In five years," he wrote, "I became attuned to McKinley Burke's vision of global reach through nonjudgmental coverage of the rest of the world. It seemed natural I would be considered next in line to become head of GTV through my innovative rise to become the youngest head of international coverage of any network."

He looked up and saw Dees's story on the screen, a room service spring roll growing cold in his hand. When he saw the censored section about the chemical drums, the roll dropped from his hand. He reached for the phone.

CHAPTER 7

AUGUST 24, PHOENIX

McKinley Burke wore the Blass original, the gray with minute chalky pinstripes, for the interview with CBS. NBC got the Calvin Klein black double-breasted blazer, ABC a black Armani, *Time* a Versace dark blue single-breasted, the *New York Times* a Cardin with tiny tan checks.

Burke was totally prepared for the reaction that continued even three weeks after the invasion. GTV, alone among the American networks, and alone among the world's journalists except for the BBC, Reuters, and Agence France-Presse, was in Baghdad, carrying almost everything put out by Iraqi TV in a licensing arrangement, going live twice an hour twenty-four hours a day. GTV broadcast even when there was nothing to go live with except the latest hard information supplied by the *Washington Post*, and Burke reveled in the anguish he imagined echoing off the walls of every office of every news executive on the planet whose visa requests were being sandbagged by Baghdad.

Today, Burke was wearing a gray double-breasted job that cost two grand, made by some Japanese whose name he couldn't pronounce. He clicked a computer mouse and ran it across the pad like a miniature bumper car, stopping, starting, jerking left, then right, as he went deeper into the computer files until, buried under ten other Windows programs, he got to his private file, hidden and locked with a password that changed every day. He typed in "brie." This week's theme was cheese, since *U.S. News* had called him *"le fromage grand,* the big cheese of TV."

GTV's subscription base had swollen from 180 stations to 510 in less than ten days. GTV coverage from Baghdad was being run in the Mideast, the U.K., Italy, South Africa, and forty-seven other countries.

Using some valid statistics and some puffery, GTV's research department estimated a billion of the almost three billion people on the planet had watched the network at some time during the first three weeks of the crisis.

Burke opened a file and began to clatter the keyboard furiously. From the second day of the crisis on, he had demanded a must-carry provision in every contract, each a minimum of six months, which required each station and network to air his daily one-minute editorial a minimum of five times per day. No one who wanted GTV from Baghdad said no. "Editorial" was the last thing he wanted to call every global essay, so he settled on "EcoGeo," which GTV's research department said tested well in almost any language.

Businessmen and women from Jakarta to Santiago were terrified about their investments in Kuwait, and their demand for GTV coverage forced even reluctant network and station executives to run Saint Mac—*Le Monde's* phrase—per the contract. Every day he would appear, impeccably dressed, steel-gray hair adroitly combed, on TV sets in Riyadh and Saskatoon and Bangkok, the pink morning light making the desert behind him, shot from the balcony attached to the executive dining room at GTV Plaza, look both majestic and soothing.

The laser jet printer hissed and hummed and spewed out both

pages of this morning's essay. Burke took them and turned to face the picture window.

"We hold the earth in our hands like a fragile bird," he read, his Plains twang elongating the vowels. "The only way we will not crush it is to speak to one another.

"Birds of all nations understand each other's songs." Burke smiled. He wasn't sure if it was true, but he was pleased with the metaphor. "And we must learn to understand one another. To do that we need to know one another, and to do that, we need global communication."

He added the words "such as GlobeStar provides" as his hand began to shake. He began searching for his pills.

He was reaching into the desk drawer when the phone line blinked. "Mr. Burke, Baghdad," the voice purred through the intercom. He clicked the speakerphone and walked back to the window, still studying his lines.

"Timothy," he said, his back turned to the phone.

"Mac. Problem."

Burke's hand began to shake again. "What?"

"You watching?"

Burke hadn't glanced at any of the monitors on the far wall because of the tight taping schedule for the EcoGeo. He saw a wide shot of Iraqi desert on the GTV monitor, pushed the remote button and turned the sound up.

He listened, then froze, working his jaws so that his teeth ground. Volga's voice crackled from the speaker. "Since we—"

"Shut the fuck up!" Burke growled. The line went silent. He listened some more. The jaws worked faster.

Burke turned down the sound. "Timothy?"

No response.

"Timothy!"

The voice peeked from behind a wall of static. "Sorry . . . phone lines . . . should we do . . ."

"Shut up and listen." Burke reached in the drawer and rolled a Prozac capsule in his hand as he spoke. "Get to the Information minister and apologize now. And get Dees out of there. Make him sweat."

". . . derstood," came from the speaker.

"And Timothy," he said, "make sure we can keep an eye on him. A close eye."

Burke impatiently clicked the phone off. He checked his watch. Time for Saint Mac to ascend to the satellite.

AUGUST 25, BAGHDAD

The GTV work space at the hotel was in turmoil. Two Iraqi officials from the Ministry of Information, dressed identically in white short-sleeved shirts and black pants, were talking at once, gesticulating wildly, while Timothy Volga sat on a love seat staring up at both of them. His mouth had the expression of having sucked on a lemon as he listened to a translator.

". . . affront to Iraq's . . ."

". . . endangers the GTV's special . . ."

". . . provocative and . . ."

Dees walked in with Shafir trailing him. Melinda was in a corner, headphones on, viewing tape. She looked up, saw Dees, and mouthed the word "no," jerking her head to indicate Volga and the twin officials, by now chattering without pausing for translation.

Volga shot him an acid look. Dees smiled, waved, and sat at one of the direct satellite phone receivers in the corner. Shafir looked around in a mild panic, saw there was nowhere else to sit, and took a chair beside Dees.

He leaned over. "Major fuck-up," he whispered.

Dees winced. "What can they do? Chain me to the wall of a poison gas factory?"

"Not you. Me. I'm with you. Shit, I'm dead."

Dees reached out to slap Shafir on the knee, to say it's going to be all right, but the Iraqi shifted his legs away, out of reach. Dees stared at him. Shafir didn't return the look.

His own nervousness, the racket in the room, and Shafir's distance made it difficult for him to concentrate. When he was sure the receiver was transmitting to an Indian Ocean satellite, he pulled out Miller's business card.

He read Arnie Johnson's scrawled name and phone number, punched in the U.S. access code, Phoenix area code, and the number. Volga motioned for him to come over to the love seat. Dees flashed the index-and-thumb "just a minute" sign. Volga glowered.

Dees heard the receiver pick up and said, "Arnie Johnson, please," before he realized he had, literally, spoken too soon. There was a delay of around one second between speaking and receiving on the sat phone, and, he knew, he should have paused. The word "please" had just escaped his mouth when he heard the greeting from the other end: "GlobeStar Television, Burke companies."

Shit, he thought, he was so rattled he'd dialed the GTV main switchboard, not Johnson's number. He glanced at the glowing readout on the control panel. Sure enough, he'd punched in the GTV main number through force of habit.

He opened his mouth to say "Excuse me, wrong number" and had his finger poised above the disconnect button. The voice on the other end, delayed, said, "One moment, please."

Huh? Damn. There must be somebody at GTV named Arnie Johnson, he thought, and now he was going to get him or his voice mail. What could he say? "Hi, I'm calling from the armpit of civilization and you just happen to have the same name as somebody who may be involved in selling chemical weapons and I just thought I'd leave a message to say, oops, it ain't you."

There was a click, and a voice said "Hello."

"Sorry," Dees said, speaking slowly and distinctly into the microphone to avoid distortion, "I'm actually looking for Arnie Johnson with a company called Archgate. Sorry."

Dees was preparing to hit disconnect when the voice said, "You got him."

Dees hadn't felt like this since he had sucked in a lungful of nitrous oxide at a Little Feat concert, what, fifteen years ago? His head felt like a balloon on a string, floating above the chaos in the room, looking dizzily down on Volga gesturing for him to come over; himself flashing the wait-a-minute sign, Melinda glancing between him and Volga, Shafir sulking with his back turned, and the two Iraqi officials, finally finished talking, picking through the stock of soft drinks kept on ice in a cooler.

The voice said, "Hello?" angrily.

"Arnie Johnson of Archgate?"

"Who is this?" the voice asked testily.

"I'm calling from Iraq," Dees said. "Ben Miller's okay. So are the Canadian and the Belgian. They're hostages at a factory west of Baghdad. Miller wants you to call his wife to let her know he's okay."

"How do you know?" the voice demanded.

"Because I saw them. You'll see them, too, if you turn on GTV. He asked me to call you so you can call his wife."

"On GTV?" Then, as if stunned, he repeated, "On GTV?"

"Yeah, GTV," Dees said, and sprung. "So how come Archgate has offices at GTV?"

Silence.

Dees repeated, "I said why does Archgate—"

The line went dead.

Dees hung up, and noticed his palms were sweating. Why would Archgate have offices at GTV unless Burke owned that company, too? Whoa, he thought. Maybe he does, maybe he doesn't. Even if he does, nobody says GTV knows what Archgate's doing.

Dees had an immediate urge to bolt, run to his room, and make sure Marmelstein's disk was still stuffed in his mattress. Instead he got up, went to the love seat where Volga was sitting, and plopped down next to him. Dees thought Volga was smirking, but a smirk seemed too much emotion for the taciturn wunderkind to express, so Dees decided Volga probably had indigestion. Spring rolls again, he'd bet.

Volga stared through him more than at him, as if playing with some concept in his brain while he talked.

"You're gone," he said. Dees looked around, then down at his own chest in mock horror, patted it, smiled, and wiped his brow in a burlesque sigh of relief. No, not gone. He was still here. Volga was not amused.

"Get packed," he continued. "Iraq Air may not be flying much longer, so you go to Amman."

"Why?"

Volga just stared. Dees had had enough. "Why? Your friends here upset I told the truth?"

This time Dees decided it was a smirk, after all.

"You're unstable," Volga said tightly. "Baghdad is too important. Too delicate. We can't have any more incidents."

"What incidents?"

"The French reporter," Volga said, this time looking like he was smiling, just a little. "You assaulted her in the lobby. In front of witnesses."

"Assaulted? I twisted her finger."

"That," Volga sighed, "is the kind of attitude I mean. You won't even admit what you did. So you're out."

Volga stared, briefly, at Shafir. Shafir saw the glance and shivered. Dees didn't care for the look, either.

"So," Dees said, "I'm not being shipped out for doing a story on hostages and poison gas? I'm being ordered out because I twisted the finger of some woman who was in my face?"

"That's what I mean." Volga sniffed. "GTV is global. International. We can't afford any of your cowboy incidents."

Dees began to chuckle.

Volga wasn't sharing the humor of the moment. "Go to Amman, then Cairo, then Saudi."

Dees stopped chuckling. "Saudi? I thought I was being shipped home."

Volga stared through him again. "We have too many needs to have you in Phoenix. Maybe your posturing will go over with the kinds of people in the American military. Not here."

Volga turned away and began speaking to the two Iraqi minders. Melinda translated. Shafir looked sick. Dees walked out, went upstairs, and discovered the computer disk was still safely stored in his mattress.

Later that night, Melinda came to his room. She told him Shafir had left with the two ministry goons, none of them too happy. He said it was a pity they went away mad. She said it was a pity she was falling in love. He slowly lifted her T-shirt and mouthed her erect nipples. Then he dropped to his knees and pulled her pants down with a swift tug. She let him lick the sweat from her body.

Afterward, she nuzzled his ear, and he told her somebody from Archgate had offices at GTV. As she worked her way down from his ear, she said she'd check on it. And she said the next time she saw the French bitch, she'd finish twisting her finger off.

AUGUST 28, DHAHRAN, SAUDI ARABIA

Dees had flown from Baghdad to Amman to Cairo to Dhahran in two days, and was as surprised as anyone else when he passed the minimal physical designed by the U.S. military for combat pool personnel in Saudi.

Tightly controlled pools of one print, one broadcast, and one wire service reporter—along with a still photographer and a two-person TV crew—was how the Pentagon had chosen to let the media cover Desert Shield.

Dees and Marco were part of a pool with the Second Marine Division. Marco had also been sent to Saudi because of what Dees suspected was guilt by association, since he'd been the cameraman at the Iraqi chemical plant. Both had to attend a seminar for pool members being held in a hotel conference room. The topics were chemical and nerve gas weapons, and how to stay alive if exposed to them.

"I need to renegotiate my contract," Marco muttered as a Marine medic handed him three packets, boxed in hard plastic. Popping open the small catch on one, he found two cylinders inside.

"Macanudos?" he asked hopefully.

"Atropine," the Marine told him without a trace of a smile.

Inside the cylinders were syringes. The inch-and-a-half heavy gauge needles were withdrawn into each syringe.

Dees listened raptly as the instructor explained that if you were exposed to nerve agents or chemicals, you were supposed to take a syringe in your fist and smack it against your butt, where the spring-loaded needle wouldn't encounter anything like bone. The impact released the needle with enough force to pierce an anti-chemical suit, cotton or canvas uniform pants, underwear, flesh, and muscle in half a second.

"When you inject the atropine, pull the syringe out," the Marine said. He was twenty-three, maybe twenty-four, blond, with a stubbly brush haircut and an accent that came from Kentucky or Tennessee.

"Toss the atropine away immediately, and I mean immediately. Take the syringe next to it, and inject yourself fast, using the same method.

"Atropine is an anti-nerve-gas agent, but it also accelerates your heart rate to around two hundred beats a minute. The second syringe is an animal tranquilizer."

An uneasy laugh went through the room. "We're all animals for sure," a newspaper reporter from Tampa offered feebly.

"Yes sir," the Marine said, with no trace of irony, "and you'll be dead of cardiac overload within one minute if you don't inject yourself with the tranquilizer. When you pull it out, take the needle and bend it over your belt or a flap of one of your photographer's vests, or whatever you have. That'll let the medics know how many shots you've given yourself."

Marco cleared his throat. "We have three sets of injectors here. Wouldn't just one shot of atropine and then animal tranquilizer kill some people?"

"Yes sir, it probably could. The medics have orders not to treat anyone with three of the needles bent over their belt. They figure if you've had to give yourself three shots of atropine and three shots of animal tranquilizer, you're dead even if the nerve agents didn't get you."

Silence. A few sideways panicked looks, but no one said a word.

The Marine continued, "Intell tells us to assume that any artillery shells or Scud warheads are loaded chemically. I would suggest," he added, packing his sample injectors back in their box, "that you might reconsider using the gas shelters our Saudi hosts have set up. If sirens go off, everyone will be asked to go to the shelter. And it is effective against high-explosive warheads.

"But their shelters are in the basement here. Below ground level. Gas and nerve agents are heavier than air. They sink and will try to find the lowest level, which is where you'll be. This is why the Israelis put all their gas shelters on the third or fourth floors.

"Any questions?" he said almost absently, preparing to sling a knapsack over his shoulder.

"Yeah," a sound technician from one of the big three networks gasped. "What do I do? I just accidentally gave myself a shot."

The Marine dropped the knapsack and sprinted across the room. The pasty technician lay on his back, eyes wide, sweat plastering back his hair.

"Give him the tranquilizer!" the AP screamed.

"Give him some air!" *Time* piped in.

"Give him some fucking drugs!" bellowed the glassy-eyed freelance still shooter who claimed to be on assignment for *Soldier of Fortune* and *Mirabella* simultaneously. Everyone suspected he had smuggled hash or khat or downers or some damn thing into Saudi, given his perpetually stoned stare.

The Marine uncapped the second injector in the sound tech's two-pack and jammed it into the technician's right cheek. "Oh shit!" the tech screamed. "It hurts! It hurts!!"

CNN ran to get the Saudi doctor whose office was just off the hotel lobby. ABC ran to get an official from the Joint Information Bureau—the JIB, the military information bureau set up in the hotel.

The still shooter sidled over to Dees, his crescent ear stud glinting in the fluorescent light. "Y'know," he said, "I used to pop animal tranks. I wonder if this load would do anything."

Dees shrugged, more than half hoping the asshole would kill himself. "Look at it this way—there's plenty of medical help available."

A Saudi doctor and two U.S. Army corpsmen hit the door at the same time. The shooter's eyes brightened. "Sure. *L'chaim.*"

He uncapped the tranquilizer injector, jammed it into his butt, looked at Dees dreamily, said "Oh fuck," and collapsed.

Dees stared at the photographer and saw beads of sweat forming suddenly on the prone figure's brow. He ambled over to the Saudi doctor, who was watching the corpsmen work on the technician, and tapped him on the shoulder. The doctor looked at Dees quizzically.

Dees jerked his thumb toward the still shooter. "Another accident."

The doctor looked at the photographer, then back at Dees. "You should go into the desert. It seems much safer there."

Dees lit a cigarette. "I could not agree more."

SEPTEMBER 18, BETHESDA, MARYLAND

Salah Gheta always ran before dawn. It was another two hours before he had to be at his office in the District, so he took advantage of the relative cool before the sun came up to put in a couple of miles.

After over two years on station in Egypt, even the cloyingly humid air around D.C. smelled fresh. He trotted toward the church of Bethesda, which always reminded him that Bethesda was biblical, the site of healing thermal springs. He wondered as he ran whether that was why the National Institutes of Health and so many hospitals were there, or if it just worked out that way.

He cut off the street and loped across a park, and saw another figure approaching, dressed in a dark blue jogging suit with red racing stripes. Too hot for that getup, Gheta thought. He himself was wearing only nylon running shorts and a white T-shirt with the Great Seal of the United States of America on the left breast, circled by the words "United States Embassy Cairo."

As the two runners approached each other, Gheta looked up in recognition, smiled, and waved hello, although part of him wondered what the man in the running suit was doing here at this hour, since he knew for a fact that the man lived miles away in Virginia.

It was the last thing he thought. A nine-millimeter slug zipped through the barrel and silencer behind him, entered his brain in the back of the skull, did quite a bit of damage, and remained lodged there.

Gheta plopped to the grass, consciousness extinguished, but still breathing, at least for a few more seconds. The toe of a Nike running shoe flipped him onto his back, and another slug ruptured his left eyeball.

The man in the running suit slipped the small weapon and its muzzle attachment into his fanny pack, zipped it up, and began jogging east, toward the lightening horizon.

CHAPTER 8

DECEMBER 21, SAUDI AIRSPACE, 32,000 FEET

This is the reason the Pentagon spends umpty-ump thousand dollars to buy a coffee maker, the pilot had said. Dennis Kingen was freezing, although the crew told him the plane's interior was just brisk.

He balanced himself against the roll and creak of the C-141 as it bucked through sandstorm winds. The coffee maker was bolted to a bulkhead by a set of narrow stairs. Walk up them and you were in the cockpit of the transport, where the three-person crew fought fatigue and boredom as they wrestled the four-engine jet on its endless flight from Andrews Air Force Base to King Khalid Military City.

Kingen managed to slosh acrid coffee into a polystyrene cup, dispensed from an urn that could be nearly frozen, almost broiled, turned upside down, or rocked back and forth with the force of a car wreck, and still make a cup of halfway decent coffee.

The inside of the jet's body was mummified in olive drab, from the insulating tape that wrapped vital pipes to the paint scheme on the bulkheads. The rear two-thirds was jammed with pallets of some sort of cargo, separated from the makeshift passenger compartment by layers of superstrong nylon webbing. The one splash of color came from the incongruously orange seats slapped into tracks on the floor and secured, the Military Airlift Command's bow to passenger travel.

"Passengers are just cargo that pee," the loadmaster at Eglin, back in Florida, had told Kingen. The fuselage was pressurized but not heated, so from Eglin to Andrews, and from Andrews to Saudi, he was bundled up like an Eskimo.

He plopped into an orange seat by a window and scraped the frost off with a fingernail. Occasionally, the ochre dust filling the air would thin, and he could glimpse the beige sand twenty thousand feet below, undulating like a brown ocean, the dunes lasting hardly any longer than waves in the scouring wind.

He got up and steadied himself, walking back through the plane, making sure for the third time that the four-foot-by-eighteen-inch, six-inch-thick aluminum Halburton case was still firmly fastened in the overhead cargo area.

Below stretched Saudi Arabia, Arabia of the House of Saud. Kingen's War College master's thesis had traced the expulsion of the Hashemites from the Arabian peninsula. Shareef Husain, the grandfather of Jordan's current king, had controlled the holy sites of Mecca and Medina under a grant first issued to the Hashemites in 1840 by the Ottoman Turks. Old Abdul Aziz drove out Husain in 1924, and appropriated for himself the title of Shareef, Guardian of the Holy Places. The Hashemites fled to Transjordan and Greater Palestine and took over.

Kingen's thesis had argued that the United States should exploit the natural tensions between Jordan and Saudi Arabia to stop the flow of Saudi cash to PLO training bases inside Jordan. King Hussein was already upset that sixty percent of Jordan's population was Palestinian. He had driven out the PLO once already, in the 1970 Black September War. So, Kingen had theorized, exploiting

Hussein's opposition to the PLO on his territory, plus ancestral resentment against the family of Saud, was the best way to short-circuit both terrorism and Pan-Arabism. And the key, he had concluded, was Iraq.

Saddam Hussein ruled a country that was traditionally Hashemite, making him a sort of first cousin pretender to the title of Shareef. Jordan and Iraq had united, briefly, in 1958. The Saudis were afraid of Iraq's military muscle. So the United States, he had written in the last chapter of his thesis, should foster tension between Iraq and Saudi Arabia as a way of crippling the PLO financially and keeping the region from uniting in an anti-Israeli front.

Kingen had even explained, the same way Lawrence of Arabia had explained seventy-five years before, that there was, technically, no way to misspell an Arabic name in English. English spellings were merely phonetic transcriptions of the way Arabic sounded. Therefore, Kingen had written, old Husain and Jordan's King Hussein and Iraq's Saddam Hussein might or might not have the same name. Saddam was assuming they did, and was claiming he was King Hussein's cousin. That meant some legitimacy, however speculative, to Saddam's claim that he had a right, one day, to reclaim Mecca and Medina as the Guardian, which worried the Saudis, Kingen had written. So use the tension to American advantage.

His thesis adviser had scribbled "Too clever by half" on the title page. B minus.

The plane shuddered as the speed brakes were deployed beneath the massive wings. The whine of the engines changed in pitch as they were throttled up. The C-141 slid into a left bank as it dropped below the windblown sand.

Kingen looked at the monochromatic landscape, relieved only by distant winking lights at KKMC. He stared north, toward Iraq.

In the hours he had in D.C. before he left for Saudi, he visited DIA at the Army-Navy Club. The old man, muted in winter tweeds, had motioned for him to sit, and laid the dog-eared master's thesis on the polished table.

Kingen had looked and said, "Where—"

DIA waved his hand. "Psychic ability suits you, Dennis. This was before the Gulf Tanker War, 1980." He paused. "Dennis, I've found your account in Costa Rica."

Kingen had shifted in his seat.

DIA squinted. "Are you being bought?"

Kingen shook his head, expressionless. "Wife's trust from her grandmother. It had to be joint tenancy, with my name on it, too. We may retire in Costa Rica."

DIA sighed. "I'll be checking. I don't like subcontracting. You have one employer and one job description. Remember. Your job is to keep the lid on."

Kingen had stared into his glass. "And I'm the human screw top."

The C-141 leveled for final approach. Kingen had crushed the polystyrene coffee cup in his fist.

JANUARY 3, SAUDI-IRAQ-KUWAIT BORDER

It had taken Dees four weeks to be assigned to a combat pool with the Second Marines. It took three weeks on top of that to convince the Second's public affairs officer that Dees was the most honest journalist he would ever meet, and one of the dozen or so most upright people he would ever encounter in any circumstance.

Which is how Dees found himself in a Humvee with Carl Odell and Robert Hopkins, without a camera or cameraman, a good fifteen kilometers in front of the front lines for Operation Desert Shield.

"The deal is this," Dees had told the PAO. "You let me go

along with a psyops unit, just for the ride, only a few times, just me. I don't report a goddamn thing I see until the war's either well along or completely over. If you decide you can't trust me, you don't let me take a camera crew out later."

Normally, the PAO would have taken ten seconds to say fuck you and let it go at that. But the Marines had been getting most of the good publicity so far—and he wanted to keep it that way. So he decided on his own to let Dees go, a decision that could either mean a bonanza of positive publicity or the end of his career if Dees violated opsec and gave away any details about anything ongoing.

So, there he was, blasting along in a Humvee with a salt-and-pepper team of kids—one was twenty-three, the other twenty-five—listening to "Between a Rock and a Hard Place" full volume from a portable CD player rigged to a pair of Fostex speakers just like those the nets used in their edit bays.

Odell was black, wiry, sinew wrapped tightly over bone, from Los Angeles. Hopkins was taller, heavier, brush-cut blond with arms like a first baseman who could hit forty homers a year, which is exactly what he had been for his American Legion team in Palatka, Florida.

The alarm on Odell's wristwatch went off. He checked the odometer and clicked off the CD player. As a kid in Compton, Odell had read L.A. city maps, California maps, *National Geographic* maps, the same way his cousins studied the labels of forty-ounce malt liquor bottles on the street corner. So he was able to combine the plastic map folded on his lap, compass readings, and an almost innate sense of direction to more or less find his way across the featureless desert at night like a Bedouin.

Hopkins didn't even have to set up the wire mesh umbrella-sized antenna for his transmitter to check their position with a global-positioning satellite. Odell hadn't been more than half a klick off in four months.

The rules of engagement said they were in Saudi Arabia. Odell and Hopkins knew they had crossed into Iraq five minutes before. Dees guessed as much.

The only sound the three heard was the wind whistling around their helmets and goggles, and the surprisingly low growl of the Humvee's V-8. It plowed across the sand and up the back side of a dune ridge before Odell drifted it to the right, parking it at an angle heading back down the dune.

Hopkins and Odell climbed out and unbuttoned the rear hatch. Inside were ten small, powerful speakers, three spools of speaker wire, and three audiocassette players. Their mission was to make life miserable for the Iraqi grunts dug in behind sand berms and trenches several hundred meters east, just inside what the maps said was Kuwait.

This was technically Iraq, but it was actually Allied territory, or more specifically, the property of three companies of Rangers who had been operating in the area for weeks. The Iraqis, except for the occasional wanderer who was taken prisoner almost immediately, had remained dug in behind sand berms and trenches filled with light, flammable oil, living inside dugouts excavated from the desert, burrowed down like animals, coming out at night, and then only briefly.

So every night at around 0330, when REM sleep is at its deepest for those who sleep, and concentration is at its lowest for those who don't, Odell and Hopkins, and for the last two nights, Dees, had visited sections of the Saddam Line and serenaded the troops.

Odell took four speakers and a spool of wire and walked to the top of the dune line. Hopkins took four more speakers and another spool and walked in the opposite direction. Eight speakers were placed in pairs, twenty meters or so apart, capable of producing a line of sound across a front roughly the length of a football field. In the desert, sound carries for miles at night.

The black speakers were attached to three-foot-tall black aluminum tripods. The wires were run to a four-channel amp in the back of the Humvee. The battery pack would push enough power to drive the speakers at distortion volume for two hours. Cassette players running off rechargeable ni-cad batteries had sufficient muscle to run looped ten-minute cassettes for about the same amount of time.

Hopkins smiled tightly as he picked tonight's selection—messages and curses in Arabic. The boys and girls who ran psychological operations had figured, correctly, that most of the Iraqi troops were conscripts, probably from villages rather than cities. They were probably at least moderately religious.

Hopkins's favorite tape contained the high-pitched voice of a man screaming in Arabic that the Americans buried all their enemies' bodies sewn inside hogs' skins, and no one could ascend to heaven and join Allah wrapped in the flesh of a pig.

Odell was partial to the guitar heroes feedback loop. He'd helped splice together ten minutes of howling guitar distortion and feedback, including everyone from Eddie Van Halen to Metallica. It was a nice juxtaposition to the pig sermons. Odell dropped a cassette into the player. Within seconds the nasal voice screaming about what Dees called Iraqi wrapped in bacon filled the night.

Elements of a Ranger company were less than a hundred meters behind them. Odell and Hopkins slipped on their night vision goggles and crawled to the top of the dune. Dees sidled up next to them, unable to see shit.

The bait was set. If the Iraqis open fire, withdraw. If they send out a scout, capture him. If nothing happens, nothing happens, and you just sit and imagine those poor bastards not being able to sleep.

Dees felt his heart beating, felt it through his undershirt, turtleneck, shirt, battle dress uniform coat, and flak jacket. It resonated in his chest. When he rolled over in the sand, onto his back, it pulsated along his spine, keeping time with the stars' waltz above him.

If he crossed his eyes, he could imagine the stars left trails as they moved, that he could actually trace their tracks with his eyes like a time-exposure photo.

Odell lay five meters away, watching the phosphorescent green night through the night vision goggles. The Iraqi tanks beyond the berm glowed faintly from the residual engine heat. Three were idling, their pattern glowing more brightly than the others.

It was the smell, Dees thought. Sometime in his life, he'd smell the combination of iron-hard cold, his own sweat, and the musty uniform smell, and he knew he'd be right back here. Smell, the psyops trainers had told them, was an overlooked part of psychological operations. It triggered response more powerfully than any other sense.

If he could atomize the smell of bacon frying, would it cause them to shiver, he wondered, the same as the *mullah*'s message about the pig skins did? Or would it just make them hungry?

Odell drew in a sharp breath. Something was moving this side of the berm. He zoomed the goggles in for maximum magnification. It was a man.

He scooted over and tugged on Hopkins's arm, pointing. Hopkins, adjusting his own goggles, nodded. They watched and saw a figure clambering down to the bottom of the sloping berm. It crouched at the berm's base, then straightened up and, crouched, moved toward them in a half sprint and half waddle.

Shit, Odell thought. He's in the mine field.

Hopkins thought the same thing. The Iraqis had laced the areas in front of their berms, as well as most of Kuwait, with what intell estimated to be three to five million mines. Most were a nasty Chinese-made variety that sold for about two dollars each, a variant of Vietnam's Bouncing Betty, a mine with a spring-loaded charge. It clicked when you stepped on it. The spring propelled the canister anywhere from knee to chest high, and either blew off your legs or shredded everything from your gonads to your chest with dozens of jagged pieces of metal, or ball bearings, depending.

Both men reached for their M-16s, equipped with flash suppressors to eliminate most noise and light when they fired. CENTCOM was so worried about lights at night that no fires were allowed, and that meant morning coffee consisted of a packet of instant coffee from rations, known as MREs, emptied between the cheek and gum and washed down with cold water. It tasted terrible, but provided a serious caffeine jolt.

Dees's gut tightened when he saw the rifles. He tapped Hopkins on the shoulder and shrugged. Hopkins pointed toward the Iraqi berm, and made a running sign with his index and middle fingers. Dees nodded. Great time to have that camera he didn't have, he thought.

The figure scuttled across the sand. Hopkins was hoping he'd make it so they could snatch him and pick his brains—not that he would tell them anything they didn't already know. Still, it was always nice to get a little human intelligence to go along with what the technogeeks got from their satellites. It had been almost two weeks since he and Odell had snagged a prisoner.

But this was different. That had just been some cowering conscript hunkered down in a sand bunker who got freaked about reconnoitering this close to Allied positions, and gave it up like a little girl when the speakers started thumping. This guy, though, was humping across a mine field at least two hundred meters wide, a mine field laid down partially to slow down Allied troops but mainly to keep Saddam's draftees from doing the chicken run. Odell wanted to capture him, too, but was also wishing he'd make it for the plain old hell of him making it.

A sudden white strobe went off, and Dees could see the berm and the mine field and a figure arcing through the air for an instant, before everything went black again. Odell and Hopkins could see clearly through their goggles once the white flash cleared.

The sound followed, a concussive *thwauumpp*, followed by the screams of unspeakable agony, gargling high-pitched shrieks coming from a piece of meat with the brain still attached, blood puddling and then sinking into the sand, leaving rust-colored granules on the surface. A tendril of intestine, still steaming with life, lay in front of the Iraqi as he howled.

Hopkins put the rifle to his shoulder, elevated the muzzle, and fired, one round. Odell saw it kick up sand near the figure. "Two feet off," he whispered.

Hopkins adjusted a fraction of an inch and fired again. Odell saw the body twitch. It was hit, but he didn't know where. Close enough, Hopkins thought. Four more rounds cracked off, the M-16 set on single fire.

Five rounds on target. The screams stopped. Maybe he'd been put out of his misery, maybe he'd just bled to death.

"Shit," Hopkins said softly. Shitshitshitshitshit.

SOUTHWEST KUWAIT

"Megadeth. They're playing Megadeth. Megadeth sucks," he muttered. But at least they mixed it in with Van Halen.

Machmoud Shafir leaned against a T-55 tank two hundred

meters behind the sand berms and oil moat. Stretched in front of him were trenches filled with troops trying to sleep under roofs of timber and corrugated tin covered with four feet of sand.

The secret police had hustled him out of the Baghdad Sheraton and slapped him around a few times as he was being driven to the Ministry of Information. He'd been hit harder in his life, so the slaps didn't bother him so much as the speculation between the goon who was driving and the one guarding in the backseat as to which one might succeed Shafir in minding the American journalists.

It was a good life, the two agreed. Fine food and a chance to fuck the *sharmuta* American women who probably bucked like goats in heat. They had prodded Shafir, asking him about the photo of the blonde in the power suit standing in front of the Harris Bank building in Chicago. "So you fuck her?" they asked and laughed. "Say good-bye to your soft American whore and your soft American job," they said, and laughed some more.

And so he'd been moved from the Ministry of Information to an army barracks in one night, put in a unit with farm boys and slum dwellers on what would probably be the front line. "The Americans will execute you for us," he was told.

Shafir, corporal, drew night duty near the circle of tanks behind the berms. A ring of tanks, turrets pointed outward, was placed every five hundred meters or so. Anyone trying to breach the berms would find pits of flaming oil in front of them, ignited by electric charges. Moving past that, they would be pulverized by cross fire from dug-in tanks.

He sat heavily on top of an ammunition box, wiping grains of the powdered, blowing sand from one eye. Megadeth had segued into the Saudi *fakir* screeching about being buried in pigskins. A number of the rubes in his unit were unnerved by the noise. Shafir didn't mind it.

He planned to surrender the second the Americans came raging over the berm. He had planned the speech. "I am an American. Here are my papers. I have a job on LaSalle Street in Chicago. When can I go home?"

A breeze blew over the berm in a sigh, almost as if the echo of something alive and breathing out there in the dark crouched, waiting.

Shafir kept his Illinois driver's license, a folded copy of his resident alien work permit, and his bank ID card in a plastic bag sealed at the top with twine and tied around his neck with a plastic strip. He would surrender with a blast of colloquial English, proffer his bona fides, and go home. But first he had to keep from getting killed. At least, he had told a private, Americans were out there, somewhere. The Egyptians, facing the Iraqi lines southeast, would insist on killing everyone.

A *cruuuummp* from about four hundred meters in front of him snapped Shafir back. He slid behind the tank, hacking as he inhaled exhaust, clutching the bag around his neck. Coming? Already?

After a half hour of confusion and yelling, it became clear that some private had tried to escape to American lines across the mine field. A couple of recruits were jabbering that the Americans were using the corpse for target practice.

The wind picked up, carrying a flurry of distorted guitar notes with it. Cool. Eddie Van Halen.

JANUARY 16–17, RIYADH, SAUDI ARABIA

Dennis Kingen sat in a corner of the basement at the U.S. embassy in Riyadh. Two video monitors faced him, and he, in turn, faced a small TV camera.

The shadows of faces and chairs in the familiar Washington conference room filled one monitor. The other was blank except for some wavy hash and static. In his lap was a small switcher, about the size of an audiocassette player minus headphones. It enabled him to switch between his own image and images on the second monitor.

The faces in the D.C. conference room peered at him, displayed on a six-foot monitor. "Gentlemen," he said, "this is real time."

Surveillance satellites skidding through the vacuum of space a few dozen miles up would slide above a target area, aiming their high-resolution lenses. A tiny antenna beamed the signal to the nearest military communications satellite parked in a geosynchronous orbit almost 23,000 miles away.

DIA had once told him the briefings were like mass. Priests of mass destruction, the old man had said, celebrating on a video altar. And the body and blood to be served to the seated acolytes, he had said dryly, was delivered by remote control.

"The screen will show Baghdad and its suburbs for a few minutes," Kingen said into the camera. "After a brief blackout, we'll acquire the signal from another satellite, this one above Iraqi ammunition stores near Wafra."

He hit a button on his lap, and the huge screen in Washington hissed to life with the same image he saw from the satellite.

"Please concentrate on the lower part of the screen. That's the location of a fertilizer plant in the southern suburbs."

"Fertilizer?" State snorted. Each chair had a lavaliere microphone attached, running into an earpiece Kingen wore.

"Fertilizer as in phosgene, we think," Kingen replied.

The screen's image was a ghostly green. The bridges spanning the Tigris appeared as parallel black lines, clearly visible across the ancient river as it snaked through the city, north to south.

Three spots of greenish-white flickered and moved along the lower right of the screen.

"Cruise missiles," CIA said needlessly, "probably from the *Wisconsin* in the Gulf."

The subsonic missiles crept along the screen. Then, light flashed from the lower center of the picture. "Bull's-eye on the fertilizer plant," Kingen said.

More lights danced in the screen's center. "Probably the Defense ministry," he continued. "The F-117s from Taif."

The Stealth fighters stationed in southern Saudi, far away from possible Iraqi counterattack, were dropping laser-guided bombs, Kingen knew, and left the Iraqis shooting at their tailpipes.

The picture flickered and disappeared, replaced a second later with an image of featureless terrain with what appeared to be clumps of buildings dead center.

"The Wafra ammo dump," Kingen said.

Black dots spiraled above the buildings. They disappeared in white splotches.

"What exactly was stored there?" State demanded.

"Best estimate is artillery ordnance," Kingen said. "Possibly one-twenty millimeter or larger shells. Also rockets for their Astra launchers."

"Warheads?" CIA asked.

"High explosive," Kingen replied. "And very probably chemical and possibly some nerve agents. All destroyed, as you can see."

A chair squeaked in Washington, heard by Kingen in Riyadh. It was DIA. "And everything in it's airborne? Including chemical and nerve residue?"

Kingen shrugged. "Winds in the area are unpredictable. Our closest troops are two dozen kilometers away. I recommend MOPP Four."

MOPP, Mission Oriented Protective Posture. MOPP One

meant merely donning chemical suits. MOPP Four meant going all the way, suits, hooded gas and chem masks, rubber boots, gauntlets.

SecDef's chair spoke. "Not your call. Our people are well-prepared."

Kingen shrugged again. "Multiply this several hundred times over the next few days. Or weeks. Or months. We could have toxic clouds all over the KTO." The Kuwaiti Theater of Operations.

"Some theater," DIA said. "Curtain going up."

CHAPTER 9

NORTHEAST SAUDI ARABIA

"Hey, Pete," Odell yelled over the *whoosh* of predawn desert air, "wanna go airborne?"

Dees smiled and nodded. Dawn was twenty minutes away, and pink light was already overtaking the purple sky in the east. Day began softly in the desert, but quickly became blinding daylight when the sun popped out of the Arabian Gulf with the force of a rock through a plate-glass window.

Odell gunned the Humvee, pushing Hopkins, tight-lipped, and Dees back in their seats. It picked up speed, roaring toward the top of a dune, and went flying over the crest, all four wheels off the ground, arcing toward a sky the color of a fresh bruise.

The three camels plodding along just below the top of the dune line had time only to look up and see a tan thing hurtling toward them before the Humvee pitched nose down. Two snorted and managed to trot away.

The third stared at the thing and spit. Behind the Humvee's wheel, Odell yelled, "Oh shit!" and closed his eyes as the reinforced front fender and spinning front tires plowed into the dromedary.

Viscera, fur, and blood splattered across the front of the vehicle as if shot from a hose. The Humvee fishtailed briefly and slid to a halt, spraying sand in the air.

Hopkins, who loved animals, hopped out, ready to use his M-16 to put the camel out of its misery. But the camel was already dead.

Dees pulled his goggles off and stared at Odell standing over the mutilated animal. He reached inside his flak jacket, pulled out a cigarette, lit it, and inhaled deeply.

"So," he said tiredly, "you owe somebody a few grand."

Odell, out of the driver's seat and standing next to Hopkins, turned. "Huh?"

"They're worth a few thousand bucks each. It's how the Saudis still count their worth, especially with the Bedouins."

Hopkins stared at the corpse. "Y'know, they're related to elephants and llamas."

Odell turned and scrunched his brow.

"Take a look at the lips," Hopkins said. "They're split in two. Kind of like weird fingers. Same as a llama. They use their upper lips to grab things."

"Fuck it," Odell muttered, using the arm of his BDU to clean the blood and entrails off the windshield. "Let's go home."

He ground the gears, and the Humvee leapt forward again, tearing toward the Second Marines desert encampment. The sun was already blistering a half hour later when they drove past sentries, electronic motion monitors, dugout emplacements, razor wire, and arrayed Bradley fighting vehicles and M-1A1 tanks, and Dees saw Melinda Adams.

Tan or brown or khaki, they said. Wear anything except desert colors and you don't go on a combat pool, they said. She wore khaki pants that fit a little too tightly for the comfort of Marines who had been in the desert for four months. Otherwise, she was standard desert issue—a baggy brown T-shirt underneath a chocolate-chip camo battle-dress uniform jacket.

Dees wiped sand from his cheek as he trudged from the splattered Humvee. His face felt like sandpaper. He heard a guttural "hooo-rahh" from Odell and Hopkins behind him. He flashed a thumbs-up over his shoulder.

She eyed him coolly. "I see they still haven't put enough saltpeter in your MREs."

He smiled, face coated with dust and dirt except for the patch around his red-rimmed eyes, which had been covered by his goggles. "Where the hell did you come from?"

"Baghdad. Phoenix told me you needed help out here."

He looked puzzled. "I never called Phoenix. I have enough trouble getting copy cleared through the JIB in Dhahran."

All stories and scripts from reporters in the field were first transmitted or hand-carried several hundred miles south, to the Joint Information Bureau in Dhahran. But since Dhahran was only a branch office, all approval actually came from CENTCOM headquarters in Riyadh. So by the time the field, to Dhahran, to Riyadh, back to Dhahran, back to the field reporters loop was completed, the stories were censored to pieces, or outdated, or both.

She shrugged. "Maybe they just thought you needed help. Want me to leave before I deliver your mail?"

He shook his head as she handed him a bundle of mail and a newspaper, secured by a rubber band. "Stay. It'll give you something to tell your grandkids. You happen to deliver water along with the mail?"

Without saying a word, she handed him a liter bottle of water. He splashed it in his hand and rubbed his face, smearing the dust into mud. Three more splashes and his face was almost clean.

As they walked past a line of Humvees, each painted tan, each with a black inverted V on the side, he looked for someplace in the shade, and finally settled on the rear of an empty deuce and a half—the two-and-a-half-ton truck that was the workhorse of the U.S. military. Still without a word, they climbed inside. It smelled military, he thought, canvas and desert dust.

"Remember the disk you told me about in Baghdad?" she asked. "Forget using it. We can't use any of the laptops GTV sent over. The sand's wrecked two Toshibas already. It gets in through the keyboard and disk port. I sent word back to Dhahran for them to buy up every manual portable typewriter they can find. We should have six or seven here in a couple of days."

He stared, and could see her cheeks starting to glow even redder under her sunburn. She looked at him, and quickly scooted across the floor and kissed him, hard. After a few seconds she pushed away.

"No passion. You been here too long?"

"You're beautiful and smart," he said. "You've got a great body and a tongue like boiled okra."

"What!"

"Old expression from down home. It means I'd love to, but so far I've been focused on everything but sex. For once. Like Arnie Johnson's Archgate office at GTV?"

"I checked," she said tiredly. "No office, no phone extension, no record of anyone with a name remotely like Arnie Johnson."

He nodded, and dumped much of the remaining water in the bottle on his head, letting the cool water trickle down his neck and inside his shirt, making tracks of delicious coolness across his chest.

He looked at her and she winked. "I've got an idea what else we can use this truck for."

"Here? Now?"

"Why not here and now?"

Dees took a swig of water. "No reason. Just something else to remember when that bullet catches us in Kuwait. Or the helicopter goes down in Salvador. Or maybe we get lucky and we die of a stroke in the shower at home, where the walls are covered with all the artwork we got from all the shitholes we've covered, except that nobody else remembers where they were, not even in the history books."

She sniffed. "My, you know how to inflame a girl's passion. What brought that on?"

"Dead people, dead camels, dead body parts scattered like trash. This is the first bang-bang for most of those kids out there. None of them have seen any of their friends dead yet. This is my seventh war, eighth if you count two rounds in Nicaragua. Friends die in wars, and I can deal with that, sometimes better than others.

"But Dick and Saed and the dwarf and Christ knows who else? Uh-uh. That I can't deal with until I figure out why. Or who."

She wrinkled her nose. "You sure as hell won't figure out who in the next few minutes. So you can clean yourself up and I can find someplace to clean myself up and we can get a couple of sleeping bags. Unless you object, which is not how I remember you. Or unless you want to wait until dark."

He snapped the rubber band on the mail bundle. "This time of day is as private as any. Most of the activity here's at night. Most people are just now turning in."

She looked at him with half-lowered lids. "Then it's just a matter of hygiene. I'll get some sleeping bags and some soap. You don't move. Yet."

He grabbed her head and kissed her, wetly. He felt a slight shudder. She pulled away. He sighed. "You want to clean up? One of the mechanics rigged a solar shower over by the PAO tent. You go use it. I'll get my kit and clean up and meet you back here."

She kissed him on the nose. "Deal. Ten minutes."

As she climbed down the back of the truck, she stuck her head up above the tailgate. "By the way, do you have any idea where we are, more or less?"

"Twenty-seven thirty by forty-six thirty and change," he said. "At least as near as the wonks here can figure and will tell me."

She nodded, winked, and disappeared. Dees ambled over to the Humvee festooned with camel innards and pulled his small duffel from the rear. He unzipped it. Soap. Toothpaste. Clean socks and underwear.

He climbed back into the truck, dropped his pants around his ankles, and scrubbed as well as he could with soap and cold water from the bottle. He pulled up his pants, shed his shirt, and lathered himself, splashing the water sparingly until dust was replaced by tanned flesh.

He stepped over the tailgate, sat on the truck's bumper, and felt a stirring desert breeze across his cool skin as he brushed his teeth, glancing down at the mail. It was a bundle of a dozen letters, two weeks old, from viewers either praising or complaining about the stories he had filed. He opened the paper, an *International Herald-Tribune* dated January 2. He glanced lazily at it, leisurely turning the pages until he saw an item at the bottom of page five. He stopped brushing and took the paper in both hands, toothbrush still in his mouth.

EX-HOSTAGE FOUND SHOT, the headline read. It was dated January 1.

> Pensacola, FL. (AP)—A chemical engineer who was held hostage by Iraq for six weeks, and then released, was found murdered this morning in his home.
>
> Benjamin Miller, 56, was held from August 5 until September 17 as a "special guest" of Saddam Hussein's government. He had been held at a fertilizer plant west of Baghdad, and was released in September along with twenty-one other hostages.

He was found in the front room of his Pensacola home shot twice. The body was discovered by his wife, Doris. Robbery was the apparent motive, police say, since the home was ransacked.

Miller had worked for Archgate, Inc., a St. Louis chemical firm, for ten years. His wife told police, "He survived Iraq, and now this. What is happening to this country?"

Police say the robbery was apparently the work of professionals, since Miller was shot execution-style twice, once in the back of the head and once in the left eye.

Dees reread the article, toothbrush still in his mouth, the hair tingling on the back of his neck.

Melinda came around a corner carrying two sleeping bags under her arm.

"Bad news," she said. "The medic wants us over at his tent. And since pleasure deferred is the name of the game, we'll just have to—" She stared at him. "Is that a toothbrush in your mouth or are you just glad to see me?"

He shoved the paper at her while he finished brushing and rinsed. She whistled, low. "What'd you think?" she asked.

He stuffed the toothpaste back into the small duffel. "I think a dead Haitian and a dead source and a dead producer with eyes shot out make me nervous. Not to mention what could be World War Three out there someplace. I'm a wreck. The love of a good woman could calm me considerably."

Her laugh tinkled. "Not until we keep our pals in the medical unit happy. C'mon, let's take some pills and have some shots before they kill you. Then we'll try to find someplace cool to lie down."

They trudged to the medical tent, where they were given a

vaccine against anthrax and a tablet of pyridostigmine bromide, which had to be taken before exposure to chemical or nerve agents. Dees had been taking the pills every day for three days. They made him feel as if he had a mild case of the flu, but it was better than having no resistance at all if there were chemical or nerve or biological agents set off by Saddam. And, clearly, someone thought there was a good chance of that happening soon.

The sun was starting to heat the sand under their feet, even though the orange disk was still low on the horizon. The area around the truck they had left was deserted.

"In," she ordered. He climbed in, turned, and was amazed to see her on her knees, deftly unfastening the buttons on his pants. She took him in her mouth and he groaned softly.

He tumbled to the sleeping bags, pulling her T-shirt off in a swift movement, unsnapping her bra strap, taking first one erect nipple then the other in his mouth.

He pushed her on her back, peeling off the khakis and her panties. He tried to force her legs apart. She resisted, smiling. He bit the inside of her right thigh. She yelped, softly. He parted her legs and put his tongue inside her.

Her back arched and she began to moan. She suddenly swiveled, turning him flat on his back, sitting on his face, making soft gasping noises as his tongue flickered.

She scooted down his body, straddled him, and began to grind, slowly. Her rhythm quickened, along with the intensity of the thrusts. She opened her mouth, wide.

"Shhh," Dees said. "Opsec."

She moved faster, not making a sound, mouth still wide, until her body stiffened and shuddered at the same instant he climaxed.

She was glistening as if sprayed with water as she rolled off him and laughed.

"You know one of the best parts?" she said. "That we might be discovered doing it, here."

He stared at her. "You may be crazier than I am."

She nipped at his earlobe. "By a factor of ten. You make me that way."

He reached for his photographer's vest. The microcassette recorder in one pocket fell to the floor with a clink. Dees reached for it, and she grabbed the vest.

"Got any smokes?" she said, rummaging through the Velcro-sealed pockets.

"Yes, but you don't smoke."

She felt a pocket and pulled out a flat, thin object wrapped in several sealed Baggies, secured with two thick rubber bands. She stared at it in her hand. "The disk."

Dees nodded, took it out of her hand, and stuck it back in the vest pocket.

She picked up her wadded T-shirt, pulled it on, and said, "It's dangerous carrying it with you."

"Au contraire," he said, pulling on his pants. "I always know where it is. I don't have to worry about it."

"So," she asked, "any progress? On the story and the loose ends?"

Dees sighed. "Nothing but. Loose ends, I mean. Three people with eyes shot out. I'm almost killed. The disk has no whys, plenty of who's, and nothing connecting any of them. Except Archgate, which may have offices at GTV. Or it may not."

She kissed him lightly on the cheek, and pulled the canvas tailgate flap open, letting in a rush of oven-temperature air.

"Don't get paranoid," she said as she climbed out of the truck. She paused, looking thoughtful. "But then," she said, "you aren't paranoid if they actually are out to get you."

CAIRO

"Twenty-seven degrees thirty minutes by forty-six degrees thirty minutes. No, I do not know seconds."

Timothy Volga was exasperated. He sat on the balcony overlooking the Nile, a balcony now shaded with a large green canopy and equipped with two cushioned chairs.

He glared at the power supply for the satellite phone he was using, bypassing Egyptian, American, or Iraqi operators, linked directly by satellite to the satellite phone in Baghdad.

The GTV work space in Baghdad was now perpetually filled with Iraqis. Before leaving a week earlier, Volga had delegated operational control to a producer and two correspondents still there. But real control, agreed to with a very few sentences, had passed to the Iraqi Ministry of Information.

The only burp in the plan had been the sudden loss of Melinda Adams, the bureau's best Arabic speaker. The same day Volga left Baghdad, he had been astonished to see her at Saddam International Airport, waiting in the departure lounge. She had waved and come over. She gave him a hug that flustered him momentarily.

"Dees," she had said happily. "He called Phoenix begging for a producer. I'm the only one the Saudis will let in on short notice because Dad used to work for Aramco. Got the call an hour ago. By the way, I hear you're going to Cairo. Must be nice. Oh hey, I have to finish schmoozing my new friend at departures so I can fly first class. Maybe I can get you a seat, too? Oh, I see you're already in first. See you there. 'Bye."

Now, sitting in Cairo staring at a laminated map in his lap, Volga was forced to deal with Sadoon on the phone. Sadoon was the top minder for the Iraqi MOI, and therefore GTV's ex-officio bureau chief in Baghdad, but he had a barely workable command of English. So Volga stared at the map, pinpointing an area just inside Saudi Arabia, slightly below the corner where Kuwait and Iraq meet.

"That is correct," he repeated, slowly. "Forty-six thirty, twenty-seven thirty. I would imagine slightly north of that."

He paused, listening. A Fiat horn bleated on the Corniche below. Volga loved Egypt. With cases of electronics, he could rule his Middle Eastern kingdom from here, technically in the Middle East, yes, but out of range of any Iraqi missile except for their most advanced, retrofitted Scud models, which Volga had been told were not yet ready to fly.

"That is absolutely correct," Volga said. "We hope it is useful."

The line hissed, and went dead. He turned and signaled the newly hired office boy for *chai*, sweet. The young *boab* shuffled across the recently installed carpet toward the kitchen.

Volga stretched, yawned, and punched another series of numbers into the keypad. The tea arrived. Volga, without looking at the office boy, took a sip, grimaced, and said, "*Mish quais.* No good. Too sweet. *Mish quais.*"

The office boy looked confused. As the phone connected on the other end, Volga smiled thinly. Confusion, he had once been told by a man eight thousand miles away, was the best management tool.

PHOENIX

The color monitor glowed with a four-color map of an area bounded on the north by Baghdad and on the south by Dhahran. It showed every GTV employee along with a rough location. Mac Burke noted the names "Dees/Marco" lumped together somewhere in northern Saudi Arabia, southwest of Kuwait.

The satellite phone made a gargling sound, like a phone ringing underwater. Burke answered. "No, no computer entry. No tracks at all. Seen him yet?"

More silence.

"Umm. Let's wait. Things happen in war."

Another pause. "But not to you," he said huskily. "Ummmm-hmmmm. Any time."

He had barely hung up when the phone gargled again. He listened, then scowled. "So that's as close as you can pinpoint them? That covers a few hundred square—"

He paused to listen.

"And our friends know we can only pay for three? No more."

More silence. Burke nodded once, and hung up the receiver. He absently stroked his right sideburn, then clicked the intercom.

"Josephina?"

"Yes, Mr. Burke?"

"Arrange to transfer half a million from Hong Kong to the UAE special account." He clicked off and accessed the GTV computer. He had spent maybe five minutes studying flight characteristics of the Scud B when the intercom buzzed.

"Mr. Burke! We're bombing Baghdad! It's war!"

Burke turned and stared at the row of monitors. He reached for the remote and turned up GTV, seeing a slide with the picture of one of his Baghdad reporters, listening to the satellite phone circuit hiss and crackle. But even through all that, he could hear the thump and rumble of explosions in the background.

He suddenly caught his breath and looked down at the dark stain on his trouser front. He had peed in his pants.

CHAPTER 10

TWENTY-FIVE KILOMETERS
WEST OF BASRA, IRAQ

At a shade over thirty-five feet long, and weighing six and a half tons, the missile was roughly the size and weight of three medium-size automobiles laid end to end. It was the six feet of nose cone that worried the crew.

They were dressed in rudimentary chemical protective suits, primitive by NATO standards, which the crew guessed would not protect them from what they also guessed was inside the warhead.

The driver of the Soviet-made MAZ-543 eight-wheeled transport and launch vehicle drove with the warhead suspended above his cab. The missile lay flat on top of the wheeled chassis until it was time to launch. Then a carriage hoisted it upright while the vehicle inched forward. Much like a dump truck of death, the driver mused. Following behind him was an armored personnel carrier arrayed with antennae, a meteorological mobile unit that used radar to gauge upper atmospheric conditions so a trajectory could be determined and programmed.

Not that it made any difference, the driver thought as the dome light in the cab flickered on and off, stroboscopically illuminating the picture taped to the dashboard of a plump woman, his wife, and two equally plump little girls, his daughters.

He called the Scud B suspended above his head *sharmuta*—slut—because it might go down on anyone at any time. These missiles, he knew, could never be aimed so much as pointed, the rest left to luck and Allah. So said his cousin in the rocket corps, who had participated in a failed experiment two years before to put chemical warheads on one of these.

Thirty-seven people had died, horribly, when the nose-cone canister containing sarin under pressure, to be released as an aerosol, ruptured seconds after ignition.

The Scud roared skyward all right, his cousin had told him, leaving a plume of death behind it along with the rocket exhaust. And since then, Baghdad had been trying to perfect a warhead with chemical or nerve agents, or so the story went, with more or less the same results in a dozen laboratory and field tests.

Three weeks before, his unit had received new nose cones and new warhead canisters. Nothing was said, but all eight men in the launch crew had been handed the Warsaw Pact surplus chemical suits.

The bombs had started falling less than an hour ago, shaking him from his cot with their rattle, even though the explosions were coming from Basra itself, twenty kilometers away. Fully awake within moments, he had walked to his vehicle inside the garage, which was actually not much more than a giant piece of pipe buried in ten feet of sand. The crew had run, some with panic in their eyes as the walls shivered from the concussions. But he had walked. Save your energy, he always told the draftees, stay calm, never run unless absolutely necessary. The less you panic, the better your chances of staying alive.

So he and the companion radar truck drove along, watching the flashes from the northeast and Basra while they went southwest, blacked out, steering over rutted roads by memory since there was no moon, craning their necks every so often to hear or see jets. They would have done neither, since the damage was coming from Tomahawk cruise missiles launched from an American battleship over a hundred miles away, and from aircraft-launching laser and radar-guided weapons from a distance well beyond the range of antiaircraft.

But the driver did not know that, although he would probably have figured it out had his attention not been riveted on keeping on the pavement in the pitch-black with the world's largest air force somewhere overhead.

The driver thought the flashes behind him illuminated the sky in front of him like desert lightning. He remembered, as a boy, traveling west from Basra with his father, camping in the rocky desert, watching with awe as a rare summer storm rolled in from the mountains to the far north and lit up the world with flashes that froze everything for a second in the light of day, much as the shorted dome bulb in his truck cab flashed a visual counterpoint to the light from the bombs. It illuminated the faces of the ones he loved more than life itself, it sometimes seemed, taped to his dashboard.

They reached the coordinates on the map, and the launch officer in the seat behind the driver began barking instructions. The driver ignored him, found a flat, slightly elevated hillock, pulled the MAZ on top of it, and stopped.

The crew piled out and began loosening the bolts that held the rocket and its carriage to the truck body. When they were unfastened, the driver pushed two levers and gunned his engine. The vehicle sat still, but the rocket and launcher rose slowly, until the missile's tail fins began to scrape the ground. Slowly, the driver put the vehicle in gear and inched forward. Just as slowly, the rocket settled onto flat ground and locked in place, missile and carriage.

The driver's work was done. He left the cab and began walking. Twenty meters away he stopped, sitting on the ground, keeping out of the way and also surveying for anyplace he could hide if the launch failed.

The weather radar inside the other vehicle clicked to life, pulsing toward the sky overhead, reading barometric pressure, wind speed, and upper air currents. Its pulse was picked up by an American electronics plane circling just inside Saudi Arabia. By the time the launch officer had plotted a trajectory for the Scud and locked the coordinates in the unreliable nose-cone inertial computer, the Americans had relayed the information to one of their F-16s, which had illuminated the launcher with its radar and locked in a flight solution for its own missiles.

The driver moved behind a tall rock and pulled his mask and chemical hood over his face when the launch officer signaled it was time. A few seconds later the Scud rumbled, shook in its carriage, and with amazing speed began to climb straight up. The driver did not see any of his crew mates gasping on the ground, and was mildly surprised.

The missile heeled over to the south-southwest, still climbing toward the apogee of a great caternary arc. The liquid fuel in the rubber-lined tanks burned smoothly. The inertial guidance system was working as accurately as could be expected, which meant tracking reasonably close to what it was aimed at.

Wind whistled around the nose cone, which maintained its structural integrity despite the forces buffeting it. Unless it passed through a cloud and was thrown off course by the turbulence, this missile might actually land in the vicinity of the target.

Gravity and the engine combined as the missile reoriented itself, nose down on a fifteen-degree angle. The rocket picked up speed.

Almost two hundred kilometers behind it, and twenty thousand feet below, the driver's last thought was about whether he and his plump wife could afford to have another child. He had just decided that they should wait until after the war, to see if Saddam would be replaced and what it could all mean to his army career.

At the second he nodded to himself with satisfaction at the practicality of his decision, his right foot was on the running board, his right hand clutching a hand grip, preparing to hoist himself back into the truck cab.

At that precise moment an American missile collided with the weather truck almost twenty meters away. The fiery blast was preparing to engulf him when a second missile punched through the roof of his truck, creating a fireball that vaporized metal, ignited gasoline, evaporated aluminum, and left only the driver's right foot still encased in his boot, found scorched but intact over a hundred meters away, as proof that he had ever existed at all.

JANUARY 17, NORTHEAST SAUDI ARABIA

Night again, trackless desert night with breath coalescing like crimson steam, illuminated by a flashlight's red gel. Sand froze in the desert winter night, granules locked together by icy dew.

Dees picked up a clump of sand with his hands and crushed it, feeling the rough granules roll between his fingers. He had fought a headache all day. His joints ached. He figured it was the result of the anti-nerve-agent pills. He had awakened at 1800, fighting off dreams of flying low over the desert, arms outstretched, as his face melted. A Marine medic had told him his British Aerospace gas mask would probably work fine against nerve agents, but if he weren't wearing his full chemical protective suit, any chemical agents would simply permeate his skin and kill him.

Chemical weapons, the medic noted, would probably just melt

the rubber and plastic on his mask anyway. So he had dreamt of his face melting away in globs, like a candle. The image stuck with him through his MRE breakfast of gelatinous corned beef hash.

It remained with him as he asked Odell about night patrol, and was told everything had been canceled. It came back to him as Melinda pointed out that this was the first night of the dark of the moon. It had been rumored for days as the starting point of an actual move against Saddam.

"Something's up," she said, standing next to a Bradley Fighting Vehicle in the cold and dark.

"Yeah," he replied, "no psyops dance party tonight, either. Everybody's been told to stick close."

"I'm scared," she said flatly.

He felt his knees go to rubber. "I'm scared of something else," he said. "I think I'm getting very fond of you."

She stared, then chuckled. "Whoa, cowboy. I'm not that scared."

He stroked her hair and suddenly kissed her, hotly, tasting sweat and salt and sandy grit. She kissed back, relaxing. They both let it go on just long enough to not be caught, then pulled apart slowly.

"I may be scared of this," she said, "but you scare me even more."

He smiled. "Those of us about to die lust after you."

"Infidel asshole." She grinned. "What time is it?"

He glanced at the luminous dial on his watch. "Midnight at the oasis. A little past, 0015, to be exact."

"Send your camel to bed," she said with a small laugh. "I'm going to try to talk to Dhahran to see if the last two days' worth of pool tape made it on the air. A couple of jarheads from Phoenix want to know if the feature we shot on them has aired there yet."

She brushed his face lightly with her fingertips and walked toward the PAO tent where the satellite phone was located. Dees backtracked to his tent site, unrolled his bag, and tried to sleep.

He was just starting to dream of the ocean when the *braappt* of an air horn blasted him awake. He heard shouts, "Incoming! Missile incoming!"

He heard more yelling. "MOPP Four! MOPP Four! It's MOPP Four!"

Dees reached into his small duffel packed with his sleeping bag and unfurled a pair of forest-camouflaged pants. It was the only chemical suit GTV had available. Sorry, they had said, none in desert camo.

He was hopping on one leg, jamming the other into the pants, when he heard a massive *baanng*, followed by a roar and a *whoosh*. Then another. Then another. As the Patriot antimissiles exploded from their launch tubes, he jammed the other leg into the pants, tied the blouse cords around his boots, slipped on the chem suit jacket and buttoned it up. He unrolled the hood from the jacket collar and made it snug. Around him Marines in full MOPP—including the rubber boots that he didn't have and the long gauntlets—scurried to their vehicles or to defensive fire positions.

He saw Melinda and Marco—he in complete MOPP, she with the pants and suit on but with her hair and face exposed—scanning the skies with the high-eight-millimeter camera equipped with a two-foot night scope.

"There!" Melinda yelled, and pointed.

Dees looked, and saw a bright light falling toward them. Fast.

12,000 FEET OVER SAUDI AIRSPACE

As the Scud's warhead, aimed by its creaky computer, angled downward, the liquid-fueled motor kept firing, accelerating it toward the dark desert below.

The missile passed through a layer of clouds, typical for the Arabian peninsula in winter, bouncing and shaking. Inside the nose cone a large, pressurized cylinder began to leak. If the Iraqi rocket was the ballistic equivalent of a used, battered family Chevy out for a Sunday drive, then the MIM-104 Patriot roaring toward it was a Porsche leaping through a straightaway at Le Mans.

The Patriot's phased-array radar had been the reason the missile was overbudget and behind schedule throughout the 1970s. Now, almost two decades after it had first been proposed, the complex radar was tracking the Scud almost perfectly as the antimissile accelerated to almost three times the speed of sound while pushing upward at a sixty-degree angle.

But the Scud was now wobbling, its trajectory interrupted by successive layers of clouds. It amounted to an evasive maneuver, something that could not yet be accomplished by sophisticated American technology but was standard for a poor Iraqi copy of an unreliable Soviet missile that had once been described by one of its designers after too much vodka as having "the aerodynamic characteristics of a flying bathtub."

The Patriot guidance system plotted a solution almost instantly, but still lost precious seconds in the calculation and course correction.

The Scud's nose-cone altimeter guessed it was at around three thousand feet when the Patriot tore through its fuel tank. The warhead detonation enveloped both missiles in a white-hot fireball.

The nose cone was first torn open, and then ripped loose entirely from the Scud's body. The four-foot aluminum and stainless-steel pressurized canister inside the Scud's nose cone exploded in the heat, blowing most of its atomized contents into the churning air, but leaving a thin trail behind as it rode the shattered nose cone down toward an empty stretch of desert precisely eleven kilometers west of where Peter Dees was standing with his mouth open.

CHARLES JACO

NORTHEAST SAUDI ARABIA

Pedro Marco pulled back with the eight-millimeter to reveal the flash of light overhead, and then followed one especially large, glowing piece of wreckage as it spiraled across the sky above him.

"We're gonna fucking die," he kept repeating, quietly, almost to himself. "We're gonna fucking die."

Melinda had tried to jerk away, but Dees roughly unrolled the hood from her chem suit and forced the gas mask on her face.

"Inhale," he yelled over the sounds of falling metal, the *braaapp* of alarms, and shouting men. He blocked the two air vents on her mask with his hands. "Inhale!"

She did, and the mask drew in tight, fitting snugly. Dees unblocked the air vents, gave her a thumbs-up, smiled, and pulled his own mask down.

A new sound, a high-pitched shriek, joined the cacophony. Then another. Then another. Three sniffers, alarms designed to detect the presence of a variety of chemical weapons, had gone off. Dees froze at the sound. He reached in his chemical suit's jacket pocket and pulled out a pair of gloves. They were cloth, not rubber, and gloves, not gauntlets, but at least they were some protection.

He grabbed Melinda's hand. Her eyes still on the flashes overhead, she tried to jerk it away, but Dees held on. He jammed one glove over her right hand. She turned and stared through her gas mask.

He forced the left-hand glove on, flashed a thumbs-up, and jammed his own hands in his pockets.

The flashes stopped. One by one the howling alarms died. Hopkins, although Dees wasn't sure who it was because of the hood, mask, gauntlets, and rubber boots, was half waddling, half sprinting near the camera position when he saw Dees reach for his mask, hands bare.

Dees was merely going to block the air intakes for one breath to tighten up the mask. Hopkins thought he was about to remove it. He trudged over, through the sand, and grabbed Dees's hand, forcing it back into a pocket.

He shoved his mask next to Dees's hood. "Stay buttoned up! We got chemicals! You understand?"

Dees stared, then nodded. Hopkins clapped him on the shoulder and resumed his double-time trudge.

Twenty minutes passed. Melinda, Marco, and Dees walked across the area near the tents and bunkers, sweating inside their masks, scanning the skies. Nothing.

Dees saw a Marine nearby remove his mask. Another did the same. "All clear!" they yelled. "All clear!"

Several dozen meters away from the camera crew, Odell and Hopkins emerged from a sandbagged bunker. They removed their masks almost simultaneously.

Odell weaved slightly. "Shit."

Hopkins looked at him. "What?"

"My face feels numb. I can't feel my lips."

Hopkins bit his own lip. He didn't feel it. "Me, too. Like novocaine."

Odell nodded. "Maybe we had our masks on too long."

"Shit," Hopkins said. "Maybe. But I can't feel nothin' in my face."

They stared at each other. Seconds later the numbness and tingling began to subside.

Odell felt the feeling return. "My nose is cold. Must've been the mask."

Hopkins nodded, but looked dubious. He sniffed, testing his own nose. "You smell that?"

"What?"

"Dunno. Smells like ammonia."

The faint aroma from his childhood of his mother scrubbing down something or other with ammonia twinged Odell's nose. "Yeah. Wanna button up?"

Hopkins looked at the other Marines undoing their masks and hoods. "Nah. Nobody else's dying."

"Odell! Hopkins!" a gunnery sergeant nearby yelled.

"Yo!" In unison.

"Saddle up. Something big landed due west. Recovery team."

When they got to the Humvee, they found the PAO, Marco, and Dees waiting. Odell squinted. "Where's Melinda?"

Marco grimaced. "Medic tent. She took her mask off and starting puking her guts out."

Odell looked at Dees and asked quietly, "She okay?"

Dees exhaled. "Medic says it's probably nerves. No other signs of exposure. And the chem tape we tacked up is still green."

The chemical detection kit included an olive-green strip that looked like flypaper. Strips had been taped to tents and trucks and tacked to poles. Red dots appeared if it was exposed to a variety of chemical agents. Three near the camera position had stayed all green. Others were being torn down for analysis by a decontamination unit.

Odell hadn't seen any of them. The alarms and the numbness were enough evidence, as far as he was concerned. Hopkins figured he was alive, which was a plus.

Three Humvees headed west through the night, along a series of goat, sheep, and camel tracks. Because of the misty rains, scrub filled the desert, so tribesmen would bring small flocks to graze, even with a war on.

Forty-five minutes later the caravan turned right into some small dunes, around where the AWACs and tracking satellites had spotted a large piece of debris plummet to earth.

Odell, driving the lead Humvee, stopped. A large sheep,

eighty pounds or more, lay in his path, its eyes open, tongue lolling, legs as stiff as steel rods.

Marco powered up the night scope on the camera, panned around, and said, "Shit. They're all over the place."

The residual heat from the corpses glowed ghastly green in the viewfinder. Seventeen sheep lay scattered, dead. A hundred meters away, metal too cold to show up on the thermal lens was illuminated by the red beam from a Marine flashlight. The splintered nose cone's largest remaining fragment was half buried in the sand.

CHAPTER 11

JANUARY 18, RIYADH, SAUDI ARABIA

Dennis Kingen was wearing chocolate-chip BDUs over a khaki T-shirt. The blouse sleeves were starched, neatly folded, and buttoned above the elbows. There was no insignia, not even a name.

ABC had reported chemical attacks in Israel. False alarm. CNN had reported possible chemical releases near Dhahran. False alarm.

The Scuds that had fallen near Riyadh had conventional high-explosive warheads. No traces of chemical or nerve agent residue at all. This left the lean man in the Riyadh basement rubbing his temples as he hunched over a long folding table, staring again at the two dozen single-spaced pages of reports fresh from the computer printer. Each reported a suspected incident of chemical or nerve gas exposure. He took the Jerusalem and Tel Aviv reports—five of those—and put them in another stack. Then the three Dhahran reports, then the two panicked reports filed by the Saudis themselves in Riyadh on top of those.

That took care of ten incidents, each confirmed negative. Fourteen left, including two from the Second Marines, two from around Jubail, and ten more from King Khalid Military City to Hafir al-Batin, from the First Cav to the Egyptian army. Those hadn't been sniffed and reported yet. Intell disagreed about them, except for four confirmed. But you could never be sure. Maybe they all had been hit, after all. Or maybe Saddam was too scared of the wrath of *Haji* Bush even to consider using his arsenal.

He looked at his watch, and walked over to the stool positioned against a wall covered in gray fabric. The camera on its tripod automatically focused on him as he sat down. The controller he held on his lap would make preloaded graphics seem to appear behind him. They were inserted automatically through the chromakey process, the same way weathermen and -women on TV appear to walk on maps of the United States.

He inserted his earpiece and waited. The red light on the camera clicked on, and the TV monitor sitting on a small table just below the camera came to life.

The signals between him and Washington were scrambled, audio and video, bounced off a military communications satellite and reconstituted. Like Kool-Aid, DIA had once said. Add water and stir.

Kingen's screen winked on, DIA's face filling it. "Dennis. What've you got?"

What DIA and the others in the Washington conference room saw was the chromakey map displayed behind Kingen. It showed fourteen red stars scattered across northern and eastern Saudi Arabia.

"These are reported chemical or nerve agent attacks," Kingen said. "We'll get sniffer reports soonest. None are confirmed yet. We believe—"

"Dennis," DIA interrupted gently, "stand by."

DIA was replaced in close-up by NSC. He nodded to Kingen. "Our assessment is there were no chemical or nerve gas attacks.

We don't want a panic. Until we analyze every chem strip, every sniffer filter, and every grain of sand for contamination, we have had no chemical attacks."

"But," Kingen said, "we have a half dozen that may be positive—including a pair from an area nowhere near Scud attacks."

The graphic behind Kingen changed with a click of the button, replaced with a map of Kuwait, southern Iraq, and northern Saudi Arabia. Several wavy arrows moved from northwest to southeast. Others moved almost directly north to south.

"These are the latest upper atmosphere winds," Kingen said. "Common for this time of year. Particles won't travel more than a few hundred miles because of the moisture in the air. There's a possibility of fallout from some of the air strikes, especially if Wafra or any other targets contained chemical or nerve agents."

NSC's mouth tightened. "Kingen, we need analysis. Fast. But the official position is that all—repeat, all—of the incidents are false, including any where equipment registered positives. Use the CNN and ABC reports. No chemicals after all. Use the Riyadh strike. Explosives only. Leak the word intell confirms no positives. We'll take care of the on-the-record part."

NSC stepped aside. DIA reappeared. "Dennis." That same soft, avuncular voice. "Dennis, I'd like you to go north. Seems the Second Marines have found a little something. Nose cone and canister. Coordinates follow."

The screen blinked off. Kingen sat, immobile, for over a minute. He removed the earpiece, switched off the hand controller, and walked to the secure phone.

He would call the *Washington Post* and *New York Times* in Riyadh and the "intelligence sources say" lead would be spread to those that mattered within a day. Kingen had just started to punch in an altogether different number when an army colonel opened the door and came in. He was short, not more than five-nine, and looked like a beige camouflaged fireplug.

"Sir," the colonel said stiffly, "we have tapes and sniffer results. Three confirmed. Eight negative. Still waiting on the other three."

Kingen blinked. "Thank you, Colonel. Those results are my eyes only, soonest. And if anyone asks, there are no positives. No confirmation at all."

The colonel's face showed no emotion, except for a single twitch in his left eyelid. "Yes sir." He turned and left, shutting the door so hard the wall rattled.

CAIRO

The satellite phone unit gargled, once.

"GTV. Volga."

He spent the next four minutes and thirty seconds not speaking, listening, nodding absently as morning traffic began to snake its way along the Corniche below the office balcony.

"Understood," he said at last. "Call me back in exactly a half hour."

Volga bit his lower lip as he punched in the Denver access code. "Mac. Timothy. We have a problem."

He repeated what he'd been told, then paused and sipped his now lukewarm tea.

"Understood," he said finally, after listening for a full two minutes.

Ten minutes later the phone gurgled again. He picked up the receiver without speaking and listened.

"Use your special talents," he said. "We need this resolved as soon as possible. If *it* didn't work, *you'd* better."

CHARLES JACO

JANUARY 21, NORTHEAST SAUDI ARABIA

Odell absently scratched one of the scaly patches that had appeared on his arm two days before. His unit had had the shit scared out of it, then found out its detection equipment must have been defective because the brass said there were no chemical attacks. And now a dozen people he knew of had some sort of this desert crud somewhere on them.

It was night. Odell was standing next to a huge tank. He had been fascinated ever since he discovered that the M-1A1's fired uranium. He had visions of small mushroom clouds erupting over each target. Then he found out it was depleted uranium—DPU—stuff that had been run through reactors for so long that nothing was left but a slightly radioactive husk.

The uranium was used to make shells for the M-1A1's 105-millimeter cannon, shells so hard they'd tear through tank armor like a knife through cloth. But Odell still wondered if one of the shells going off inside an Iraqi tank might radiate the tankers inside so they'd emerge from the turret and end up growing like Arab Godzillas, three hundred feet tall, swaggering through Allied lines, popping tanks and Humvees in their mouths like after-dinner mints.

Odell had been warned another arc light mission was coming, so he stood by one of the sixty-ton Abrams tanks to watch. Arc light was a name left over from Vietnam, much like the lumbering B-52s that would pound areas in overlapping arcs, making sure that nothing that walked or crawled inside those arcs would survive. Before an arc light, he and Hopkins pulled their speakers and themselves back a few miles, trying to give plummeting half-ton chunks of high explosive and shrapnel a wide berth.

Odell and Hopkins had found themselves suddenly on temporary duty with a new unit, the Tiger Brigade, a union of the Marines and the Army, an amalgam of soldiers, jarheads, and tanks from both services. Their mission was unknown as yet but pretty well suspected—to be the point of the spear that was supposed to tear through Iraqi defenses.

Odell checked his watch and braced himself. Suddenly the entire horizon was on fire, geysers of sand, shrapnel, machinery, and body parts a hundred feet high, blazing at first and then fading into pale light. At about the same time the shock waves shook the Humvees and even the mammoth M-1A1s, rocking the tanks on their suspensions, causing the sand to wiggle and dance. Odell tried to keep his feet, and finally turned his back as the concussion shook his internal organs like so many lumps of Jell-O.

A few thousand meters away, another flaming sandstorm erupted. He tried to think of what this was doing to the poor fucks underneath it. His imagination failed. He simply and firmly decided that nothing could live through this. Nothing.

SOUTHWEST KUWAIT

Shafir screamed, but no one heard. He couldn't even hear himself. Once again the American bombs were falling. And once again his captain told the men to scream. It was the officer's theory that it would help equalize the air pressure inside the ears, and perhaps keep the bomb's concussion from rupturing eardrums.

The screaming raised the tension inside the underground dugout five meters below the surface, a sand cave supported by steel plates, corrugated tin, and wood braces, buried under more than fifteen feet of the best insulating and shock-absorbing material—sand. But anyone near the top of the gentle incline that led up to the bunker's entrance on the surface would scream for real when the shock waves from explosions actually did rupture their eardrums. Some recruit from Basra had done just that, bleeding from the ears two days before.

The bunker was packed with eighty-seven soldiers. Feeble flashlight beams floated like clouds of fog in the fine dust stirred up by the *thumpthumpTHUMPTHUMP* on the surface. The tomblike bunker was humid because of the respiration of so many bodies squeezed into a space roughly the size of a railroad boxcar but half the height. If anyone had been able to hear anything but themselves screaming, they would have heard eighty-seven voices howling, some like a roar, some like a woman's shriek, all mixed with the explosions' rattle and thud.

Standing almost at the start of the incline to the surface, screaming, his hands covering his ears, Shafir saw a soldier stagger down the incline, his mouth wide, his eyes closed in pain, his hands tearing at his ears, alternately clawing at an earlobe and slapping the other ear with his flat palm. Shafir's stomach turned when he saw blood leaking between the soldier's fingers, blood from his ruptured eardrums. The soldier was in excruciating pain. He rolled on the ground, clutching at his ears, curled in a fetal ball, screaming and screaming and screaming.

Shafir felt an almost electric shock course through his body. He was going to vomit. He panicked, thinking that if he did throw up, he might choke to death, because if he stopped screaming, his eardrums, too, would become bloody little flaps of skin and he would never hear anything again except the thump of his own heart.

He suppressed the urge to vomit and closed his eyes, tight. The screaming went on for another five minutes, until the last flight of B-52s wheeled and turned for King Khalid Military City in Saudi Arabia.

DEAD AIR

JANUARY 24, KING KHALID MILITARY CITY, SAUDI ARABIA

Dennis Kingen had watched the bombers take off and land at KKMC for forty-eight hours. It had taken that long for the last of his three reinforced aluminum Halburton cases to arrive from Riyadh. Two had caught up with him almost immediately. The third, four feet by two feet by one foot, had been bumped from helo after helo until it arrived, still securely locked and apparently not tampered with.

He had scrounged a Humvee and driver, had finally received everything he needed—and now this.

The Czech captain who stood before him in the beige light inside the tent had uneasily but competently ridden the waves of change washing over Eastern Europe. He had been seven when Russian tanks crushed the Prague Spring in 1968. He had never forgotten.

Captain Vlad Klavel, chemical weapons specialist, graduate of the Warsaw Pact chemical training center in the Soviet Union, was ten percent of Czechoslovakia's entire contribution to Desert Storm, commanding one of two chemical and nerve agent detection teams in this part of the desert.

"No need to stand at attention, Captain," Kingen said, motioning for him to sit on a folding chair. "Technically, I have no rank."

Klavel sat, and in American-accented English with only the slightest tendency to hiss his s's, said, "Do you mind if I smoke?"

Kingen shook his head, and Klavel lit up one of the delicious Marlboros the American troops had in great abundance. He stroked his wiry mustache with his right index finger. It was an absent gesture, but allowed him a few seconds to study the American intelligence officer to whom he had been told to report.

"So what can I do for America's intelligence community?" he

asked, sibilant s's ruining what was otherwise a perfect Cleveland accent developed as a chemical engineering major at Case Western Reserve.

"I understand you have something to report."

Klavel nodded, and pulled two sheets of paper from his breast pocket. He loved to read, and appreciated the crinkle and feel of paper in his fingers. He spread the papers on his lap, glancing at them, then at Kingen.

"At 0800 our tests thirty kilometers northeast of here detected traces of mustard agent. Samples from the ground and from the dust off one of your Humvees in the area were positive."

Kingen's eyes narrowed slightly, and he sighed so softly that Klavel didn't hear it.

"At 1400," the Czech captain continued, "we were roughly in the same region, this time, oh, say, thirty-five kilometers from here, and detected traces of yperite."

He paused. Kingen asked, "And yperite is?"

"Also called sulfur mustard gas. A dichlorodiethyl sulfide. It's a blister agent and can cause skin lesions now, or later, especially later if it's part of the *novachoks*."

Kingen interrupted. "*Novachoks?* Newcomers?"

Klavel smiled. "Congratulations on your Russian. The *novachoks* are newer binary agents. Combine yperite as one half, say, with a dioxin compound as the other half."

He put down his cigarette and clasped both hands together. "They combine. Dioxin compounds infiltrate lipids, body fats. They are stored there. So you could also get small amounts of yperite stored in the body's fats when combined with a dioxin compound. And that could mean symptoms, serious symptoms, later on, for years perhaps."

"Captain Klavel," Kingen said, "I will pass this on to Riyadh immediately. May I have those reports for reference?"

Klavel nodded and handed over the sheets of paper. He rose and extended his hand. Kingen took it and said, "By the way, one other matter."

Klavel's hand was still held by the American. Kingen smiled, but kept his grip firm. "Report only to me. And do not mention this or, ah, any future results, to anyone else. Anyone at all."

Kingen released the hand. Klavel flexed his fingers discreetly, said, "Of course," and left. He had notified Prague two hours earlier.

JANUARY 27, NORTHEAST SAUDI ARABIA

She was sitting in the sand, her legs spread apart like a man's, laughing. Three Marines, transfixed, sat and laughed with her. She was pretty, they had all agreed. She could probably rupture your spleen, one of the Marines, a medic, had whispered to another.

She had overheard and replied, "Not so's you'll ever find out," and they had all laughed some more.

"So," Melinda continued, "a bottle of Pepto and some Tagamet, plus some Immodium to keep me from shitting my brains out, was all it took. Plus some rehydration from an IV."

"And water," the medic said. "We had ten other cases like you, and eighteen more with lousy vision and dizziness, all temporary. At least we got you out of the medic tent in forty-eight hours. But these . . ." He nodded toward two small scaly patches on Melinda's right arm.

She shrugged. "Desert crud. I figure I need more water and some Oil of Olay."

"Any word about Khafji?" Odell asked.

"I heard," Hopkins added, "the Saudis ran like chickens."

"You heard right." Hopkins, Odell, the medic, and Melinda looked up. Peter Dees was thumbing through his reporter's notebook. "You'll love this," he said, reading through his notes. "I'm just back from the PAO tent. A Saudi colonel and the public affairs officer spent the better part of half an hour arguing, like this . . .

" 'We believe journalists should see what the Iraqis have done,' says the Saudi.

" 'But sir, the city hasn't been secured yet,' says the PAO.

" 'Our Saudi troops and your Fifth Marine Expeditionary Brigade have retaken the city,' says the Saudi.

" 'But I can't take responsibility for releasing our pool reporters to travel to Khafji,' says the PAO.

" 'My government will be glad to oversee the trip,' says the Saudi.

"And on and on until the Saudi colonel spots me sitting quietly in a corner, and orders me to leave.

"By that time," Dees said, sitting down in the sand next to Melinda, still staring at his notebook, "your obedient servant determines that between statements of mutual affection and respect, the Allies despise each other.

"Seems Iraqi armor punched through Saudi lines like they weren't even there. Saudi soldiers took off. The Marines let them run behind Fifth MEB lines, and then had to listen to them demanding the jarheads retake the city. One British general," Dees continued, studying his notebook, "said he'd have ordered his troops to shoot the Saudis if he'd been dug in behind them when they ran. But he wasn't.

"So the Saudis hid behind the Marines and demanded the Marines go in and dig out the Iraqis house by house. The Saudis said there were two full Iraqi divisions on the way from Kuwait to Khafji, and the Marines had to go in now. Turns out the Marines knew something the Saudis didn't. Besides how to work."

Snickers all around. "So now I give you today's pool report."

He paused and read from the notebook. " 'For the first time in military history, a mass movement of armor has been crushed from the air. Tuesday evening, high-altitude flights of B-52s and low-flying A-10 Warthog tank killers destroyed over a hundred Iraqi tanks without any Allied losses.

" 'The tanks were reinforcements for the Iraqi troops who still hold the Saudi port city of Khafji. Those troops are now cut off, since the reinforcing tank columns were destroyed, according to Allied sources.

" 'The main highway leading south from Kuwait to Khafji, from Al Jahrah to Al Ahmadi, is described as being littered with pieces of the armored column's shattered spine.' That's it so far."

Melinda whistled, low. "You're good."

"Thankee vous. You see what graphics Phoenix can design to cover it. I'm going to try to find out about any tests on those Scud pieces."

He and Melinda exchanged glances. He had told her about the sheep. While she still lay on a cot, rehydrating, they had agreed that the official explanation, death by concussion and blast fragments, didn't seem logical.

Odell squinted. "So what about the speed bump colonel?" Allied troops generally referred to the Saudi army contemptuously as "speed bumps."

Dees shrugged. "He wants to arrange a field trip to Khafji. Seems the Iraqis keep sticking their noses out and keep getting killed. The Saudis figure there may be only a hundred or less left alive. The Marines think they may be snipers and don't want to haul us in there. But the Saudis want the coverage."

As Dees and Melinda rose, a Sea Stallion helicopter coming in for a landing cast a long shadow over them. They didn't notice. A passenger in the helo, looking down at just that moment, did.

—

As Dennis Kingen's helicopter settled onto the landing zone, pounded hard and flat on the sand by Marine engineers, the Humvee and deuce and a half he had ordered, along with five Marines, were waiting on the ground.

Carrying a duffel bag and his long aluminum-sided case, he hopped into the rear of the Humvee. The two vehicles tossed up dust as they rattled half a kilometer across the compound and stopped in front of a tent where two sentries stood guard.

The three Marines turned to look at Kingen. One said, "Sir?"

"You all have MOPP gear?" he asked.

They nodded.

"Then go to MOPP Four, and put the metal inside that tent in the polypropylene bags in my duffel. Fill each bag half full at the most, then secure it with the tape, put it inside another bag, and seal it. Give the bags to the drivers with these instructions." He handed a folded sheet of paper to the closest Marine, then turned to his Humvee driver. "The containers I requested?"

"Got 'em, sir," the young man said. "Four of the heavy sacks the big tents come in. Rubber-lined canvas."

"Yallah," Kingen said. "Let's go."

An hour later Kingen watched the Marines remove their sweltering MOPP gear and the deuce and a half grind down the road toward KKMC. There, the drivers would toss three sacks into a C-141 that would transport them to Andrews Air Force Base. From there they were to be hauled in an Army truck with four cars of MPs as escort to Fort Detrick, Maryland.

Kingen turned and, just outside the area around the tent that was staked and roped off with orange plastic tape, saw Dees leaning against a Bradley, arms folded, staring.

From the waist down Dees looked military: chocolate-chip pants, blouse cords tied neatly around tan boots. From the waist up he was strictly civilian, brown T-shirt under a tan safari jacket, pockets bulging with pens, notebooks, and a water bottle, all topped by a sunburned face and a bristle-cut goatee.

Kingen walked over, ducked under the tape, and stood in the shade next to the Bradley. Dees didn't move, didn't blink.

"Peter. Good to see you again." He didn't extend his hand but instead tried to return the languid stare.

"Opsec, Dennis? Or is this national security? How about social security?" It was Kingen's turn to just stare. Dees continued. "So where are your boys taking several bags of scrap metal?"

"Can't say. We need to analyze them."

"Mmm-hmm," Dees said, "to Fort Detrick, maybe?" A muscle high in Kingen's right cheek twitched. Dees saw it and pretended he hadn't. "I mean, where else would a trade attaché send half a nose cone? Especially when it kills a couple of dozen sheep. But they died from concussion and the explosion, except that there weren't any blast marks and no wounds, only blood and some foam from their mouths.

"So we load it in a truck with minimal MOPP gear since, shit, it's simply high explosive. Except we arrive here, and all the pieces are quarantined like Typhoid fucking Mary.

"And then you show up in full spook, and jarheads in moon suits load up the pieces. Which is just what you would do with harmless metal in a desert that already has enough scrap scattered around to start a junkyard."

"Every positive field report has turned out to be negative. But, ah, that doesn't mean we stop checking everything that might even possibly be chemical. So we're running tests to make sure. Besides, I understand almost none of your M-8A1s went off."

"Bullshit," Dees said. "The ones that went off shorted out. That's the official line. The ones that didn't go off worked fine, they said."

Kingen squinted. "We need to talk. I've got a billet over here. Let's walk."

The two walked among two-and-a-half-ton trucks, Bradleys, tanks, tents, and Marines, hundreds of Marines, all dressed in tan camouflage. Dees put on his sunglasses.

"Funny thing," Dees said, "you get plenty of time to read out here. You read anything. The other day, I'm in the medic's tent. My producer's sick, so I'm sitting with her."

Dees remembered Melinda lying on a cot, an IV saline solution running into her right arm, her fine hair plastered by sweat against her brow, her lips quivering slightly as she slept. He kept his anger under control.

"So I pick up something to read. It was a stack of material safety data sheets on how to handle chemicals, and a manual for the M-8A1. Funny thing. The safety sheets tell me for, let's say, sarin, that one ten-thousandth of a milligram in a cubic meter of air can be hazardous. Then I read that the sniffers detect sarin at a minimum concentration of a tenth of a milligram. And so I do the math figuring, shit, there's nothing else to do since my producer's just lying there wheezing, but I figure, hey, it's because she's been vomiting and shitting her brains out, it can't be exposure to chemicals, or otherwise all of our trusty sniffers'd be wailing."

Dees's words became clipped, sharp, brittle, like glass being crunched underfoot.

"So I do the math, and figure out your fucking M-8A1s aren't designed to go off unless they're exposed to a thousand times the level of sarin that's supposed to hurt you. Ain't that swell?"

The two entered Kingen's musty tent. Kingen sat on a cot. Dees sat on the edge of the long hard-sided case and looked down. "So you always carry an electric guitar to the desert?"

Kingen smiled thinly. "Measuring equipment for preliminary readings on whatever we find."

"And?"

"Inconclusive. That's why we're testing more. Meanwhile . . ." Kingen paused. "Meanwhile, any word of this causes, um, a panic. We don't want that. We don't want Saddam to know anything about any effects their weapons may have. This is numbah one opsec."

Dees stared at his hands, and looked up. "Numbah one? You in Vietnam long?"

Kingen didn't change expression. "Generic expression."

"Right," Dees said. "You could tell me, but you'd have to kill me."

Kingen cracked a smile. "So," he said, still smiling, "are we on the same page?"

Dees smiled back. "Not even the same chapter."

Kingen's smile faded. "You violate opsec on this and—"

"I'm a fucking star," Dees said flatly. "I'm kicked out of Saudi, and I'm a hero in America. I've whipped up patriotic outrage over a psycho Arab dictator who gassed our boys, and I make a fortune on the speaking circuit. And just maybe whoever supplied the stuff to him comes running out from under the baseboards. And I'll get even richer and more famous.

"Go ahead, threaten me some more, Kingen. It gets better." Dees spread his arms. "At least three people are dead. A spook calls me in a basement in Cairo and gets cagey about why somebody wants to kill me. A GTV Egyptian says he did it, only he gets blown up by the incredible hulk you provided me."

He paused, cocked his head slightly to one side, absently stroked his goatee, then stopped. "The movie rights alone are worth millions."

Kingen spread his palms flat on his knees and cleared his throat. "You are in a war zone under our protection. You violate opsec and the Saudis pick you up and you disappear for a little while, or the Marines do the same. Or you piss people off and something happens in the field and they're not watching your back like they should."

Dees heaved himself off the metal case and grunted as he felt both knees crunch and pop. Arthritis? Any doubts he had vanished with the sudden rush washing upward from his creaky knees, an adrenaline surge that came from the thought that flashed across his mind: He was, no joking, too old for this, and time was evaporating in front of his eyes.

He looked down at Kingen. "So we have nothing to say. You lock me up for two weeks, six weeks, hell, six months. The story's even more valuable. I get killed, somebody else does the story." He began to improvise. "There are documents and videotapes detailing everything stashed safely in several places outside of Saudi. And a number of people know how to get to them.

"So here's the deal. I blow the whistle now, naming names. Or you help me, I hold it until the war's over, and you appear exactly nowhere. I'll cover—"

A fuzz-faced lieutenant from the public affairs office rapped his knuckles on the tent pole and lifted the flap.

"Excuse me, sir." He paused. Kingen nodded. The lieutenant turned to Dees. "The pool's going to Khafji. Not our idea. The Saudis want to. We don't think it's safe yet, but . . ." He shrugged.

Dees said, "Thanks. I'll be ready in fifteen minutes."

The lieutenant left. Kingen exhaled deeply. "Tell you what, Peter. We have plenty of time. After we get back from Khafji, we can talk some more."

"We?"

Kingen smiled. "It seems like Khafji might be interesting to, ah . . ."

"A trade attaché?"

Kingen glared again.

"You ever hear of Wilfred Owen?" Kingen shook his head.

Dees continued. "No reason you should have. A Brit. Minor poet. Enlists in World War One and gets himself killed a week before the Armistice. Writes some nifty stuff about war. He wrote one about a gas attack. Funny thing, I used to know all of it. But all I remember now are a few lines, when he sees some soldier dying: 'In all my dreams, before my helpless sight/ He plunges at me guttering, choking, drowning.'

" 'If you could hear, at every jolt, the blood come gargling from the froth-corrupted lungs, obscene as cancer.' Like it, Dennis?"

Kingen stalked out of the tent.

THE ROAD TO KHAFJI, SAUDI ARABIA

Dees and Melinda sat next to each other. Marco was in the seat across from them, next to an AP photographer. Kingen was in the front, next to a Saudi colonel and across from two Saudi soldiers. Two Marines sat behind him.

The night was as black as the asphalt that the 1960s vintage American-made school bus creaked over, headed toward Khafji. By looking through the viewfinder on Marco's night scope, Dees could see the smoldering hulk of an armored vehicle next to a Marine roadblock, people and machinery turned into glowing green ghosts.

Ahead several miles, the horizon suddenly appeared in flashes, as if monstrous strobe lights were pulsing, illuminating each section of sky and earth for a second or two. The school bus began to vibrate, the windows rattling. The old Bluebird bus creaked and swayed on its springs.

"If Khafji's so bloody secure," a correspondent from the BBC said, "why are we bombing just north of it?"

"Practice," said the AP shooter. No one laughed.

The bus turned to the right and drove under a shell-pocked

cement arch marking the Khafji city limits. The two Marines simultaneously racked shells into their M-16s. The Saudi soldiers noticed, and pretended not to. The bus lurched and shook as it negotiated the dark road littered with chunks of concrete, random pieces of steel girders, bits of tank tread, and the odd body part left over from a battle that took place in an apparent ghost town.

The bus stopped, suddenly. The Saudi colonel announced, "We are here," but waited for the two Marines to get out in the inky blackness before he exited. The journalists piled out in crowded confusion.

Dees could see barely three feet. He could only hear the spasmodic rumble of the still-idling bus, and the scraping crunch of dozens of boots stepping on thousands of bits of broken glass, fallen masonry, and random pieces of metal. But there were enough smells twisting through the black air to make up for the loss of his other senses.

The acrid aroma of burned things was all he smelled at first, but the scents slowly sorted themselves out into charred wood, the bitter hint of overheated metal, the foul odor of cooked rubber and plastic, and the occasional whiff of partly cooked meat.

Dees tapped Marco on the shoulder and nodded toward what appeared to be a smoldering Iraqi armored personnel carrier. A Marine noticed. "Careful of mines and booby traps, sir."

Dees, Marco, and Melinda all bobbed their heads. The cameraman reached into one of the dozen pockets in his tan vest and produced a small flashlight with a red gel taped to the lens. Dees took it, clicked it on, and began to lead the way across the street through litter and debris.

At first he thought he'd kicked a wet sandbag, sodden and lumpy. Dees froze, convinced himself that if it was a booby trap, he would have been dead by now, and aimed the flashlight at it.

It was a head, the dried black blood that had run from the mouth and ears made red again by the ghastly light. The eyes were rolled upward so that only the whites showed. The tongue—at least Dees thought it was a tongue—was coal-black even in the red light, protruding between the lips underneath a bushy black mustache. Flesh hung in shreds around the severed windpipe, and a pair of thoracic vertebrae lay next to it, partly immersed in a coagulated lump of dark gelatin. Two flies sat on top.

With a *whoof*, Dees felt the air go out of him. He was going to vomit. Marco saw the head and began rolling, the night scope converting the head in the viewfinder to glowing green and white pixels. Keeping the camera on his right shoulder, Marco gestured with his left arm to get Dees away. Something this gruesome wouldn't get on the air if it was shot too tight, so he was attempting to frame a medium shot and make sure it didn't include a barfing reporter.

Suddenly, the guys from the BBC and the AP arrived, the Beeb shooter rolling with his night scope, and also waving Dees away. A pudgy Saudi cameraman, whose sole television experience consisted of shooting office-training videos for Filipino workers hired by the Saudi government, waddled up. His wife's uncle, an army colonel, had been persuaded to let him chronicle the Saudi army's Khafji victory, so when he saw the head, he hoped it was Iraqi, not Saudi. He hoisted his camera on his shoulder and turned on the floodlight.

"Motherfucker!" Marco yelled as his night-scope picture was bleached totally white by the light.

"Shit! You asshole!" the BBC cameraman bellowed.

"Kill the light! We still have snipers loose!" one of the Marines yelled.

"Whoof," Dees croaked, and doubled over.

"My hero," Melinda said as she held Marco to keep him from attacking the Saudi shooter.

Dees bent over, and the Saudi camera followed him, panning down to record Dees's expression, the vomit, and stopping at the severed head.

The Saudi suddenly lurched backward. Dees thought the BBC guy had cold-cocked him when he heard the *crraack* of a rifle shot ricochet off the walls. The Saudi fell, hard, flat on his back, the entrance wound on the bridge of his nose considerably smaller than the exit wound in the back of his skull. The camera slammed to the ground, the floodlight breaking free of its mount. It bounced in the air, still attached to the cable hooked to the dead Saudi's battery belt. It leaped like a snake, lighting the walls of the ruined city, the smoldering personnel carrier, the Iraqi head, Dees's gray face, and the BBC cameraman, his mouth wide open, before the Marine raced over and stomped on the light, crushing the filament and plunging the block back into darkness.

"Everybody in the bus! Now!" one of the Marines yelled. The Saudi colonel barked at his soldiers, and they grabbed the cameraman by his shoulders. The colonel sprinted toward the bus. The soldiers dragged the body about ten feet, looked at each other, dropped it, and followed their leader.

Dees looked at Marco. "Still rolling?"

Marco nodded, stopped, and panned around one last time. "I don't know how much I got since the dickhead turned on the light. I hope it didn't burn out the lens."

The bus was running as Melinda arrived at the door at the same time as Kingen. "After you," he said.

"You see all that?" she asked over her shoulder.

"The whole thing," he replied as he wedged his way between the two Marines with their weapons at the ready. Their Saudi counterparts were already aboard.

Dees and Marco were the last on board. Marco tripped on something.

"Sorry," Kingen said. He bent over and shoved an aluminum container that looked like a long, thin suitcase under the seat.

The bus groaned and clattered, crunching over the wide street until it was turned around, heading away from Khafji.

"Hey," Dees said, "where's the body?"

The bus was silent.

"Damn," Dees said.

"You always carry out your dead?" Melinda asked.

Dees shrugged. "Only when they have tape of me puking."

CHAPTER 12

JANUARY 27–28, POW CAMP, NORTHEAST SAUDI ARABIA

He could close his eyes and imagine thunder, followed by a gentle *whoosh* as rain crawls slowly down a mountainside and into a valley. *Wadis* become torrents, thick ochre water colored by clotted sand gushing forward until the *wadis* widen and slowly begin to absorb it. Eventually, the roaring liquid would become nothing more than damp earth and then not even that, so all traces of the flood would disappear within a few hours, a day at most.

Colonel Ali Jassim was convinced that the Americans, French, British, and even the Czechs and Chileans, for God's sake, were the river, and Kuwait and Iraq were the *wadi*. He lit another of the intoxicating American menthol cigarettes, then closed one eye and pressed the other against the window of the purring Mercedes bus, its engine humming with German precision to operate the heater. Outside, he could see a berm, a ring of sand fifteen feet high, with Saudi soldiers every ten meters.

Inside the ring, in a sand bowl thirty by twenty meters, several hundred Iraqi prisoners were huddled, some so hungry that they tore into the American GI rations, wolfing down packets of beef stew, applesauce, spaghetti and meatballs, corned beef, or whatever else happened to be inside. Several of them ate the coffee creamer and sugar, and the hard candy—cellophane and all.

Jassim was an intelligence service colonel who had been interrogating Saudi prisoners in Khafji, waiting for the armored column from Iraq that had never come, when the battalion of farm boys to which he was temporarily assigned decided to surrender. He had looked out the ground-floor window of the ruined building in which he'd set up office, and seen dozens of the dirty-faced, hungry conscripts tossing their rifles by the side of the main boulevard, lifting their hands over their heads and running at a trot for the archway at the city limits, beyond which were American Marines and food.

Another man with the official rank of colonel had been in the room with him, but his powers went far beyond Jassim's. The other colonel was with the *Mukhabarat*, Ba'ath party intelligence, the most feared of Iraq's three security agencies. He was also a tribal kinsman of Saddam's from the area around Tikrit, Saddam's birthplace and his power base, a town on the great looping Aqaba-to-Basra railway.

Ali Jassim was with the *Estikhbarat*, military intelligence, and had risen through the ranks despite being a member of an unrelated clan from the south, near Basra. He'd been trained in Moscow and East Germany in the refinements of chemical warfare. In the 1980s he supervised murderous barrages of chemical artillery shells hurled at Iranian human wave troops in the marshes around Abu al Khasib. And, at least until he was called back to front line duty, he was head of internal security at Al Fallujah, the "fertilizer plant" west of Baghdad.

And he'd done all of it without family or tribal connections, but with a ruthless pragmatism. He had bought, stolen, or threatened until he had a nest egg of roughly half a million pounds sterling in an Emirates bank. Every step of the way, he thought Saddam might take it all away before he could escape to enjoy it.

He was thinking that very thing while in the room in Khafji as he watched the *Mukhabarat* colonel stride past him, stare out the window, and turn toward his Kalishnikov, leaning against the wall. It was clear he meant to stop the surrender by shooting a few unarmed soldiers in the street, to cow the rest.

In a fluid motion, Ali Jassim had unsnapped his holster, raised the Czech nine-millimeter pistol shoulder high, turned it sideways in his hand, since that was how he preferred to shoot, and fired two rounds into the back of the *Mukhabarat* colonel's head. The hollow-eyed stragglers in the street seemed not to notice the two tinny pistol shots.

Then Jassim opened a desk drawer and stuffed his military ID, his intelligence ID, his pass allowing him free access to any part of any Iraqi theater of operations, and his military passport into a blouse pocket of his field jacket. After unbuckling his holster, he placed it on the desktop alongside the pistol and strode into the street, his colonel's insignia plainly visible. His clean, well-fed face was in sharp contrast to the troops all around him.

It took the Americans roughly thirty-six hours to figure out who he was, separate him from the rest of the prisoners, isolate him inside one of the Mercedes buses they used to transport prisoners from Khafji, and question him twice. The second session was with a slim civilian who nodded repeatedly when Ali Jassim traded information for a guarantee of political asylum in any country where wire transfers from numbered Emirate accounts were routine.

Now, he looked through the bus window and saw a filthy yellow American-made school bus lurch to a stop. Two American Marines got out, leading a line of people with cameras and notebooks toward the prisoner pen. Then the slim American got out. Beside him another American, shorter, heavier, with a goatee.

Ali Jassim banged on the bus window and waved. Kingen's head snapped up. He glanced tiredly at the bus, and walked in the opposite direction, toward the Saudi and American officers supervising the prisoners.

Dees looked quizzically at Kingen, then followed him over to the Saudi colonel in charge, to whom he spoke in rapid-fire Arabic. Dees could only pick out *sahafi*—journalist—and *Amerikee*—American.

A Saudi guard's hand on his chest prevented Dees from following Kingen into the tent. Kingen turned and looked at him almost disinterestedly.

"Look, I have to take care of some business about having a dead Saudi in Khafji. We'll talk. Later." He disappeared inside.

Dees looked at the guard, then down at the hand still pressed against his chest. "If you're going to be this fresh you could at least introduce yourself."

The guard looked at him stolidly. Dees grunted. "The strong silent type, eh? You see too many Clint Eastwood movies?"

Silence. Dees turned and started back to the bus. The Saudi army, he thought. What a concept. The Saudi air force was a gentlemen's service, well respected and well trained, populated with royal cousins, more than an even match for any Mideast air force except, maybe, the Israelis.

But the enlisted ranks in the army tended to be filled with men who couldn't make it in Saudi society, even with cradle-to-grave benefits and a $100,000 cash gift from the royal family to every citizen on his marriage day. All of which went a long way, he thought glumly, toward explaining the rout at Khafji. He glanced over at the Mercedes bus, at the Saudi guard trying repeatedly to light a cigarette with a failing disposable lighter.

Dees walked over and snapped open his brass Zippo, engraved with the seal of El Salvador's army. The guard looked at him and smiled. "Many thanks."

Dees fished for a smoke of his own. "Your English is very good."

The Saudi smiled even more. "I picked it up from my father. He imports your videotapes, the ones that get past our censors. I have seen every movie America has made for ten years. Except the ones with the sex parts. No one gets to see those."

Dees laughed. "Except maybe the censors."

The Saudi nodded vigorously. "Exactly right. Exactly."

Dees glanced inside the bus at the Iraqi officer, who waved again. He stared at the Saudi. "So why is a man of your education here?"

The Saudi looked pleased. "You are very kind. My father's business will go to the eldest son. I am the youngest. I was a little—how you might say?—undisciplined at home, so . . ."

Dees nodded sympathetically. "I can see that would limit your prospects. By the way," he said nonchalantly, "why one prisoner in here?"

The Saudi laughed. "He seems to be a special one. Very important. A parade of people in and out. High, high in Iraqi intelligence. And you are?"

Dees flashed his military-issued ID card. The journalist's card and the military ID card looked exactly alike if you saw them only for a moment. "Official business."

Dees bent down and undid the Velcro on his ankle wallet. He counted out five hundred-dollar bills. The Saudi stared. Dees looked at him earnestly.

"My translator is busy calling the palace in Riyadh on your satellite phone." The Saudi looked impressed. Dees nodded. "But I need to talk to this man quickly, and I need a translator quickly. And the government of the United States of America authorizes me to make this payment for translation. It is standard. Do you know anyone who can translate for me?"

The Saudi looked at the cash. He licked his lips. Dees's face brightened. "I have it. Could you translate for me? This is official business. My government and your royal family would appreciate it."

The Saudi nodded rapidly several times, gently took the bills and placed them in a pocket, and opened the bus door. The Saudi sat directly across from the Iraqi, and Dees sat down on the bus bench to the Saudi's right.

Dees took his Marlboro pack out and shook one out for the prisoner, produced the Zippo, and lit his cigarette. Their eyes locked for a second. Dees lit his own Marlboro, inhaled, clicked the lighter shut, exhaled through his nose, stared through the smoke, and said, *"Quais"*—good.

The Iraqi smiled faintly.

"Do you know who I am?" Dees asked.

The Iraqi nodded. He spoke through the translator. "You are with Mr. Dennis."

Dees exhaled and nodded. "I need to ask some questions."

The Iraqi looked confused. "But I have already made statements to Mr. Dennis. Three times."

Dees laughed. "But you know how governments are. One more time, if you would be so kind."

Ali Jassim shrugged, and went through his name, rank, assignment, and his surrender. Dees scrawled in his notebook, then looked up.

"What do you specifically know about chemical weapons being used in Kuwait or Saudi Arabia?"

"I know they have been used," the Iraqi said. "I know most units have refused to fire them because of fear of revenge from your air force. But some have been fired. Mostly Scuds. I also know we lost most of our supply of agents when your air force destroyed the storage area at Wafra. Hundreds of pounds of agents blown up and blown away on the wind."

Dees scribbled furiously, underlining the word "fallout," then asked, "But why were Scuds fired if you fear air power?"

Ali Jassim jammed the Marlboro out in the armrest ashtray. Dees fished out the pack, put the lighter on top, and placed them on the armrest in front of the Iraqi, who smiled thinly.

"Because Scuds are mobile, with less chance of detection than stationary artillery or tank units." He looked at Dees. "And because once we were asked to launch at one particular target. At your Marines and some *sahafis*."

Dees stopped writing. *"Sahafis?"*

Ali Jassim looked very tired. *"Sahafis."*

Dees felt bile rise in this throat. "Why launch missiles at *sahafis*?"

Ali Jassim spread his palms open. "Because the great GTV asked."

"What? They asked what?"

"Asked us to launch missiles with chemicals."

The information made Dees's stomach ache.

"The *Mukhabarat* directorate in Baghdad receives a call from the presidential palace," Jassim explained. "They pass the message to the *Estikhbarat*, and we arrange three missiles from around Basra to be fired at the coordinates provided. It was said to be in exchange for the favors of the GTV. A late colleague of mine was assigned to the palace when the original request came from the GTV's top man in Baghdad." He paused, frowning. "The man was maybe in Egypt . . . or elsewhere."

Dees scrawled "Volga" in his notebook. He took a shot in the dark. "When you were at Al Fallujah, did you hear of an American company called Archgate?"

The Iraqi looked puzzled. Dees said slowly, "An American company. Named Arch—gate. Anthrax. Growth mediums. Experiments to put aerosol canisters in nose cones or artillery shells."

Ali Jassim smiled. "Ah, yes. Suppliers to the Salman Pak facility, mostly. We attempted at Al Fallujah to synthesize anthrax. It was a failure. But yes, this Archgate was most reliable for a number of years. They were our most regular suppliers of the precursors for sarin. They and several others seemed to have all the export licenses they needed.

"Which means, of course . . ." He trailed off, shaking his head from side to side. The young Saudi translator was so intent on every word that he began shaking his head, too.

"Which means your government knew of the shipments, and approved of them," Jassim continued. "Or at least most of them, which was most helpful to us. Can you imagine how difficult it is to buy anthrax and botulism, laboratory grade, on the black market? Or to remove them directly from the laboratory?" He shook his head. "Very difficult indeed."

The bus door banged open. Dennis Kingen took the three entrance steps in one stride, grasped the shoulder of the seated Saudi corporal, pulled him to his feet and growled, *"Emshee!"*

Wide-eyed, the soldier scooted out of the bus. Kingen was breathing slowly, deeply. He spat out a few dozen words in clipped Arabic. Ali Jassim looked worried and bit his lower lip.

Dees glanced up languidly. "Y'know, we may not need to have our conversation anymore."

Kingen's nostrils flared. "Oh, we will talk. We most definitely will talk."

FEBRUARY 22, CAIRO

The *felucca* tacked, its triangular sail shifting to push it upriver against the Nile currents. Timothy Volga watched, holding a plate of fried squid in his right hand, the satellite phone receiver in his left. A belching Fiat bus on the Corniche underneath the balcony sent up a cloud of blue smoke, temporarily obscuring Volga's view.

He spoke softly into the receiver. "I've tried, but they claim they don't know when it will start. They claim not even to know exactly where they are."

Mac Burke's voice barked through the static. "So how do you propose we find out?"

"Our pool in the water," Volga said, referring to the GTV combat pool assigned to the preparations for an offshore landing, "seem to think they're the ones. One punch, the shortest distance between two points."

"Our friends seem to like the beach, too," Burke said. "What do we tell them?"

Volga put the plate on the desk, picked up a string of fried squid, and crunched on it. His nose wrinkled at the amount of oil in it.

"We should tell them our best estimate is that they should prepare for a beach party. And we don't know yet if they'll play in the backyard sandbox."

Burke snorted, his version of a laugh. "I have another call to make."

The line went dead. Volga replaced the flat handset in the satellite phone console. He watched the river until the *felucca* disappeared under a rusting iron bridge.

SOUTHWEST KUWAIT

A major from the Ba'ath party had delivered a lecture that morning about the puppets of George Bush meeting a flaming death in the oil trenches between the sand berms, and about how concentrated fire from the tanks would catch them in a cross fire that would have them pleading for mercy.

A fine rain of sand from the bunker's roof fell on Shafir as American planes pounded another target. "Chicago," he said under his breath, like a prayer. "Chicago. Sweet home Chicago."

One fourth of all the troops in his unit were dead. In pauses between bombing they dragged corpses to hollowed-out sand pits. Body parts sometimes rained down when the pits took a direct hit from a five-hundred-pounder.

Amazingly, most of the tanks had not been destroyed, since the high-altitude runs were aimed at the trenches and the men in them. Shafir's hearing, along with that of about half of the survivors, had been permanently damaged. Several other soldiers cowered near him, farm boys from villages like his. Someone in their families, maybe a generation ago, had not shown sufficient loyalty to the party, so here they were, watching other troops being mangled physically or mentally, slowly going insane themselves.

And going hungry. The tins of rancid lamb left over from the war with Iran were long gone. Crumbs of flat bread, and whatever water was still available, were the limit of their diet. Shafir had become friendly with a conscript from near Al Amarah who still had a few handfuls of figs.

Three figs a day, and he had stopped complaining about hunger. His friend from Al Amarah eyed him suspiciously.

"You are never hungry," he said. "Are you stealing food? Are you hoarding food?"

Shafir smiled. "No. I just believe this cannot last much longer. Meanwhile, we make the best of it. What the mind of man can believe, the hand of man can achieve."

The recruit looked puzzled. "The Koran?"

"No," Shafir replied, "Norman Vincent Peale. A great philosopher. My success in America I owe to the giants of civilization. Norman Vincent Peale. Earl Nightingale. Richard Evans. They have tapes I have listened to. I have read all of their books. Each man is responsible for himself, they say. A man can achieve greatness only if he believes in himself. All this," Shafir said, waving his hand to indicate the underground bunker, "this is a distraction. We must plan for the future."

His hand went quickly to the plastic pouch with his American identification cards tied around his neck. That was his future, literally, in his hand. What he could believe, he could achieve. And Shafir believed in himself.

His friend from Al Amarah nodded dubiously. "But our future may be here with the scorpions and spiders," he said, "unless the Americans get here quickly so we can surrender and eat."

FEBRUARY 24, NORTHEAST SAUDI ARABIA

Carl Odell slipped on the pants of his chemical suit. Robert Hopkins, behind him, helped Odell give the pants a final tug. Odell pulled the waistband tight, slipped on the suspenders, and turned to help Hopkins into his chem suit.

"Go to MOPP Two," they'd been told. "Tonight," they'd been told. "It's tonight."

Before they slipped on their gauntlets, Hopkins and Odell shook hands, soul style.

"Rock and roll," Hopkins said.

"Motherfuckers," Odell replied.

Dees had fought off headaches and mild nausea for days. Melinda's symptoms seemed to have cleared up—except for the dried, gray patches on her arms. He'd secured his chem jacket above the protective pants, as Phil Collins's lyrics ran through his head. Yes, indeed, he could feel it coming in the air tonight, oh Lord. He looked at Melinda.

"Cocksuckers," she hissed. She'd been told, bluntly, to forget about filing any video for Christ knew how long. Any pool video would be cleared, as usual, and then uplinked as soon as possible from the nearest available site.

"That means Dhahran," she'd fumed. "All the traffic's moving north, so the roads are jammed. So unless they fly it out, which they indicate strongly they won't even consider, we're fucked. No tape feed. For days."

So much for being Mencken's eyewitness to history's first draft, Dees thought. The journalist's job wasn't done until he'd told somebody, and he couldn't tell anybody if he couldn't transmit.

This was the way the world ended, he thought. Not with a bang, nor a whimper, but with silence.

SOUTHWEST KUWAIT

The silence wrapped itself around Shafir like a soft blanket, silence between bomb runs, silence so he could come out of the bunker and lean against the side of a tank.

He dragged in a deep lungful of air. How sweet it smelled. How clean.

CHAPTER 13

SAUDI-KUWAIT BORDER

Ka-RANG. Ka-RANG. Ka-RANG.

The mine-clearing line charges were all launched at once, whirring as they soared over the mine field leading to the first sand berm. The lines snapped taut and fell beside each other, four parallel tracks across the sand.

Each MCLC was a length of cord with explosives attached every few feet. It was blown out over a mine field. When it had uncoiled and landed, one end of the cord was still attached to the launcher. The parallel lines of explosive cord detonated, setting off any mines nearby, clearing a path through the mine field for men and armor.

Dees, watching through a night scope from a Humvee just to the rear of the engineers' launch vehicles, had always thought "miclick," as the MCLC was called, sounded like Irish oral sex. The four lines running through the mine field in front of him exploded simultaneously, setting off secondary explosions for five seconds as land mines in every direction went off.

At the same instant there was a *whooooosssshh* overhead as explosions lit up the area behind the nearest sand berm. Multiple-launch rockets fired from a mile or so behind the Americans were pouring into the area behind the berm where Iraqi tanks and troops waited. Each launcher was firing a dozen of the thirteen-foot-long rockets per minute.

The warheads were loaded with either contact mines that could take out tanks, or the lethal M-42 bomblets, 644 of the M-42s per nose cone, a single charge capable of shredding a human being. The warheads detonated twenty meters above ground, sending whistling explosives by the hundreds in all directions, going off seemingly all at once.

To Dees and Melinda in the Humvee, the howl of rockets overhead followed by the nose-cone detonation followed by the howling *poppoppoppoppop* of antipersonnel and antitank munitions sounded like tearing fabric, followed by the bang of a car crash, followed by the concussive pows and bangs of mammoth cherry bombs.

As the explosions ripped and howled in front of them, armored bulldozers began to lumber forward through the mine fields along paths cleared by the miclicks. Behind the berms were trenches filled with oil fed by pipes running from nearby oil fields.

The Iraqis had planned on using electric igniters to set the oil ablaze. But the incessant air strikes had destroyed most of them, as well as the pipes feeding the trenches. Now the bulldozers were shoving the berms into each oil-filled trench, creating bridges over which the M-1A1s could slice across.

Explosions tore through the mine field. Whether it was incoming from the other side or stray mines popping because of the vibration, Dees couldn't tell. With a series of bangs and flashes, more lines of miclicks were fired all along the front of the berm, setting off more explosions and sending clouds of talcum-fine sand into the night sky.

Bulldozers were gunning their huge diesels four abreast, grinding tons of sand back into the trenches. Small-arms fire began to pop and chatter. There was a shrill whistle, followed by an explosion ten meters from one of the Abrams tanks.

Marco, eye glued to the eyepiece of the high-resolution eight-millimeter camera, yelled at no one in particular, "At least now we know those assholes are shooting back!"

The bulldozers churned forward through a sand fog. Two disappeared into the smoky darkness on the other side of the filled trench. There was a slamming explosion, which lit the entire field of battle like a flashbulb for about a second. In the strobe flash Dees saw a flame like a blowtorch erupt from one of the 'dozers, followed instantly by a thick cloud of jet-black smoke where it had been hit by an antitank rocket.

In the strobe effect of flashbulb-popping explosions, Melinda saw the second bulldozer place its blade along the right front of the flaming earth mover and shove the smoking mass, slowly, until it tumbled off the side of the makeshift causeway and into the oil. Pausing just the other side of the demolished berm, an M-1A1 began firing a cascade of 105mm shells and .50 caliber machine-gun fire to cover the second 'dozer's exposed rear.

The bulldozer pirouetted to put its nose to the Iraqis, and the M-1A1 leapt across the bridge, firing as it went. Three more Abrams tanks followed. Behind them, three Bradley fighting vehicles scooted across the berm.

The Humvee carrying the GTV crew began to inch forward. Once inside the initial berm, now almost completely collapsed into the oil trench, Dees thought the sand was lit like a disco dance floor, streaking yellows and oranges from some explosions, the white-hot *thumpthumpthump* from others, all illuminating the world in brief flashes.

Inside the first berm were three more, with a trench behind each, concentric circles to hold troops firing low, while the tanks in the very center of the ring laid down a cross fire. There was fire coming from the other side, all right—cannon fire, antitank rockets, machine guns, Kalishnikovs—increasing in volume almost each second, until the sky was lit by tracers.

What looked like a miniature tank scooted along the base of the outermost berm. It was actually a glorified armored car with an oversized ninety-millimeter gun attached to the top, made in South Africa and sold all over the world.

It exploded in an orange flash and a dull *thuummmppp*, and all Dees could hear for several seconds afterward, despite the roaring chaos surrounding him, was a scream.

FEBRUARY 24, SOUTHWEST KUWAIT

Hopkins gunned the Humvee, TOW launcher rigged to the back, and drove straight for the flames coming from just on the other side of the breached oil berm. Odell hunched in the seat beside him, fastening the huge rubber boots required at MOPP Three. Hopkins had merely tucked his chem suit pants tight into his desert boots. MOPP Three required the rubber boots and gauntlets, but not the hoods and gas masks. Both men had their gloves tucked into a handle on the dashboard. Hopkins needed to drive, and Odell wanted to be able to get at his M-16 or the TOW launcher.

Their radio screeched to life. "MOPP Four," the voice yelled over the speaker. "MOPP Four. Chemical attack! MOPP Four!"

Hopkins stared at Odell. Odell stared back. Both saw the infantry supporting the tank columns jerk off their Kevlar helmets, slip the hoods in place, lock the drawstrings, and plop the helmets atop the hooded masks.

Driving with his knees as he undid his Kevlar, Hopkins

snatched the mask and hood from a nylon bag, yelled, "Take the wheel," and slipped the hood down quickly.

Odell held the steering wheel with his left hand until Hopkins resumed control. He then tightened Hopkins's drawstrings, locking the mask in place. He took Hopkins's helmet, mashed it in place atop the hood, and flashed a thumbs-up.

Hopkins slowed the Humvee to a crawl and, again steering with his knees, helped Odell jerk down on his hood. Before it was tight, a fusillade of artillery shells landed about thirty meters away. Odell whiffed a faint hint of ammonia just as Hopkins pulled the hood taut and locked the drawstrings. Their hands slid easily into the oversize gloves, and Hopkins accelerated.

Through the hood's lenses, Odell saw the first two Abrams tanks disappear behind the farthest sand berm. The sky above where they slid into darkness was suddenly laced with orange and yellow light.

Captain James Forrest heard the squawk to go to MOPP Four over the radio, but he and his crew were already mummified inside their chemical suits, snug inside the huge Abrams tank's air-conditioned cocoon.

The bulldozer immediately in front had just compacted its last swath of sand, and veered out of the way as Forrest guided the M-1A1 up the side of a sand berm at almost thirty-five miles an hour. Bits of shrapnel and rifle slugs thunked against the Abrams's reactive armor. Small-arms fire clattered as the tank zipped past.

Annoyed, Forrest keyed his radio. "Cobra Six. Small-arms fire from the trenches between berms. Small-arms fire from the trenches."

"Cobra Two. Same here. Lots of bad guys with small arms."

Forrest was jolted, briefly, as the entire tank bounced from side to side. A badly aimed antitank rocket had angled off the turret, leaving only a black blast mark on the tan armor. The Abrams hopped over the top of one of the defensive berms and angled downward.

"Holy shit," Forrest's gunner whispered. There were fifteen or sixteen Iraqi tanks, arrayed in a ragged semicircle.

Two of their muzzles flashed simultaneously, winking like flashlights in the darkness. The shells both hit the Abrams in what would have been a slamdance of death before reactive armor was invented. The M-1A1, like all of the world's most modern tanks, had rectangles of solid explosive stitched together and fitted snugly to the tank like so much chain mail. A shell would strike the plastic explosive and physics would take over. The shell exploded at the same time as the plate. The reactive armor blast scattered the shell's kinetic energy, so the shell never penetrated the tank. Forrest and his crew felt the Abrams vibrate and rattle, nothing more.

"Hard left," Forrest barked.

The tank ground at forty miles an hour across the talc-like sand, kicking up the kind of gritty dust that clogged everything from turbines to computers to rifles.

The turret moved evenly to the right, firing once every six seconds, obliterating Iraqi tanks trying to reload and set up a cross fire. The Abrams turned 180 degrees, the turret following evenly and never letting up fire. Its shells, encased in depleted uranium, tore through Soviet-made armor and detonated inside the T-62s and -72s, welding skin and steel into a burning gelatinous mass.

Moving parallel to the uneven line of Iraqis, the M-1A1 picked off more as they reloaded. Some tanks were still running, from desperate attempts to engage their diesel engines and move. Others sat, silent, as their crews bailed out of the hatches and sprinted for the relative safety of the trenches.

"So?" It was the gunner.

Forrest grunted. "Ten. Maybe more. In one minute."

The tank was gliding back and forth in front of the Iraqi armor. The firing had stopped completely. Suddenly, the Abrams bucked forward.

"Engine's cutting out," the driver yelled into his microphone. "Stalling. Losing power!"

As it had done since Desert Storm was merely the waiting game of Desert Shield, the powdered sand was scouring the turbine blades and fouling the air intake of the M-1A1's engine. The tank shuddered and stopped.

"We could have a friendly fire problem if we're stalled." It was the driver.

"I'm on it," Forrest said flatly. As he prepared to key his microphone to warn other friendlies that he was stalled, the tank rocked, violently. Off to the right, an Iraqi T-62 was still firing, its shell exploding on the reactive armor below Forrest's turret.

"Take him," Forrest said, but didn't have to bother, since the gunner had already locked on the laser sight and fired, causing the Iraqi tank's turret to separate from the body. At the same instant, another M-1A1 hopped over the berm and depressed its cannon toward the smoking Iraqi tanks. In the green glow of his night scope, all the tank commander saw was a flash from a turret opposite, leveled in his general direction.

The tank's gunner instantly fired a 105mm shell. Its depleted uranium casing sliced through the reactive armor on Forrest's tank. It exploded inside the main compartment, killing the gunner, loader, and driver instantly.

Forrest screamed, not from the explosion, but from grabbing the emergency hatch control with raw hands that had been flash-burned. He shoved himself through the hatch, hit the ground on a badly lacerated left knee, howled again, rolled free of any explosion from the burning Abrams, and passed out in the sand.

—

Shafir stumbled up the ramp from the underground bunker as explosions tossed gritty sand in front of him. He intended to stay on level ground and surrender the first chance he got.

He reached the top of the ramp, and his mouth dropped open. Over a dozen tanks were burning not fifty meters from him. He stared and then looked down, slowly, at the AK-47 he held by the barrel. He tossed it away and tugged at the cord around his neck, making sure the plastic bag stuffed with his IDs and his work permit was in place. He crouched, and crab-walked across ten meters of sand, and slid feet first into a trench.

To his horror, he discovered the six-foot-deep ditch was packed with men. He inched down and found he was immediately pinned so tight that there was nothing to do but stand. Shafir was jostled forward by several more bodies piling in behind him. It was becoming difficult to move his arms, so he reached inside his shirt, tugged at the cord and broke it, clutching the plastic bag that held his entire life.

Some soldiers in the trench had thrown away their weapons as Shafir had. But most still had theirs and were firing blindly into the night, pinging bullets off the giant sand-colored American tanks as they rolled across a sand bridge that had been shoved into the trench.

He craned his neck, and his eyes grew wide. Arms and legs were sticking out of the sand, most still wiggling desperately on the edge of a pile of sand eight or nine meters across. The tanks were gunning across a causeway built of sand and bodies.

"Stop firing!" Shafir screamed. "Stop firing! Stop!"

Whether it was from panic or duty, dozens of the conscripts elevated their weapons and kept firing. Shafir tried to twist his body to turn, attempting to slither toward the edge of the ditch. Some men were already able to claw their way up the side of the trench and run into the night, hands above their heads. But Shafir was pinned.

Above the *brrraaaattt* of AK fire, above the explosions and the pounding of his blood and the wheeze of his breathing, Shafir could hear a clanking sound, the grinding clank of a huge tread, not the trucklike automotive hum that came from the M-1A1s crossing the sand bridge.

Ten meters away, where the trench ended in the bridge, where still-moving limbs protruded from the sand, a wall of moving sand suddenly appeared. It cascaded down the slope and onto the men below, and a portion of a huge earth-moving blade appeared briefly poised over the trench before it clanked away.

The first load filled the trench waist-high as the men, packed like toothpicks, tore at each other. Some howled. Some twisted above the waist, screaming. Shafir's eyes bulged in terror as the clanking became louder and more sand plopped down as men fired impotent rounds at the sand or clanged rounds off the bulldozer blade.

Only one head remained above the sand now, and Shafir heard another clanking, directly above him. The sand, lit by the stroboscopic flashes from exploding shells and grenades, seemed to fall in jerky slow motion.

As the sand reached above his waist, Shafir thrust both hands in the air, waving his plastic bag. "I'm an American!" he screamed. "No! I'm an American!"

A second blade, immediately behind the first, filled Shafir's mouth and nostrils with sand and left only his right hand, closed in a fist around a plastic bag stuffed with documents, exposed.

Hopkins steered the Humvee across the berm shoved into the oil trench, as Odell took his position with the TOW in the rear. The sand, or what they could see of it in the dark illuminated by headlights, was streaked black.

The Humvee ground forward, across a sand bridge shoved into a second trench. Hopkins looked to his left and gagged. Several hands and arms stuck out of the sand. One of the hands was clutching a plastic bag.

CHAPTER 14

FEBRUARY 25, PHOENIX

McKinley Burke was pleased with the ratings, and pleased with himself. So after only one trank to bring him down from an amphetamine and adrenaline high that had been on the verge of making him loop out, he was able to purr into the phone.

"No, our problem can't wait. And I'll tell you what you'll do. You'll take care of it personally."

Burke paused, listening with no expression on his face, then shook his head vigorously.

"No, and I'll tell you why, Timothy. One, they'll empty out Kuwait City soon, so I'm told." He smiled thinly. "Two, we'll need to have you there to oversee things. Three, we have a professional to take care of the . . . ah, details. And four, no, let me finish, no, no, let me—*shut the fuck up, you little asshole!*"

Burke stopped, took deep breaths, and, composed again, spoke evenly. "You think we lifted you out of some Tulsa shithole because of talent? You and fifty other people who applied had talent. But you had the will. And you followed orders better than the rest of them put together, none of that 'But Mr. Burke,' or 'I'm not sure, Mr. Burke,' or any other rat shit. So keep dancing with the one what brung you, Timothy, and you'll be fine."

Another pause. Burke's lips tightened. He snapped into the

phone, "I don't care about your problems! You see, I have my own. Do you have any idea how much those fucks in Indonesia want for a satellite that we need to cover about one-sixth of this planet's surface? No, I don't want you to guess. Let's just say you can't count that high.

"We get it, we complete a network that can beam GTV to ninety-five percent of the people on the earth. Without it, we don't cover south Asia and parts of China, which is where all the growth's gonna be over the next couple of decades. Now that's power. *Power, goddammit, you understand? Power!*"

Before the voice on the other end could interrupt, he raced on. "And to get that power takes money, the kind of money that you can't imagine and even I have trouble adding up. So it's simple, Timothy. Very simple, really. I get the rest of the money if you take care of our problems. We get the money, we get the satellite, we get the power.

"And we're already changing history. We've been making history, and getting paid for it besides. So you stop your whining and get the job done and our friends finish paying us and we have the entire fucking planet shoved in my hip pocket."

He glanced at the printouts on his desk. He had already added the figures. A shade over a billion people so far. Another half billion, and GTV and he personally would be in the eyes and minds of the roughly half of the earth's population that would ever go near a television set. And the other half would follow along, like they always had, like they always would. And the majority of that chunk he had yet to reach lived in the footprint of the satellite and its dozen transponders that he was this close, *this close, goddammit,* to having.

He turned his attention back to the phone and cracked a half smile. "And besides, if I have to remind you, you're in the fast lane to become president of GTV. If you want it, you personally supervise Kuwait."

He paused again. "Good. See? I knew we'd agree."

FEBRUARY 26, MINAGISH OIL FIELD, KUWAIT

Dees sat on the Humvee's bumper and poured the rest of the bottle of water over his head. The small bar of soap next to him was almost jet-black. As he scrubbed his hair, he felt small gritty lumps. Sand? Or maybe lice?

Staring down at the dirty sand, he saw a pool of gray water soak into the ground, leaving behind a dark, filmy sheen on the surface. He studied the water rolling off his head, which had the consistency of the oil he used to empty from the crankcase of his '58 Dodge as a teenager in Arkansas.

He picked one of the pieces of grit off his scalp and looked at it. He gave it a squeeze, and felt the hard crust crack as it oozed out black gummy goo. Tar balls. His hair was soaked with airborne oil residue, and filled with pinhead-sized tar balls. He squinted at the horizon, toward the smoldering oil wells in the distance. He coughed, and tasted a tickle of petroleum in the back of his throat.

What passed for the rainy season on the Arabian peninsula consisted of vapor clouds that hung close to the ground at night and vanished in the day. The billowing smoke he could see from miles off mixed with the mist, creating an oil sheen that coated everything. He coughed again, twice.

The white wooden sign lying faceup near the road said SALAAM AL MINAGISH. Welcome to Minagish. The road was dotted on both sides with orange tongues of flame, erupting from the cracked wellheads the retreating Iraqis had broken open and then ignited.

A few feet above the flames, viscous clouds of boiling oily soot shot skyward. Fifteen wells at Minagish were roaring, three dozen at Ahmadi, and twenty at Umm Qudayr. In all, a dozen flaming oil fields with hundreds of burning wells tossed opaque airborne petroleum into the hazy blue sky. A KH-11 reconnaissance satellite scooting overhead at the exact moment the Humvee entered the inferno sent back an image showing eighty percent of Kuwait obscured by oil smoke.

Dees coughed again, a deep, racking cough that shook his entire body and caused his eyes to water even more than they already were. He finally caught his breath, wheezing, when he heard the same sound behind him. He looked, and saw Odell almost doubled over, coughing and gagging in the front seat of the Humvee.

The deal hadn't worked out so badly, Dees had thought at first, as the Humvee plowed along a packed-dirt road surrounded by otherwise trackless desert. The public affairs office couldn't provide a vehicle. With no way of feeding any tape anyway, Dees, Melinda, and Marco no longer needed to be under the supervision of the harried public affairs officer. So everybody agreed after about ten minutes of haggling that Dees, Marco, and Melinda could squeeze into the Humvee with Hopkins behind the wheel and Odell either standing at the TOW launcher or sitting in the passenger's seat up front.

They were in the forward advance unit for the Tiger Brigade, and had been driving full throttle toward the port town of Al Jahrah, about twenty-five miles west-northwest of Kuwait City. All five were coated with powdered sand and oil mist.

The parked Humvee's fender rocked slightly. Dees looked up, and saw Melinda sitting beside him, her face still streaked from using a dirty bar of soap and a pint of cold water to try to remove the gummy residue.

There was a gargling snore behind them. Marco had fallen

asleep, mouth open, in a rear seat. Hopkins had a map unfolded on the steering wheel. Dees turned his head.

"So, where are we?"

The map rustled as Hopkins answered, not looking up. "Near as I can figure, either a few klicks ahead or behind the front, maybe. This thing's moving so goddamn fast I can't tell."

He looked up and around at the roiling well fires. "I guess behind the front, unless the ragheads just ran away and left this place open. Who the fuck knows? I figure we're safe anyway unless they hit us with a chem attack, but since everybody's telling us none of it ever happened, we'll live until we're a fucking hundred."

He went back to studying the map. Dees felt a tug on his sleeve.

"You said you had something to tell me about something," Melinda said dully. "That was—what, a year ago?"

He looked at the streaks on her face. "Do I look as bad as you?"

"Worse, lover boy, unless you count whatever this is on my arm that's about to itch me to death."

Dees got up. "Walk with me in the desert, my princess, where we will eat honeyed figs and drink sweet camel's milk."

She got up and wiped her eyes. "I'll settle for water that doesn't have oil in it and something besides an MRE."

They had taken three steps in front of the Humvee when Odell yelled hoarsely, "Hey!"

They both turned. He jabbed a finger straight ahead. "Stay in the rutted tracks. This place is lousy with mines. See?"

He pointed to the right. About twenty meters away Dees saw a small orange speck in the black and gray sand. He looked more closely and saw more, counting eight dots of orange barely visible in the thick air. The wind and light rain had exposed the tops of some of the land mines.

Odell pulled out his M-16 and sat with it on his knees. "Intell told us eight million, maybe ten million. You know they were able to buy them for about two bucks apiece from the Chinese?"

In one fluid motion he raised the rifle and fired. The most distant orange dot, thirty meters off, exploded with a *whumpfh*, tossing powdered sand into the air.

"Goddammit, Odell," Hopkins said, not looking up from the map. "I've already got a headache."

"Yeah," Odell said quietly, clicking the safety back on and sliding the weapon back into the Humvee. "I got one myself. Remember you two, stay in the tire tracks."

The only noise besides the squeak of compacted sand under their boots came from the white noise *whoosh* of compressed gas erupting from distant wellheads and the grating sound of Marco's snoring. They walked carefully ahead a few yards and stopped.

Melinda looked around. "Welcome to Hell, population five."

"You've worked with him in Phoenix," Dees said quickly. "I've just yelled at him on the phone. Why would Volga want us dead?"

She stiffened. "What?"

"The Iraqi colonel in Khafji claims he was an intell officer. Told me they launched the Scuds at us because of a direct request from GTV, and the guy he described as having made that request sounded one hell of a lot like our very own Timothy."

"What?" Her eyes grew wide. For some reason, Dees thought she might panic and start running, so he grabbed her shoulders.

"Everybody who knows anything about Archgate or chemical shipments has ended up dead. We get killed here, it's fortunes of war. Archgate's got offices at GTV, or had offices there. So it doesn't take a genius to figure out there's a connection, and I've got the only evidence of it on the computer disk. Now, back to square one. I was saying, you've worked with him. What—"

"That little fuck," she said through clenched teeth. "He thinks if Mac gives up direct control of GTV and just becomes Mister Gazillionaire CEO that he gets control. He thinks."

Dees cocked his head. She shook her shoulders free and suddenly smiled. "Hey, at least that's the office rumor. He's the most ambitious person I've ever met next to D—"

She was racked by a coughing fit, wheezed, then smiled again. "Duh. Sorry. Next to Mac, the most ambitious person around."

"So? What? He's running a chemical arms ring on the side? Getting people killed? Trying to kill us?"

She shrugged. "What'd you want to do now? He's still in Cairo as far as I know. You figure to blow the whistle on him?"

"More than that. I figure we still have a war to cover and get out of here. Keeping alive until then is the best idea. Out of this hellhole, we take what we know, the murders, the prisoner's statement, the disk, the fact that everybody's being cagey about chemical attacks, and tie it all together and blow the lid off."

She squinted. "With what? You've got some facts and a lot of supposition. I've seen slices of Swiss cheese with fewer holes."

Dees wiped a particle of grit out of his left eye. "Yeah, well. Back when I was stringing for the *Daily News* in Chicago, back when there was a *Daily News*, a desk editor told me that at some point you go with what you've got. So we go with what we got."

"We?"

He looked at her. "Yeah, we. Unless you figure I'm more trouble than I'm worth."

She laughed again and touched his filthy face, lightly. "Cowboy, you are trouble personified. Okay. We."

"Hey! Hey!" It was Hopkins, looking over his map. "Over there! By the road! Past the antipersonnel bomb!"

An empty ten-foot canister, looking like a smashed torpedo, lay by the side of the road. It had disgorged hundreds of antipersonnel bomblets across the area. But there were no bodies, except for the three along the road ahead, dressed in soiled white djellabas.

They were lined up, on their knees, alongside the left shoulder of the road, facing southwest. Toward Mecca, Dees thought, death and sacrilege.

Hopkins got out of the Humvee and pulled his goggles atop the Kevlar, looking like a negative image of a raccoon, a brown-and-black-streaked face surrounding a goggle-shaped pink mask.

"Kuwaitis," he said. "A Palestinian worker wouldn't be dressed this well. Maybe the supervisors here."

Melinda glanced at Hopkins, impressed. Dees saw the look. Okay, he thought, I'm impressed, too. Odell rolled one of the corpses over with his foot, then stepped back.

"Mo-ther-fuck-er! They stuffed his cock in his mouth."

Dees bent down to look. The front of the djellaba was covered with a red stain. The Kuwaiti, eyes lolled back in his head, lay with a severed penis, presumably his, jammed into his mouth. Dees didn't gag, which surprised him. With a toe, he rolled the corpse back over. Its hands were secured behind its back with what looked like duct tape. Sticky matted black hair didn't quite cover the entrance wound in the back of the skull.

Marco, awake and with the camera in hand, took a white balance from one of the bodies. Before taping, every video shooter anywhere in the world except the totally incompetent aimed the lens at something white and took a balance reading. That way the camera knew what pure white was, so other colors would come out true. Otherwise, the sky could be green, skin could be purple, and the video could be worthless.

Hopkins stared at the bodies. "Why?"

Dees shrugged. "Why not? Why not torture prisoners?

Why the hell not? A little rape, a little pillage, a little poison. A little—"

"Hey," Marco yelled. "Look. Look!" He pointed toward the horizon, where the road ran out of the oil field.

Marco clicked to his extender lens at the same time Odell hopped up by the TOW launcher and looked through his binoculars. Dees could see only a dark mass of something in the distance.

Odell began laughing. He tossed the binoculars to Hopkins. "Check this out."

Hopkins looked. A smile cracked the caked oil and sand around his mouth. "This we gotta see up close and personal."

They piled in the Humvee and drove down the road as the dark mass began to distinguish itself. It was people; dozens, maybe hundreds, Dees thought, of people. As they drew closer they saw spread in front of them, like an extra scene from a biblical epic, hundreds of men, arrayed in three more or less straight lines, trudging along, most with their hands over their heads.

Six Humvees, machine gunners at the ready, drove slowly outside the mass, three on each side. They were marching through the desert, just west of the road. Marco stood in the TOW position and began rolling. Hopkins steered his Humvee next to one of the lead vehicles, barely moving parallel to it at five miles an hour.

"Tiger Brigade," Odell yelled out the window. "Got a media pool here. What's up?"

Both Humvees stopped. A wiry sergeant got out, and as Dees and Melinda talked to him, Marco shot a series of slow pans, right to left, left to right, filling the viewfinder with the surrendering Iraqi army. He pushed tight to a knot of walking men, then slowly pulled back, revealing a screen filled with trudging prisoners, stretching now from left to right, filling the horizon.

The sergeant shook his head. "We can't keep up with it. They've been surrendering to anybody. Us. The media. The French, the British.

"When we were getting here to round all of them up, one Iraqi popped out of an APC, his hands up. We were too busy, so we took his AK, gave him an MRE, sat him down and drove off. He was still there when we marched these prisoners back, and just fell in with the rest."

He shook a cigarette from a pack, lit it, and exhaled a luxurious cloud of smoke. "They're running in all directions. They've emptied out Kuwait City. Hell, we even heard CBS is already broadcasting from there."

Melinda and Dees looked at each other, then back at the sergeant. "CBS?"

He nodded.

"So when did the Allied troops get there?" Melinda asked.

He laughed. "We haven't. We're clearing all this up and still fighting the Republican Guard around the airport. It's an open city. We've got time. All we have to do is cut off their retreat."

He flicked the butt into the sand, got back in his Humvee, and resumed the plodding guard duty for prisoners who didn't really need to be guarded unless it was to keep them from running over each other in their rush first to surrender, then to cooperate.

Dees motioned to the two soldiers and Melinda and Marco. They faced each other: Hopkins and Odell leaning against the Humvee, Dees and Melinda facing them, Marco craning to listen from the TOW launcher.

"We need to get to Kuwait City," Dees said. "If CBS is there, GTV will be soon. That means the dish from Dhahran, so we can feed the tape we've shot. If you guys can help us find a ride—"

"Yeah," Melinda chimed in, "if we keep heading toward Al Jahrah, you can drop us off once we—"

Odell held up his hand. He looked at Hopkins, who nodded.

"No can do," Odell said. "We're tasked with providing transportation and protection for this pool."

Hopkins squinted. "If we drop you off," he said, "we'll end up like those guys." He jabbed his index finger toward the Humvees escorting prisoners.

"We'll be babysitting Iraqis. We'd rather babysit you assholes."

Dees grunted. "Roger that."

CHAPTER 15

FEBRUARY 27, KUWAIT INTERNATIONAL AIRPORT

Built with American engineering, British supervision, and Palestinian labor, the Kuwait International Airport very recently had been one of the most modern airports in a region riddled with modern, petrodollar airports. It sat southwest of the city center, just outside the Fifth Ring Road. The only military action on its tarmac until now had been the day Iraq invaded, when three Kuwait Air 747 crews had managed to lumber their jumbo jets off the twelve-thousand-foot main runway toward Cairo, directly ahead of the Iraqi tanks that smashed down the perimeter fence.

And now, Marine infantry supported by M-60 tanks were trying to dislodge the Iraqi Third Armored Division and its T-72 and T-64 tanks, each tossing 125mm shells at the advancing Marines. It was the first time the Marines moving in from the south had encountered organized resistance. The Third Armored was showing no inclination to surrender, or even retreat, so the Marines were being forced to advance inch by inch under a barrage of tank and machine-gun fire.

Hopkins's Humvee had hauled along the debris-littered highway at close to sixty miles an hour. Every few hundred meters he'd been forced to steer around blasted remnants of Iraqi armored vehicles, body parts, and an assortment of unexploded shells, grenades, bullets, and mines, blown across the motorway when Iraqi ammunition trucks were ripped apart by A-10 Warthogs.

Hopkins steered toward the sound of explosions and the flashes of light streaking across the sky. At the airport perimeter a Marine captain, face streaked with grime, eyes swollen from exhaustion, had refused to let them past his roadblock. Dees and Melinda sympathized, and talked about how the Corps commander had come up through the public affairs branch, and that he seemed very happy that the majority of the war video so far had featured the Marines and not the Army.

"We'll stay well out of the way," Melinda had purred, "and we'll be able to tape the Marines pounding their way into Kuwait City."

It might have been thirty-six hours without sleep. It might have been battle fatigue. It might have been Melinda's soft, persistent argument that they already had been through hell and were in the company of two of the Corps' finest. Whatever, the captain finally agreed.

As she climbed back into the Humvee, Dees said, "You're good."

She nodded, and arched one eyebrow with a sultry look. Dees wondered if she was trying to flirt in the middle of all this. She winked. Later, he thought.

Hopkins crept the Humvee forward. Odell manned the TOW launcher. Marco sat in the front seat, rolling, while Dees and Melinda sat in the back. Everyone wore their Kevlar and flak jackets.

With a *ka-raaannnng* that echoed off the ruined walls of the airport buildings, a top-of-the-line T-72 tank blasted away with its cannon. Asphalt and dirt erupted to their right, where the shell had missed a Bradley Fighting Vehicle. A Marine rifle squad emerged from behind the Bradley and began advancing toward a terminal building. Windows were outlined with flashes of light as small-arms fire erupted from inside. The Marines returned fire and flattened themselves on the tarmac.

There was a *faww-thummppp* behind them as one of the M-60s fired on the T-72. A tearing sound was followed by the *clanngg* of metal hitting metal as the American 105mm shell ripped into the Soviet-made tank and exploded inside. Smoke billowed from all sides of the Iraqi tank.

"Hoorah!" Odell yelled, pounding the Humvee roof with his fist. "The Army's got the Abrams but the Marines got the M-60 and balls!"

While Army armored units were slicing through Iraqi defenses with the M-1A1, the Marines preferred the war-horse they had ridden since Vietnam. The Abrams looked like something out of science fiction, Dees thought, but the M-60 looked like, well, a tank.

The Marines were using the M-60A1, not the more recent A3 model, and on paper were outgunned by the Iraqi T-72s. The T-72 had a bigger shell, could fire at a greater range, and had a top speed of fifty miles an hour, compared to the M-60's thirty. But in a hemmed-in area like the airport, the difference was in the tank crews. And while the Iraqis were plastering everything in sight with their 125mm shells, the Marines were firing carefully, for effect.

It showed. To the Humvee's left a Marine 105mm shell hit the auxiliary fuel tank on the rear of a T-72. The fireball washed over the treads, setting them on fire.

It was eight A.M. in Kuwait, yet dark as night because of the raining oil, thick fog, and swirling clouds of burning battle debris.

It was midnight, too, in Pine Junction, Illinois, just southwest of Chicago's O'Hare Airport. A late winter storm out of Iowa was scattering snow and gusty winds around the airport. The wind chill was eight degrees above zero.

At the Kuwait airport, where it was 82 degrees Fahrenheit with a solid petroleum overcast, Marco focused on the Marine rifle squad. Lance Corporal Lavon Williams had no way of knowing that, at that precise moment, a blast of prairie wind had sent a small oak limb through a corner pane of the south-facing window of his room in his mother's house in Pine Junction.

His younger brother surveyed the broken glass and the thick branch of oak rattling in the window frame. He shoved the limb into the yard and went to look for some tape and cardboard to patch the window until he could get to the hardware store. As he sighed, wondering when Lavon would get home, Lavon was pouring rifle fire into the terminal from his crouched position on the tarmac.

Lavon's mother asked about the sudden chill in the house. Her youngest son said, "Don't worry, Mama. I'll fix it."

She suddenly shivered very hard. It was 12:07 A.M.

At 0807 Kuwait War Time, a tumbling slug from a Kalishnikov ripped through Lavon's throat, directly above the collar of his flak jacket. Through his viewfinder, Marco saw a pair of hands clutch a throat, then spotted two riflemen grab their fallen comrade and carry him double-time, screaming something all the while. Two other Marines appeared, and the four of them sprinted around a corner, carrying Lavon gently. His screaming stopped, along with his heart, just as they put him down softly on a sidewalk. A medic placed two fingers on the artery at the base of Lavon's throat, then shook his head.

Marco panned back to the rifle company, where grim-faced Marines suddenly sprinted toward the terminal windows, pouring in rifle fire that shattered the glass to splinters.

Three rapid *whump whump whump* sounds came from the building as the Marines lobbed grenades and then rushed inside.

It had gotten so dark by nine A.M. that Marco had switched to his night scope. By nine-thirty a dark cloud, of biblical proportions, Dees thought, had settled over the city. Hopkins inched the Humvee forward, lights out, as Marco rolled.

Suddenly, there were three bright flashes that temporarily whited out the night lens. It was so dark that Marco couldn't see the outlines of whatever had fired. The flashes were immediately followed by the distinctive *ka-rannggg* of a T-72 cannon, followed by white and yellow explosions behind the Humvee, less than thirty meters away.

"Shit," Hopkins yelled, and gunned the Humvee. As the battle swirled and moved around them, they were now apparently between a row of Iraqi tanks out yonder someplace, and whatever it was just behind them that the Iraqis were trying to hit.

The V-8 engine accelerated the Humvee quickly, moving it out of the way just as a pair of M-60s behind it opened up, each firing at the maximum rate, one shell every six seconds, until each had delivered a half-dozen shells in thirty seconds.

The corner of a maintenance building was lit in flashes of explosive lightning, the concussions rolling the Humvee side to side on its shock absorbers. Melinda held her hands over her ears.

Dees stuck his helmeted head out the window, like a terrier on a Sunday drive, and through his streaked goggles saw four Iraqi tanks arrayed in a rough battle line. Two fired just as the area was lit by the tank on their far left, or Dees's right. It disappeared in a boiling cloud of flame as more explosions erupted to their right rear. One Iraqi shell had hit an M-60, tearing off the right tread.

The three Iraqi tanks began moving at once. The Humvee was no longer between them and the M-60s, so Dees felt relief. A sudden explosion went off about twenty meters in front of them, the concussion shoving Dees across the center console in the Humvee's rear and up against Melinda.

"He's after us!" Odell screamed from the TOW position. The tank on Odell's far left was churning directly toward them, just as the other two survivors moved right, trying to maintain a running fire aimed at the Abrams. It was an older T-64, not the more sophisticated T-72s that were now attempting to fire their maximum six to eight rounds a minute at the Marines.

"Track him!" Hopkins screamed, and steered the Humvee to the right to get to the side of the T-64 so it would offer a bigger target. The Iraqi fired again, but its 125mm shell merely blasted into asphalt and concrete as the Humvee leapt well ahead of the Iraqi turret's range.

Odell was ready to fire, but needed more light. He suddenly got it when one of the T-72s now directly behind the T-64 exploded in a white flash. It illuminated the other tank in silhouette. It also lit the Humvee for two seconds in the light of high noon.

"Stop!" Odell screamed. Hopkins jammed on the brakes, and before the Humvee had stopped rocking, Odell hit the fire button, and the four-foot-long TOW-2 spit out of the launch tube.

As expanding gases from the boost charge fired through lateral nozzles amidships of the missile, a foot-long probe in its nose deployed and locked rigid. It was designed to punch through armor plate to help the missile burrow inside before igniting. Four fins just forward of the launch nozzles snapped into place, locked at a forty-five-degree forward angle. The Hercules K-41 propulsion motor roared to life, so the missile was traveling over a hundred miles an hour only a few feet beyond the tube.

Twin microfine wires trailed from the missile to the launch tube. Each drove one pitch and one yaw helium-powered actuator in the tail. The four small helium jets worked on command from the optical sensor in the sight, which Odell had locked onto the spot where the T-64's turret joined its body.

The sight's laser winked on the target. The tank's turret was almost swiveled in place to fire at the stationary Humvee.

The tank commander had just inhaled before saying "Fire!" when the TOW's forward probe hit the tank at a little over six hundred miles an hour. The eight-and-a-half-pound shaped charge inside the warhead went off and started to melt the metal in its way, just as the tank's gunner hit the fire button.

The TOW was almost inside the tank a picosecond after he fired. The shell hadn't even had time to fully clear the cannon's barrel when the five-and-a-half-pound warhead went off inside the T-64, peeling the turret back like a beer can's pop top.

The initial blast had elevated the barrel barely three inches when the T-64 managed to fire. The tank exploded in rolling clouds of fire just as the shell whistled ten feet over the Humvee and exploded far off to the left, near an airport passenger concourse.

It had all taken less than ten seconds. Odell stared. Hopkins gripped the steering wheel so tightly that Marco, who had shot it all rock-steady and now couldn't keep himself from shaking, had to help him pry his fingers from around the wheel.

Melinda was hugging herself, staring at the flaming tank, breathing through her mouth. Dees fumbled for the door latch, opened it, and tumbled to the ground. The tank, some fifty meters away, was still burning.

The firing between the Iraqis and the pair of M-1A1s grew fainter as they kept up a running fight along the main runway, behind the terminal building. Dees picked himself up and leaned inside the Humvee. "You okay?"

Melinda nodded. His hand found hers and squeezed. Her hand responded, barely. Dees turned to Marco. "You all right?"

Marco nodded. "Except for the shit in my pants, yeah." He paused and looked thoughtful. "We need to feed this tape. Fast."

Dees had to get to a satellite phone, call Phoenix, and find out where, or even if, the GTV portable uplink was in the city.

Three Marines appeared out of the smoke. The sergeant, a chunky Filipino whose name strip over his breast pocket identified him as "Romero," poked Hopkins on the shoulder.

Hopkins turned slowly and gave a thumbs-up. Romero grunted. "I have a message from the captain," he said, referring to the red-faced officer Melinda had sweet-talked at the roadblock. "He says good job on the tank, and to get the fuck out of his area in half an hour or he'll shoot you himself."

Dees walked over and extended his hand. "Peter Dees from GTV."

Romero's face broke into a smile. "Shit. You're famous. We got all the A-FARTS feeds at base. It's a pleasure."

A-FARTS, or more properly AFRTS—Armed Forces Radio and Television Service—carried segments of almost all the network's coverage. Dees was aware of his ears burning. Underneath the sweat, oil, and sand, he was blushing. "Ah, um," he stammered, "we're trying to find where GTV is in the city. You know?"

Romero nodded. "I was out on recon a few hours back. CBS is by the port. CNN's up by the Hilton. GTV's trucks just got in. I saw them trying to unload equipment over by the Sheraton."

Romero unfolded a map on the Humvee hood, and using his teeth to hold a tiny flashlight with a red gel on the lens, pointed out how they needed to swing around on the ring road and head into the city center. No, he said, no Iraqis we know of except for a few snipers and stragglers, and the Kuwaiti resistance is hunting them down. Yes, booby traps all over the place, so assume everything's been mined. No, he didn't know when the Allied troops would officially roll in, since the Kuwaitis and Saudis were to be given the honor of coming in first.

He nodded toward an airport office building behind them. "Tell you what. Head over there. Take five. Use the head if you have to."

"There's a bathroom that works?" Marco asked expectantly.

Romero smiled again. "Just the ground. But don't go inside. The structure's been quiet since we pasted it a few hours ago. I don't expect anybody's alive. But it's probably booby-trapped."

Romero trudged off, waving. Hopkins steered the Humvee to the entrance and a smoking hole smelling of burned wood and metal and explosive residue where the twin doors should have been.

Marco sprinted behind the building. Hopkins and Odell slumped in the front seats. They didn't seem to notice as Dees motioned to Melinda and both stepped through the yawning hole, glass and masonry crunching underfoot.

Melinda turned on her flashlight. Light fixtures hung drunkenly from wires in the ceiling. Blackened gouges covered the walls. The stairway leading to the second floor lay in a mangled heap. Every door down the hallways to their right and left was blown off its hinges or missing completely.

Dees pointed down the right hallway. Melinda aimed her flashlight, and the two looked into the first office. Nothing except shards of glass from the window, whose metal frame, empty, had fallen into the room.

The next office was full of burned papers. A shell of some sort had punctured the wall and blown a filing cabinet apart. Rubble from the partially collapsed ceiling was piled in the center of the floor.

Melinda peered into the next office and pulled back into the hall. Dees heard her say, "Oh."

She jerked her head toward the door, and both stepped into a room, about ten feet square, where a framed picture of Saddam tilted but still hung on the light green wall.

All three were wearing uniforms. The one sitting at a desk was slumped forward, the crown of his skull sliced off neatly. The second was slumped in a corner, eyes open, a dark red stain covering his shirt from the collar to his pants. At his feet was a long piece of coat hanger, bent into a thin U shape. The bottom six inches were coated with electrical tape. At the bottom of the U a frayed electrical cord ran from the coat hanger to a wall socket. It was still plugged in.

The third body lay on its left side in a chair. Dees wondered why it hadn't slumped onto the ground. He took the flashlight and looked closer. A strip of duct tape was wrapped around the corpse's chest, fastening it to the metal chair. More tape pinned its arms behind the chair. The legs were fastened to the chair legs with even more tape. The pants had been undone and pulled down, so the body's navel, genitals, and thighs were exposed. Purple sores streaked the thighs, the testicles, and the penis.

Dees looked closely at the face. The left eye was a clotted mass of blood and viscera. He stared for a second longer and his eyes grew wide. He went from a crouch to sitting down on the concrete floor.

Melinda came over and looked. "Cattle prod, like we use on the ranch," she said. "Homemade. Our boy was being tortured, for sure. Must have been a blessing when the Marines blew the place apart."

Dees shook his head. "Those two, maybe. But he"—nodding toward the corpse—"was already dead. Somebody shot his left eye out."

Melinda drew in a sharp breath. "Shit," she said, "I don't feel so good."

Dees, hands trembling, pulled a cigarette from his pack. But his sweat-soaked matches refused to light. A puzzled expression crossed his face. Wrinkling his forehead, he reached into the corpse's left pants pocket.

"What're you doing?" Melinda yelped. Dees didn't answer. Coming up empty, he dug into the right pocket.

"That's one of the sickest things I've ever—" She stopped and stared as Dees withdrew his hand, opened a palm, and displayed a brass Zippo lighter that looked disturbingly familiar.

"I left it on the bus," Dees said flatly. "With our friend here."

Colonel Ali Jassim's remaining eye continued to stare at the pale green wall long after Dees and Melinda left.

CHAPTER 16

FEBRUARY 28, FOURTH RING ROAD, KUWAIT CITY

"Oil all over everything. It's sunrise, but we can't tell. It's like black smog. Buildings burned, abandoned. Bodies in the street. Iraqis ran them over, maybe? Note for feed—tapes are out of sequence. Airport bang bang, then street B-roll. Older tape to be fed soonest thereafter, depending on live shots."

Dees clicked off the microcassette recorder and slipped it back in a pocket of his photographer's vest. He had changed from his chemical suit into jeans and T-shirt with the vest while they had waited for sunrise to begin driving into the city.

Melinda had stripped to her khakis and a black turtleneck. Marco, Odell, and Hopkins still wore their chem pants and jackets, but had stashed the gas hoods, rubber boots, and gloves.

Dees tapped Hopkins on the shoulder. "What next for you?"

"Find our unit," he replied. "We still have all the psyops stuff in here—minispeakers, tapes, parabolic big ear dish, microphones. We may need to convince somebody to surrender with it."

"Fat chance," Marco said. He was standing in back in the TOW launcher position, shooting scenes of abandoned streets with Iraqi tanks and armored personnel carriers, empty and smoking, scattered every few hundred feet.

"They're either dead or bugged out. Those ain't Kuwaitis underneath that tank. They ran over their own soldiers."

"Whuff," Odell said, fanning his hand in front of his nose. "Man, these dudes are ripe."

The acrid stench hit Hopkins in the stomach. He stepped on the gas, trying to circulate more fresh air through the Humvee. As he sped past a cloverleaf connecting an east-west ring road with the north-south motorway he was now on, Hopkins looked to his left. His jaw sagged.

A white Chevy Caprice packed with six men in civilian clothes had pulled from the cloverleaf even with him. They were waving AK-47s out the windows. And smiling.

A bearded face emerged from a rear window. "*Haji* Bush!" it screamed at Hopkins. "Free Kuwait! *Haji* Bush!"

The driver, smiling and waving, motioned for Hopkins to pull over. Odell's right hand slid to his side, and he flipped the safety off his rifle. Hopkins pulled behind the Caprice, steering with his right hand, using his left to click the safety on his M-16.

Hopkins and Odell both got out at the same moment, each holding his rifle with the right hand, stock cradled against the right armpit, ready to raise and fire in three-shot bursts.

Dees stepped out immediately behind them. Melinda started to unlatch her door. Dees held up his palm and shook his head. Melinda ignored him.

The driver leapt from the Caprice, smiling, waving his arms. He stood in front of Hopkins, said, "We are Kuwaiti resistance! Welcome, liberator!" and kissed him on each cheek. Odell began to laugh until another resistance fighter, whose face from the nose down was completely obscured by a curly black beard, kissed him on each cheek. Odell sputtered, spitting tiny black hairs from the corner of his mouth.

"Can we be of any assistance?" the driver said, still smiling.

Before anyone else could speak, Marco asked, "How about some scotch?"

The driver barked a few words in Arabic. Dees was preparing to apologize when the driver handed him a box. "I hope Dewar's will be sufficient."

Marco reached down from the Humvee and snatched the box, assuring one and all that it would, indeed, be most sufficient.

"We actually do need some help," Dees explained. "We are with American television, GTV, and we—"

"Ah, the great GTV," the driver said. "We are already helping the GTV."

"What do you mean?" Melinda asked.

"The GTV arrived last night. We met them on the road, saw them to the Sheraton. We have other resistance people there to help.

"They tell us the head *sahafi* is coming from Saudia, and ask would we help with an escort. We are just returning from bringing him to them.

"We brought them all one hundred kilometers from the border. They came in one of your vehicles like this," he said, indicating the Humvee.

Dees furrowed his brow. How did the network get a Humvee? "Who was there from GTV?"

The driver pulled at a corner of his mustache. "It was driven by a tall man wearing your kind of camouflage." He nodded toward the chocolate-chip camos worn by Odell and Hopkins.

"And from the GTV, a Mr. Themm . . . or Teem . . . or . . ."

"Timothy?" Melinda asked.

The driver's face broke into a smile. "Yes. Exactly. Mr. Teemothy." He laughed again. "Your people with the satellite equipment say it took them two days and two nights to drive their truck from Dhahran. U.S. roadblocks, roadblocks by the army of Saudia, mine fields, exploded Iraqi trucks, bombs across the highway.

"But your Mr. Teemothy and his driver, they arrive at the border with an American army escort. Then we escort them from the border to here. What took the others forty-eight hours took Mr. Teemothy no more than six, seven at most."

He shrugged. "But by that time, there was no more danger on the highway."

Melinda pointed up the road. "And Mr. Timothy and the tall man are where now?"

Again a smile and a shrug. "Toward the city center. The Iraqis took everything they could, and what they could not take they burned, or tried to burn."

Dees nodded grimly. He assured the Kuwaitis they did not need their protection, but were grateful. After more kisses, and waves, and hugs, the Humvee pulled away.

The Sheraton, staring silently at the Arabian Gulf with smashed and blackened windows, was a few blocks to the left. They could see its upper floors as they pulled onto the Corniche, the city center to their left, the Gulf to their right.

Ahead, on the right, were the three blue neo-Islamic water towers that were Kuwait City's trademark. Dees thought they looked like three huge onions on skewers.

Melinda was now riding in the right rear seat, panning the dusky seafront with her binoculars. Flipped-over Iraqi tanks were mixed with charred civilian autos along the Corniche. On the beach, crude cinder block and mud brick blockhouses were scattered every hundred meters.

Some, she noted, had twenty-foot lengths of oil pipe jutting into the air at a thirty-degree angle from holes punched in their seaward side. They were phony cannon, aimed out to sea to fool a Marine amphibious assault that never came.

Panning left, she saw the beach turn into piled rocks, a sloping erosion barrier that ran from the ocean to the chain-link fence that topped it. Just inside the fence was a brick wall, a little less than waist high. The wall only ran along the chain-link, apparently defining the limits of a packed lot of dirt and sand that had been used as a parking lot at one time.

She focused the binoculars and saw two men, standing next to the wall, staring at the Gulf, their backs turned. As they pivoted, Melinda said, softly, "Oh shit."

Without a word she whipped off the glasses and shoved them into Dees's chest. She leaned forward, tugged on Odell's sleeve, and said, "Can we use some of your gear?"

Dees adjusted the binoculars. Timothy Volga, arms folded across his chest, was talking with a taller man in a chocolate-chip battle-dress uniform.

"Stop here!" Dees barked. Hopkins ground the Humvee to a halt behind an abandoned tank and an armored personnel carrier that was lying on its side. They were shielded from the beach, two hundred meters away.

As Dees walked to the tank's rear and adjusted the binoculars again, Dees thought that Volga and Dennis Kingen seemed too preoccupied to notice him.

SEAFRONT, KUWAIT CITY

"They were shot right here," Kingen said, his hands folded behind his back as he scuffed the dirt with the toe of his boot. "Deserters. Kuwaiti resistance fighters. Whoever.

"Look over there. Blood all over the bricks and dirt."

Volga, arms still folded across his chest, looked at the red stains splattered across the tan bricks and sand. He wrinkled his nose. "Messy."

Kingen had also paused, still staring at the ground. "But

effective. We figure they only had to execute twenty or so here to get their point across."

Volga turned. "They have a racetrack here?"

"Not that I know of, why?"

"The Kuwaitis like to ride their horses to death in Cairo out by the pyramids. I thought they might have a racetrack here. I enjoy horse racing."

Kingen looked noncommittal. "Umm. If there were horses, the Iraqis would have eaten them by now. Look what they did to the rest of the city."

Volga barely glanced over his shoulder at the crude pillboxes scattered across the beach. Dried mortar oozed sloppily from between each cinder block. The same type of blocks had been used to construct blockhouses in the middle of streets, to control traffic. Smaller versions of the scabrous blockhouses had been built on the balconies of luxury apartment buildings, giving gunners a clear field of fire down the avenues.

Volga fastidiously brushed a large chunk of ash from the sleeve of his safari jacket, which he'd had custom-made in Cairo. The ash had been falling mixed with the misty oil. "Fortunes of war."

Kingen looked vaguely contemptuous. "You have no idea what that means."

Volga dabbed his nose with a handkerchief. "It means oil. Isn't that why you're here?"

Kingen's left hand absently kneaded the air, forming and unballing a fist. "I'm here because you have a problem you can't take care of."

"First, it's our problem, not just mine," Volga said, pursing his lips as he looked up at the sky and then down at the ground in seeming distaste. "Your other employer has as much at stake. We may have sold certain items to our associates, but someone in

Washington had to approve it, hmm? And second, you're being paid well enough to do whatever's necessary."

Without a word, Kingen grabbed Volga by the collar of his unwrinkled jacket, pulling him backward. Volga squealed, backpedaling to keep from falling. Kingen shoved him against the low brick wall. Volga plopped heavily on top of the wall, his back rocking against the chain-link fence. Kingen shoved him against the fence again and squatted in front of him, their eyes level.

"How old are you?" Kingen asked. Volga tried to rock forward, but Kingen, without losing his own balance, straight-armed him in the chest, forcing his back against the fence. "Thirty?"

"Thirty-three," Volga said through clenched teeth.

"Umm." Kingen nodded. "When I was a little younger than you, I discovered the eyes are the windows to the soul, just like they say."

He stared at Volga, who kept flicking his tongue out to wet his lips. Kingen didn't blink. "I'd interrogate suspected VC or NVA who were even younger than me. We'd do it just like we are now. Sometimes they talked, sometimes they didn't.

"But I'd always know, right before the end." Kingen paused, seeming to collect his thoughts. "I'd always know what kind of man was inside the skin in front of me by the eyes. Did you know that in some Indian cultures, the left eye is considered *el ojo de Dios*? The eye of God?"

Still staring straight at Volga, still perfectly balanced in a squat, Kingen reached backward with his right hand. He pulled a nonstandard-issue hard plastic Glock nine-millimeter pistol from a holster clipped on the inside of his waistband, snug against the small of his back. He touched the barrel, lightly but forcefully, against Volga's left eye.

Volga's right eye grew wide as the pistol barrel jammed against his left. He opened his mouth to speak but only a thin wheeze of air came out.

"Right now, for example," Kingen said, "I see nothing except cowardice. No defiance. No calculations about getting out of this. No regrets. Just fear. That's good. That's very good."

He thumbed the hammer back with a click. Volga quivered sharply. Kingen sighed. "Some men might shit in their pants about now. But you're not much of a man. And you're too anal. So I figure you won't."

He released the hammer and put the pistol back into its holster. Volga inhaled sharply through his mouth. With his right hand, Kingen squeezed Volga's cheeks, forcing his mouth open.

"Breathe deeply. That's it. And listen. A hundred thousand for Port-au-Prince. A hundred thousand for Pensacola. A hundred and fifty thousand for D.C. So far, I've been paid one hundred thousand, period.

"You owe me a quarter of a million. And now you want me to take care of God knows how many people, because God knows how many know about your little operation."

A breeze ruffled Volga's hair, stirring up small dust devils, tiny tornadoes that swirled in the hard-packed grit and disappeared as they pirouetted toward the seaside highway dotted with abandoned, burned vehicles, and with bodies.

Kingen jerked his head toward the pavement. "See those?"

"Of course."

Kingen turned slightly and flicked out his wrist, slapping Volga across the face with the back of his hand.

"You snotty little piece of shit. 'Of course.' Of course, you don't see anything. Those men out there died for something. Maybe it was for Saddam's glory. More likely it was just for their families, trying to get home in one piece. But it was for something, at least.

"You, you sit in antiseptic isolation and push buttons or pull strings or whatever it is your kind does. And if you're uncomfortable you simply turn up the air-conditioning or send someone out for a Coke. Discomfort is as far as your emotional meter goes. You don't know anything about terror or longing or getting ready to die. You just sit someplace."

Volga dabbed at his red cheek with his handkerchief. "And what makes me so much different than you?"

Kingen turned and shoved Volga up against the chain-link fence again. "From you, you piece of excrement. It's from you, not than you. A coward and an ignoramus, um?"

He turned his back on Volga, folded his arms and stared at the city, at the blast marks that looked like smeared makeup across the windows of the distant high rises, at the wreckage of a small armored car whose front had collided with a median barrier and whose rear had been crumpled by an explosion, at the torso that had apparently been torn from its seat and deposited, bloody end down, on the road. It looked as if a bearded soldier had been encased from the waist down in concrete and had managed to climb halfway out.

"Do you have any idea," Kingen asked quietly, "how many men I've killed? And women?"

The only sound was the *whomp whomp whomp* of a pair of Sea Stallions flying several hundred meters out in the Gulf, parallel to the coast. "There are goddamn few of us left. It's all satellites and analysts clipping foreign-language newspapers. People like me analyze and deduce, all right. And then we do what needs to be done and keep it all very quiet."

Volga tried to straighten himself against the fence. He pushed forward and put his feet back on the ground. "The difference is we're paying you. And quite well."

"Ah, Timothy, Timothy, Timothy. Not yet you haven't. You see, my superiors have discovered my, ah, safety net account. And it's not nearly full enough yet.

"So we fill it up quickly and maybe, just maybe, I can take the money and end my career where there'll be enough money to buy enough soap to wash the memory of you and everyone else from Vietnam to Kuwait out of my mind, so I hope you understand my position *you lying cowardly little cocksucker*!"

He turned again, suddenly. Volga put his palms flat in front of him. Kingen, breathing hard, laughed. He took a deep breath.

"Ah, better. Don't worry, little man. I'm not going to kill you, at least anytime soon. What was it, little man? Six years ago? Six and a half, I think, when I first stumbled on your shipment records and wondered what some company with a mail drop in St. Louis was doing sending biologicals and chemicals to Baghdad, a few liters at a time? Luckiest day of my life when I decided to keep it quiet and take your money."

Volga was the one breathing hard now, through his mouth. Kingen cocked his head. "Careful. I don't want you having a heart attack on me."

"It's all this," Volga said, waving a hand. "Dust and oil and that stink. I keep stopping up. Hard to breathe."

Kingen sneered. "Then get your flaccid little ass up and walk. It's the smell of life, little man. The smell of death. It's what the consequences smell like when someone like you makes a decision."

Volga snuffled, and walked, unsteadily, beside the taller man. "You said they've discovered your account. Have they discovered—"

"Your records?" Kingen said acidly.

Volga nodded. Kingen massaged the bridge of his nose. "No, I hardly think they've had time. They're too concerned about the shipments they already know about. Some of them perfectly legal, too. They might find out eventually, but by that time I'll be vanished into thin air with my money, and all this will be ancient history, and no one will care much."

Kingen stopped and turned. "So. We still need to talk business. And money. Let's be optimistic and say just two more have to die. Okay, Timothy?"

Kingen reached out with his right hand, gripped Volga's chin, and moved his head up and down. Kingen nodded, too. "Good. Then you owe me, as of right now, $250,000 past due, and another $750,000 for the current contract, for a grand total of one million dollars, U.S. And I'll tell you what you're going to do, right now.

"I'm going to write down a name and an account number. I'm going to go with you to a sat phone. You're going to call your boss and have that money wired now. You do understand the concept of immediacy, don't you, Timothy?"

Again he jerked Volga's head up and down, four times, rapidly. Volga was still sucking air through his mouth.

"Good. I'm then going to call the bank. And when I'm told the money has been deposited and I can access it, I'll do what needs to be done. And there'll be no more contact between us. Ever."

He released Volga, who didn't move. Kingen pulled a small notebook and pen from a pocket and scribbled. He smiled thinly.

"You know the beauty of these accounts is you don't need a name except for preliminary identification? It's all alphabetical and numerical. Totally impersonal. Sort of like life itself."

He pulled Volga toward him by the arm, and handed him the paper. "Read this exactly as written. Have it read back to you. It should take half an hour at most. Then we take care of business."

Volga glanced at the notebook sheet. It read: "Bank of the United Arab Emirates. Dubai. 2169946. ZGRWQ. 5P37XD8. Ali Jassim."

FOURTH RING ROAD, KUWAIT CITY

Dees pursed his lips and whistled, low. He removed the headphones he'd been wearing and watched around a corner of the tank as the distant Humvee pulled away from the seafront and headed downtown.

A parabolic dish, less than two feet wide, sat on the tank's rear fender, aimed across two hundred meters of sand and dirt at the spot just vacated by Kingen and Volga. A pair of small cables ran from the dish into the back of a mini-amplifier and mixer, barely six inches across. An adaptor plug connected an output with a cable that ran into the audio input of Marco's camera. The camera, extender lens pushed to full magnification, sat atop one of the tank treads, almost invisible to anyone more than ten meters away.

Melinda listened on a set of headphones plugged into the mini-amp's headphone jack. The feed to Dees's headphones came from the audio out-jack on the camera. That allowed both to listen—and make sure the audio was actually being recorded.

Without a word, Dees disconnected the various cables and handed the dish and amp back to Odell. Odell packed them in the hard plastic case and stashed the case in the rear of the Humvee.

"Thanks," Dees said.

Odell grunted. He and Hopkins had spent the past fifteen minutes on the Corniche side of the tank, rifles ready, looking for any sign of Allied troops. So far, nothing, although the distant rumble of fire at the airport had stopped.

"We need to find our unit," he said. "Now that we've delivered you home nice and safe, that is."

Dees nodded. "Just get us to the Sheraton, and we'll make sure all this tape of you two gets fed back home. You could be heroes."

Hopkins secured his M-16 inside the vehicle. "Heroes to y'all, maybe. But how we gonna explain a PAO vehicle getting in the middle of a tank attack?"

Dees smiled. "Tell 'em you lost your orders and forgot you weren't supposed to shoot back."

Hopkins said, "Roger that," and got into the Humvee. He glanced at the tank. Melinda was taking the just-shot tape from Marco's camera and stuffing it inside a Velcro-taped pocket of Dees's photographer's vest. Her hands were shaking.

"Let's go," she said. She stared at Dees on the other side of the rear console. "What now?"

"Back to Dhahran," he said firmly. "Take what we shot, and the disk, and get to Riyadh. Fly to Cairo. Get this out as soon as we can. Sell it to somebody, anybody. Do the story. It buys us protection."

She brushed an oily blond strand of hair from her face. "And that makes sure you won't be guest of honor at an open casket ceremony? You'd look like shit as a corpse with an eyepatch."

"It puts the pressure on them. We sell it to CBS or ABC or NBC or CNN or Radio Moscow for chrissakes, anyone . . . to make sure we get the story out. It gives us enough time to release all the details as soon as we figure them out."

She nodded. "I know a *60 Minutes* senior producer pretty well. He should help."

He looked at her sourly. She said, "Yes, it's exactly what you're thinking. We used to be lovers. And I'd contact him again to get this released, and to save your life. Because I love you."

Marco, standing in the TOW position, said, "Ain't fucking romance grand?"

Dees blushed. Melinda glanced up at Marco. "What about you?"

"I'm only the shooter," he said. "I don't know nothin'. And nobody knows me. I'm gonna stay. I've got a war to shoot."

She tugged his pants leg. "Okay. You feed the war pool tape. I'll set it up. You." She turned to Dees. "You get a four-by. Grab one of GTV's and we go as soon as we drop off the bang-bang to feed."

Dees said, "Yeah," softly. It occurred to him that it had never entered their minds to not feed the combat tape, and just to pack up and run. Melinda stared at him. He said, "I know. It's the job. We feed what we came to cover, then we leave."

"Last stop," Hopkins barked. The Sheraton, pocked with shell-fire and blast points, loomed in front of them.

A ten-foot-long generator roared in the parking lot, sending black diesel fumes shooting skyward. Two orange camping tents shielded the exciters, which had once been explained to Dees as sort of turbochargers for electronic signals, goosing them with enough power to blast out of the three-meter-wide satellite dish and up to a geosynchronous satellite some 23,000 miles above them.

Grimy GTV technicians were surrounded by Kuwaiti men with rifles, a few women, and dozens of children. One GTV uplink engineer carried a small girl on his shoulder. She giggled as he took a greasy GTV baseball cap from his sweating head and plopped it on hers. It covered her eyes and came down past her ears, delighting her. Two satellite phone dishes were unfurled at the far end of the parking lot. It looked like a cross between a souk and an electronics show.

"Ah, the conquering heroes," Melinda said, climbing from the Humvee.

Dees got out and shook Hopkins's hand as Melinda planted a kiss on Odell's cheek.

"Thanks," Dees said. "Drive safely." He handed each a business card.

"Say," Odell said, "I'll be in touch. I'd like to get a copy of some of those tapes. I ever tell you I may run for office someday?"

Hopkins looked at him. "You figure being a war hero'll help you get elected dogcatcher?"

Odell narrowed his eyes. "They don't elect dogcatchers, peckerwood, 'cept maybe in Dogpatch."

"Shit, start your campaign here," Hopkins said. Someone had unfurled a tattered Kuwaiti flag and a pristine stars and stripes, and had taped them side by side on the deuce and a half the GTV crew had used to haul their satellite equipment. "It looks like an Arab county fair."

Odell poked him in the arm. "Say good-bye. We better find the Tiger Brigade and apply for the Silver Star."

Hopkins snapped a salute. "Yes sir, Mr. President."

CHAPTER 17

SHERATON HOTEL, KUWAIT CITY

Kingen had pulled his Humvee behind the Sheraton. He stood placidly by as Volga told the large engineer with the child on his shoulder that he was to hang up the phone now and give them some privacy. The technician glowered as he strode away.

Volga dialed in the phone codes and waited. "Volga here. We need to have some money transferred immediately." He paused. "One million." He stood silently. "No, it is not negotiable. We have thirty minutes to complete it, or the entire deal is off."

Another pause. "Yes. The entire deal."

He paused again. "There is no choice. Understood. Here is the information." He read from the scrap of notebook paper.

"Now, repeat it back to me." A long pause. "Exactly. I'll be in touch."

Kingen took the receiver from Volga's hand and punched in another series of numbers. "*Aleicham Salaam.* Might I speak to Mr. Abdullah, please? Yes. Most important. Jassim. Colonel Ali Jassim. Two one six nine nine four six. *Thnayn waahid sitta tischa tischa arbaca sitta. Skukran.*"

After a lengthy silence, Kingen began speaking in halting Arabic. He paused, gave the alphabetic codes in Arabic-accented English, and continued, "And I wish to wire transfer the incoming deposit, plus a large portion of my balance. Leaving, of course, a hundred thousand U.S. on deposit with you. No, it is purely temporary. Some Latin bond transactions best handled from this other account. And the amount minus the hundred thousand to be on deposit?

"Ah, yes. One million, six hundred forty-five thousand U.S. To the Banco del Negocios, San Jose, Costa Rica. A Mr. Ramon Fuentes."

He shifted back to Arabic. He nodded, said *"Afwan,"* and hung up.

Without a word he dialed in another series of numbers, and waited. *"Hola. Buenas. Esta es Senor Lopez Gomez. Senor Fuentes, por favor. Claro. Referencia nueve cero cinco jota ocho tres effe siete. Muchisimas gracias."*

After five minutes of rapid-fire Spanish, Kingen hung up. He turned to Volga. "Within an hour Lopez Gomez will be a very rich man, assuming your boss moves his wire transfer."

Volga sniffed. "He will."

Kingen nodded. "Did you know Costa Rica has rain forests within ten miles of the beach?"

"And no standing army, no extradition treaty with the United States, no open banking laws."

Kingen looked at Volga almost kindly. "You know, you and your boss should be going to prison. Or maybe you should just be killed. But should and will are two different things. Since we all know so much about each other, I'm pretty sure you'd never be prosecuted."

He paused. "No evidence, no paper trail, at least once we finish our business here. As long as you and your boss keep quiet, I'm sure no one in Washington will talk out of school. I disappear, rich.

You become powerful and very discreet." He sighed. "But you know, the more I consider it, the more I believe you both should be killed. Slowly."

Volga looked alarmed. Kingen touched his nose to Volga's.

"But not by me. Unless you ever mention my name to anyone at any time. In that case, I'll leave my, ah, splendid isolation and the macaws and tree frogs behind and will personally make sure that you'll take five days to die and you'll be crawling naked on all fours, drooling like a dog and begging me to kill you by the end of the first."

He gave Volga's shoulder a squeeze. As he turned to his left, he saw a Humvee disappear around a corner and Melinda walking toward the uplink dish.

Dees was walking in the opposite direction, around the far side of the hotel, toward the parking lot. Kingen gave Volga's shoulder a pull, propelling him around the nearby corner of the building, and shoved him toward the parking lot.

Melinda freed herself from the bear hug with a smile, looking at the uplink technician and the child on his shoulder.

"So, Dewey," she said, "recruiting them kind of young these days?"

Dewey laughed heartily. "My own harem. You look great for looking like shit."

She gave one of his huge hands a squeeze. "I'm just a war babe." She held out four videotapes. "These are in order. Notes on the labels tell where and when. Marco can help you shuttle to the best spots. We even got close-up video of us destroying a tank." She smiled proudly. Dewey beamed.

"All right! We're feeding B-roll now for one of Mac's EcoGeo's on the environmental toll of war."

She stuck her finger in her mouth, making a gagging sound. Dewey laughed and looked at the child on his shoulder. "Kaleefa, you want to see us feed videotape?"

She nodded vigorously, the oversize ball cap bouncing up and down. Dewey took the tapes in a hamlike hand. "Let me find Marco. I figure we have five more minutes of this crap to feed and then we'll show 'em some real rock and roll."

Melinda looked up at him. "Peter went to get a vehicle. Where are they parked?"

He nodded to his right. "Over behind the hotel. We got three Monteros, two Pajeros, and two pretty busted-up Diahatsus. The red Montero has the most gas. If Volga hasn't taken it."

Melinda's breathing became shallow. "Volga? He's here?"

Dewey grimaced. "Yeah, shooed me off one of the sat phones a few minutes ago."

Melinda stood on her tiptoes and pecked him on the cheek. "For God sakes, be safe."

Dewey rolled his eyes toward his shoulder. "As long as I have my good luck charm, I'm fine."

Melinda walked almost stiff-legged, trying not to appear in a hurry. She looked around at the chaos of activity but didn't see Dees.

As she turned the corner, she spotted him, window rolled down, sitting at the wheel of the red Montero, the engine running. She walked faster, and didn't notice until she opened the passenger door that the tinted windows had prevented her from seeing Volga and Kingen in the backseat. Volga merely looked at her without expression.

Kingen looked at her and nodded. "Melinda Adams, I presume? A pleasure."

The plastic Glock was in his left hand, the barrel nestled at the base of Dees's skull. "Get in, please."

She sat down and closed the door. Dees turned to look at her.

"Careful," Kingen said. The barrel was now aimed at Dees's right ear.

"You know the worst part?" Dees said.

Melinda shook her head.

"I think I'm out of cigarettes."

FEBRUARY 28–MARCH 1, NORTHWEST OF KUWAIT CITY

It took over two hours to navigate the few miles between the blackened high rises of the city center and the Sixth Ring Motorway, where the urbanized clutter gave way to open desert.

Cars and trucks full of Kuwaitis, many waving guns, had started to clog the streets. Debris was scattered everywhere, including artillery shells and small rockets that hadn't gone off. Whether they were from the scores of charred Iraqi trucks, tanks, and armored personnel carriers that littered the road, or from the Allied aerial arsenal, Dees wasn't sure.

Tan trucks and tanks filled with Saudi and Kuwaiti troops had begun to roll into the city. Occasionally, a black dune buggy would zip by with a throaty roar. The two-seat buggies, each with a .30 caliber machine gun mounted atop the roll bar, belonged to the Army Special Forces. For days, sometimes weeks, the two-man buggies had been playing hide-and-seek with the Iraqis, reporting back on their movements and snatching Iraqi officers for interrogation. The Special Forces soldiers, faces often protected by goggles and various tribal *kaffeyas* stuffed into their BDU jackets, had the grim look of men searching for something. They drove fast, staring straight ahead. Maybe, Dees thought, it's what you do after you've been sleeping in the desert for weeks surrounded by enemy troops.

Dees steered around a curve, and saw, straight ahead, a five-hundred-pound bomb sticking out of the pavement like a five-foot-tall lawn dart. The polished aluminum fins contrasted with the dull olive body. The business end had burrowed into the concrete three feet without going off.

Dees slowed and steered carefully around the bomb. Kingen, still holding the pistol at the base of Dees's skull, looked to his left.

"From an A-6," Kingen said. "Some subcontractor's going to get a nasty letter about this one."

By the time the red four-wheel-drive had navigated the last of the urban debris, the oil-streaked sky had completely disappeared into the blackness that surrounded them.

"Where to?" Dees asked out of the side of his mouth. "Iraq?"

Kingen snorted through his nose. "Hardly. There's something up here I want you to see."

Swinging around a sweeping right curve on the highway, Dees could see the overpass for the Sixth Ring Motorway just ahead. Maybe a hundred meters beyond the overpass, the divided eight-lane highway looked, on both sides, like a Los Angeles freeway during a particularly bad rush hour. All the traffic, though, had been moving in one direction—north, toward Iraq. As the Montero entered the jam, Dees saw that there were plenty of spaces to drive between the stalled vehicles, assuming he could avoid the bodies.

Melinda let out an exasperated gasp. "What happened here?"

Kingen, still balancing the pistol lightly against Dees's head, massaged the bone above the bridge of his nose with the thumb and middle finger of his right hand.

"Why don't you just look around and tell me exactly what you think happened," he said softly, without looking up.

Vehicles of every description were stalled in the road, some abandoned, some still burning. A Cadillac ambulance, the rear stuffed with rolled-up carpets, sat with both doors open, untouched, next to a large truck whose cargo of refrigerators, dishwashers, and microwave ovens was scattered across the highway. A rocket had blown the engine and cab to pieces, then blasted a shower of burning household appliances all over the road.

A Kuwaiti taxi, the rear seat jammed full of a jumble of lamps and end tables, had rear-ended a fire truck. A large cardboard box tied to the top of the bright red pumper had torn open, scattering boxes of stethoscopes, cotton swabs, tongue depressors, and thermometers on the asphalt.

The Montero crunched along through the ruins. Abandoned and blackened vehicles stretched as far as Dees could see, angling up toward the Al Muttwa ridge, where the eight-lane divided highway narrowed down to two lanes before it proceeded straight north, into Iraq.

"They looted the city," Melinda said in awe. "They took everything."

"Baby food, radios, furniture, cases of beans, carpets, lamps," Dees said, cataloguing everything he saw as he slowly drove the four-wheel-drive forward. "One projection TV, slightly burned."

He looked up the line of mangled vehicles. The Montero's headlights barely made an impression through the sooty air. The truck jolted over a length of car axle, shoving Dees's head against the pistol.

"Look," he said, "either shoot me or take that goddamn thing out of my neck. You want to kill me, shoot me in the back through the seat. I'm tired, I'm cranky, and I don't like nine-millimeter head rests."

Dees didn't hear anything, but felt the barrel draw away from his neck.

"Pull over here," Kingen said.

Dees pulled behind what appeared to be a relatively intact Iraqi army truck. Its cargo of splintered wooden boxes lay scattered around it.

"Kill the lights," Kingen ordered.

Dees turned off the lights and shut down the engine. Melinda reached her hand across the seat and squeezed his. He had never been anyplace this dark.

MARCH 1, AL MUTTWA ROAD, NORTHWEST OF KUWAIT CITY

The moon was a streaked yellow thumbprint on a dirty window. It peeked through the oily gauze just enough so that, after a few minutes, Dees could make out destroyed vehicles on all sides clearly. Across the median, a DHL courier delivery van had driven atop the trunk of a Toyota. Dees thought they looked like they were mating.

"Here," Kingen said from the rear seat. He handed Dees a pack of cigarettes and a disposable lighter.

Dees shook one out, lit it, and exhaled deeply.

"Put that out!" Volga rasped from the seat behind Melinda. "Must you smoke that disgusting—"

Dees heard an almost liquid *smacck* in the backseat, turned and saw Volga rubbing his mouth where Kingen had hit him in the upper lip with the Glock.

"Shhh," Kingen said. "You make me nervous." He acted as if he were suppressing a laugh, so only a *tcch* sound was forced out between his tongue and teeth. Dees felt the hairs on his neck bristle. He reached into the upper pocket of his photographer's vest.

"Careful," Kingen said, raising the Glock. The barrel was inches from Dees's nose.

Dees placed an object on the console. Melinda looked at it, then looked at Kingen.

"It's gum, stud," she said. "Want a stick?"

Kingen made the same *tcch* sound and lowered the pistol.

Melinda's eyes met Dees's. She looked at him, then down quickly toward his vest pocket, then back at him. He remained expressionless.

"So," Dees said, "it was you all along? Marmelstein, Miller, our friend the colonel? A little trick you learned coming in second in the Southeast Asia war games?"

Melinda gasped as Kingen slapped the gun's barrel above Dees's right eye, rocking his head back. Without a word, Dees took a final drag on the cigarette and stubbed the butt in the ashtray. "Wrong eye, asshole."

"None of that matters," Kingen said. His teeth were clenched, so he spoke in a hissy whisper. "Look outside and tell me why it doesn't matter."

"Fuck you," Dees said. "What matters is you're a psycho—"

"Shut up!" Kingen pressed the Glock against Dees's right temple. "You want murder? You want murder? How about mass murder? How about mass murder one body at a time? Do you have the brains to know what I'm talking about?"

"Why don't you tell me?" Dees said. "So we keep what brains I have off the dashboard."

"You know who they were?" Kingen said, jerking his head toward the carnage outside. "Draftees. Conscripts. Pulled off the streets of the areas where Saddam has the most opposition. He figured the Allies would hit here hardest. So they get to strip whatever they can carry, and destroy what evidence was left behind, and then run for their lives.

"You know one of the things they were supposed to destroy? A little item called the bed. The secret police had them scattered in basements all over the city. They'd strip prisoners and tie them to the bedsprings. Soak them with water and apply electricity. Instant information."

Melinda clenched her jaw. "So all of them deserved to die."

Kingen laughed sharply. Dees thought it sounded more like a bark. "I knew you didn't get it. Don't you get it? Nobody here, um, did any of that. By the time the assault on the city started, the secret police and the Republican Guard and the reliable officer corps and troops were well back in Iraq, beyond Basra. The torturers and rapists got away.

"And besides the one Republican Guard unit that was trapped at the airport, all that was left were farmers and peasants, maybe some street kids. All drafted with the express idea of thinning out opposition in Iraq by having the Allies kill them. So they looted. And ran."

"And died," Melinda said, looking out at the infernal jumble of cars and trucks.

Kingen was breathing heavily, slowly, almost sighing with each exhalation. "You know right now there's nothing between Saddam and the Twenty-fourth Mechanized Division except a hundred twenty miles of undamaged highway and the Baghdad police department? And you know what else?"

Dees said, "You've decided to take the gun away from my temple and stick it up your ass?"

Dees heard the *tcch* again, and guessed it was a laugh. "You have no idea, do you, hotshot? Saddam and all of his butchers are staying in power. A cease-fire's coming, and Saddam and, ah, all of the men who pulled all the strings get away. And you know why?"

Melinda cleared her throat. "Shiites and Kurds?"

Kingen grunted appreciatively.

She continued, "His only organized opposition. If the Shiites took over, you could have Iraq allied with Iran. If the Kurds took over, Syria and Turkey would raise hell because the Kurds want parts of their countries, too."

"Simplistic, but the right idea," Kingen said. "So we use

Saddam as a counterweight to Iran. He uses us to kill his opposition. We free Kuwait. Oil flows again. Checkmate, and only the pawns get knocked off the board."

Volga spoke thickly through a swollen upper lip. "You're talking too mufh. Juft get this over with."

Kingen ignored him. "They tried to surrender. Honest. The air controllers vectoring in the Apaches and Warthogs also accessed the Iraqi frequencies. They said they screamed over their radios as they died. They said that some Iraqis broadcast their surrender. The pilots never heard it. The controllers did. One of them told me it was like shooting fish in a barrel.

"You know what a British colonel told me yesterday?" Kingen paused, and began laughing. "Wow. You'll have to excuse me. You know what he said? This is, um, actually very funny. 'This was not combat, this was murder.' Full of bristly British indignation, too."

Dees lit another cigarette. "Look, we all work for somebody. The Iraqis. The GIs. Us. You. Me, I know who I work for. But you, who's telling you to add us to the body count?"

Dees heard the hammer click back on the Glock as Kingen increased the pressure on his temple.

"Look," Dees said, exasperated, "you want to kill me, fine, just fine." He shifted his head and glared at Volga. "But at least the Iraqis out here killed on orders from the great and powerful Saddam, not from a Pekinese in a designer bush jacket."

Kingen chuckled. "He is a miserable little piece of work, isn't he?" The chuckling stopped. "You two get out of the vehicle and move very slowly over next to that truck, where I can see you. And do it slowly. Very slowly.

"Or I'll put Mr. Dees out of his mouthy misery."

CHAPTER 18

MARCH 1, AL MUTTWA ROAD

The stench of clotted blood and bloated bodies was overpowering. Dees stepped onto the crunchy pavement gingerly, the barrel of Kingen's pistol following his head. They formed a ragged semicircle, Kingen leaning against the Montero, Melinda on his right, Dees directly in front of him, Volga, still wiping a swollen upper lip, to his left. Volga started to move toward Kingen, but with a wave of the Glock was advised to stay where he was.

"Let's juft get this done," Volga said thickly.

"Who?" Kingen said. "*Let's* get this done? Let us? Us? *Us?*" He was shouting. "*Us? We?* No, no, no. *We* will not get this thing done! *I'll* get this thing done!"

Dees took half a step forward, his palms open. Kingen lazily waved the pistol in his direction. Dees stopped. "Look, you were talking about pawns. What's that make you? Why? Why us? Why the rest of them? Why Marmelstein?"

"I didn't shoot Marmelstein," Kingen said flatly. He paused, and Dees thought he seemed surprised at himself. "He was done by a—ah . . . subcontractor."

"And his left eye?"

Kingen nodded nervously. "That. That was the sincerest form

of flattery. I'd trained a few, ah . . . assets in Port-au-Prince. One of them apparently knew about my . . . my . . ."

"Your trademark," Melinda said quietly.

"My trademark," Kingen said. "Ms. Adams, I'm very impressed with you. Very impressed. You grasp things quickly. So he was tasked to very simply remove an item from Mr. Marmelstein. And he killed him, and then, well, I had to step in and neutralize a problem."

"You shot the shooter because he killed Marmelstein and it looked like you?" Dees asked.

"Plausible deniability, Peter. You're not nearly as subtle as Ms. Adams. It may or may not have looked like my work. We couldn't afford even the possibility due to a breach like that."

"We?" Dees said, palms still open. "You and worm boy here? The boy genius who can have Scuds launched against American troops?"

"Against you, actually." Kingen sighed. "And I found out about that much too late—"

"Be quiet!" Volga squeaked from behind a lip swollen twice its normal size. He took a step forward. What he said sounded like "Phutt upp! Phill them! Phill them!"

Dees's brain had just registered. "I think he's trying to say 'Kill them,' " he said when the Glock fired with a popping *crracck*. Instinctively, Dees jumped to his left and put his body in front of Melinda's, pinning her against the Montero.

The bullet tore through the middle of Volga's right kneecap neatly. It shattered a section of the ball and socket joint connecting the femur and tibia before lodging in a thick section of bone.

Volga crumpled on his left side, screaming.

Kingen stood over him. "Timothy, you are never going to walk normally again. But you may end up living if you shut up this instant. You speak when spoken to, understand?"

Clutching his bloodied right pants leg, eyes wide with fear, a urine stain spreading warmly across his crotch, Volga nodded.

Dees felt Melinda breathing against his back. Kingen raised the pistol toward Dees's forehead. Dees's spine became erect.

"Dennis," he said slowly, looking straight into his eyes, "if you can, try to kill just me. She doesn't know shit. Just let her go and I promise I won't try too hard to make you eat that gun. Besides, too many people have copies of the—"

Kingen lowered the pistol toward Dees's crotch. Kingen's lips were pursed, as if he were trying to keep himself from laughing. "Peter, you have the balls of a burglar. I know for a fact that you have the only copy of the late Mr. Marmelstein's disk.

"I know for a fact Ms. Adams is too sagacious not to know all you know. And *I . . . know . . . for . . . a . . . fact . . .*" He paused. "I know for a fact I could break your neck with one hand."

"So get off me, you lug," Melinda said softly. She turned Dees toward her. "That way he doesn't have to shoot through you to get me."

Dees turned to Kingen. "So it's acceptable to launch poison gas against GIs on his orders?" He nodded toward Volga.

Kingen's lips tightened. "I told you I found out about that too late to stop—"

"Spare me," Dees said. "Just follow orders, just let poison gas fall like fucking rain on your own troops. We may all be pawns, but some of us pawns have been gassed and some of us haven't, right?"

Kingen's eyes narrowed. Dees pressed the opening. "And some of your own people, your own people, will die or their kids will mutate into cockroaches or who knows what the hell else. Why? Why you, Dennis? Do you know what you've done?"

Kingen looked at Volga. "We have a problem, don't we, Timothy?"

Volga simply stared. Kingen crouched next to him, motioning

with the pistol for Dees and Melinda to join him. He sat, his back against one of the Montero's rear wheels, facing them.

"You see, Timothy here decided that he wanted to launch some missiles on his own, didn't you, little man?"

Volga, still clutching his knee, shook his head vigorously. "Mac. Mac said to do it. He said our fhriens in Baghdad owed us."

Dees leaned forward. "Mac? Burke? Your friends in Baghdad owed you what?"

Volga's eyes were almost squeezed shut. He was crying. He shook his head no.

Melinda put her hand on Dees's shoulder. "Mac? Did he say Mac ordered missiles on us? Mac?" She was breathing hard.

Kingen's eyebrows arched. "I'm surprised, Ms. Adams. He is definitely telling the truth. Which is where I come in."

Melinda looked straight at him. "And why should we believe you? Look at you. You're sweating. You're shaking. You're either sick or . . ."

She paused. Kingen laughed brittlely. "Or unhinged? Crazy? Do you think *I'm crazy*?"

The shout echoed off the gutted cars and trucks. She stared at him coolly. "You said it. I didn't."

Kingen cocked the pistol again, and aimed it at the prone, shivering figure. "Timothy?"

Volga sniffled. "Mac had done bufiness with Saddam for years. Mac knows you have Marmelfein's disk. So he asked Iraq to launch the missiles."

"I reacted, ah, very badly when I found out," Kingen said. "My agreement was to clean up a certain mess. Not to try to kill American troops."

Dees flushed. "So you fed me all this bullshit in Cairo—"

"Hoping to scare you off," Kingen said. "But your producer, Saed . . ."

Dees drew a sharp breath. Kingen smiled. "Peter, you've been in enemy territory all along. Saed was working with us. He was too incompetent even to kill you in a lonely desert on horseback. He also, ah, attracted too much attention because of his relatives, who were fundamentalists."

Dees wrinkled his brow. "So you gave me a guard to finish off Saed and maybe me?"

"Definitely you," Kingen said. "But Saed goes crazy and ends up blowing himself up. And that attracts too much attention, even in Cairo, when it happens on a busy street in time for sunset prayers. So I called off Salah. And by that time you were in Baghdad."

Kingen paused. He giggled. "Funny. I never saw Salah again until I ran into him jogging in Washington."

Dees felt his throat become tight. "And I interviewed Miller," he said. "And I see in the newspaper he's been murdered in Pensacola. Who shoots out a left eye in a home invasion?"

Kingen waved the pistol toward Volga. "Timothy was very upset when you filed that story from Iraq about chemical weapons. And he wanted the source of that information . . . um, well, chastised."

Volga's breathing had become less labored. He had stopped sniffling. Maybe, Dees thought, he'd gotten used to the pain.

"It waf Mac. Mac . . ."

"Mac," Melinda said thoughtfully. "Mac. I'll be damned. That son of a bitch!"

"If we believe him," Dees said. "Or Norman Bates here."

With a familiar *crracck*, Kingen fired the Glock, aiming two feet to the left of Melinda's head, then swiveling it around and aiming it at Dees before he had a chance to move.

"Peter," Kingen said softly, "I am not delusional. *And I am not crazy, you fucking stupid half-wit asshole!*"

The shout, almost a scream, rocked both Dees and Melinda back in surprise.

Kingen took a deep breath through his mouth, exhaling through his nose. "I'm merely a paid employee, like the honored dead all around us," he said very quietly. "You know this all happened because of synergy."

He paused, seemingly pleased with the sound of the word. He said it again slowly.

"Synergy. We allowed companies to export to Iraq when we really shouldn't have done it. Shouldn't have done it at all."

Volga squirmed. Kingen seemed not to notice. "So we had to cover our tracks."

"Cover your butt, you mean," Dees said.

Kingen shrugged. "Whichever. So we needed not to make noise about chemical shipments to Iraq. And I discovered Mr. Burke had quite a healthy commerce with Iraq, healthy far beyond the bounds of what his Commerce Department export licenses allowed. And I also discovered that keeping that information to myself paid very well."

"So you blackmailed D—" Melinda broke off, coughing. "You blackmailed Mac?"

"An arrangement of convenience," Kingen corrected. "I helped him keep his commerce in chemicals out of the official and public eyes. And it made it easier to help, ah, dispose of some things."

"Like missile nose cones?" Dees asked.

Kingen stared at him. "I'm very tired. And I won't be able to sleep with the three of you making a racket. So . . ."

As Kingen raised the pistol toward Dees's head, Dees launched himself forward from his crouch, aiming the top of his head like a battering ram at Kingen's nose. There was contact, and Dees heard a soft crunch, like a foot stepping on fall leaves, before the Glock went off in the air. Kingen, momentarily blinded, clutched at Dees with his free hand.

Dees, figuring Kingen could probably very well kill him with one hand, shoved himself off Kingen's chest, rolled backward, pushed to his feet with one arm around Melinda's waist, jerked her erect, and began running.

Kingen grabbed his nostrils with his left hand to stop the bleeding and fired off one round that missed Dees by over a foot as he and Melinda scooted around the side of the Iraqi ammunition truck.

"Pfffbbbt," Kingen said as he got to his feet and cleared blood from his nose.

"Don't leaf me." Volga groaned.

Kingen looked down at him. "Stay here," he said.

Wheezing for breath, Dees pulled Melinda along with him. They ran past the ammunition truck, past a zigzag litter of vehicles of all descriptions, crunching broken glass and metal shards under their feet.

Hugging the side of a smoking tank, they nodded at each other and sprinted across twenty meters of unlittered roadway, toward a jumble of cars surrounding another Iraqi truck.

Just short of the maze of automobiles, Dees saw what appeared to be an undamaged AK-47 on the pavement. He bent to pick it up, wrapped his hand around the stock, heard a *pinnnggg*, and saw concrete dust and debris fly in the air not three feet to his right. At almost the same time, he heard a familiar *crrracck*. Pushing Melinda in front with the palm of his free hand, he dove headlong between a Mercedes flipped on its left side and the upright Toyota four-wheel-drive in front of it.

They lay flat on their stomachs, listening. All Dees could hear was a creak of metal on metal as a stirring night breeze rubbed a bent fan blade against a radiator. He thought he could hear a hissing from somewhere to his left, but couldn't be sure.

Melinda looked at the Kalishnikov lying between them. "You know how to use that thing?"

"I can figure it out."

"So you don't—"

"Not the foggiest."

She scooted the AK up, removed the clip, saw it was full, and clicked it back into place. "Look," she whispered, "here's the safety. No, down here. Click it up, safety's off."

He squinted at her. "Horses and guns. What're you, Calamity Jane?"

"Daddy has one on the ranch," she said, "one of these, an AR-15 that's actually a full auto M-16, although we don't tell anybody, an old Enfield, a—"

"I get it. So we have bullets and the safety's off."

She nodded, racking a shell into the chamber. "Trouble is, I don't know if it's set on single, three-shot burst, or auto. Don't know where the switch is for that."

"And we don't have time to find out," Dees rasped. He took the rifle. "Sooner or later some Allied troops will come along. We'll just stay on the road."

"Why not run for the desert? It's dark out there."

"It's also mined. We run out there in the dark and—" Dees heard a distinctive soft sound in the darkness beyond his feet, like a vehicle rolling across the highway with the engine off.

"Shit!" he said. Melinda barely had time to look puzzled when he grabbed her arm and shoved her to her feet. Dees was still on one knee, stumbling erect, when the darkness turned to floodlit noon. He grabbed one of Melinda's belt loops and pulled her out of the glare, stumbling on all fours, just as the *cracck* of a pistol ricocheted off the scattered wreckage. The slug pinged off the concrete barely an inch behind Dees's heel as he scooted out of the light.

They flattened themselves against the tires of an overturned tow truck, its cab pounded flat with the ground. Dees heard the grind of an engine starting, swung the rifle barrel around the tire, and took aim at the twin headlights just as they were shut off. He sighted on one of the fading lights and squeezed the trigger.

He was surprised at how little the AK-47 kicked as it fired a single round, followed by a pop and the tinkle of glass. Dees swung himself behind the rear twin tires of the tow truck just in time to hear a thunk followed by a whistling hiss as a bullet from the Glock penetrated one of the tires.

"He must've pushed the Montero here," Melinda said.

"What's he, fucking Superman?"

"It's a slight downhill grade, cowboy. Rolled it up and—"

"Move!" Dees yelled, and pulled her along as he sprinted toward what appeared to be an undamaged BMW sedan, both front doors open. Just as they reached it, the rear glass shattered into a giant spiderweb.

"Oh fuck you," Dees said. Turning, he raised the AK to his shoulder and quickly fired three rounds in the direction of the faint crunching behind them. He heard a bullet hitting metal, and a squeak, like brakes being applied suddenly.

"The keys are in it," Melinda yelped.

The keys were nestled in the steering column ignition. In the off position.

Dees yelled, "We don't have time to—" as Melinda leaned across the passenger seat and turned the key. Nothing happened. Another bullet whistled into the windshield, fracturing the glass just below the rearview mirror.

"Will you get the hell out of there!" Dees shouted, firing a round in the general direction of the pistol shot. Melinda looked down, saw the console shift was in drive, jammed it forward into park, and turned the key again. The engine ground, stuttered, and hummed to life.

"No shit. No shit!" Dees jumped into the driver's seat as Melinda dove into the passenger's seat. The ratchet keeping her seat back upright stripped as Dees slapped the car into gear and punched the accelerator to the floor. Melinda fell into the backseat as the BMW jumped forward. The passenger door smacked off an upright truck axle in the road, slamming shut.

As he attempted to steer without lights, Dees thrust the rifle into the backseat. "Here. You know how to use this thing."

She glared at him when the car leapt a few inches in the air, front end first, and then crashed down. Dees kept control.

"What the hell did you hit?" Melinda yelled.

"It could be anything!" he shouted over his shoulder as he tried to steer. "I have to use the lights!"

"He'll see us!"

"And I can't see where the hell I'm going. We could hit an artillery shell, or a rocket, or any damn thing."

Taking a sharp left around a truck, Dees didn't see the palm tree until a second before he hit it. The ten-foot royal palm had fallen, four-hundred-pound root ball and all, from the back of a truck emblazoned with a coat of arms from the Royal Nursery of the Kingdom of Kuwait.

The car lurched to a sudden stop with a crunch of metal. Dees's head bounced off the steering wheel.

"Or you could hit a potted palm," Melinda said dryly.

"Cute," Dees said, grinding the car into reverse and steering around the palm. He snapped on the headlights, which threaded a filmy yellow beam between smashed vehicles.

Through steam rising from the BMW's apparently punctured radiator, Dees could see that the road twenty meters ahead was completely clogged with jumbled cars, trucks, and military equipment. There was no place to drive except into a three-foot-high concrete median, or sharply to the right, out into the mine fields.

"Uh-oh," he said.

"Uh-oh? What uh-oh? I don't want to hear uh-oh!"

The car's left rear tire exploded with a sharp pop. Looking through the veins of the shattered rear window, Melinda didn't see any headlights. But she did see a wink of light a moment before the glass in front of her collapsed like a rain of icicles and the BMW's rearview mirror exploded.

Aiming at where she thought the wink had been, and correcting for a vehicle moving straight toward her, she cracked off three quick rounds.

Dees heard a dull thud and crumple of metal behind him. Then the BMW's radiator erupted in a *whoosh* of steam. He slammed on the brakes, killed the lights, shut off the engine, opened his door, and grabbed Melinda at the waist and pulled her after him in what seemed to him like one continuous motion.

Sheltered by a panel truck that had hit a median barricade head-on, they listened. All Dees could make out was the hum of an engine.

"It's still running," he whispered.

"It's an automatic transmission," Melinda said. "If he hit something slow enough . . ."

"The engine would still run."

Dees peeped around the side of the truck. Yep. Dark, all right. And not a sound except for the steady noise from the Montero's four cylinders.

"So?" Melinda whispered.

"He's either hit or it's a trap. Either way, we need that truck. Let's slip behind him."

Melinda let out an exasperated sigh, but didn't have time to object as Dees sprinted on the balls of his feet toward the cover of a flipped-over police car. She followed Dees, then crouched behind him at the left front tire.

Peering over the top of the upended car, Dees could make out the Montero, its passenger side window shattered, pushing gently against the running board on the cab of some sort of tanker truck. The four-wheel-drive didn't seem to be damaged. Rifle held at waist level, he duckwalked behind the Montero, motioning Melinda to follow. He paused for one beat behind the truck, then sprang up, jerked open the driver's door, and leveled the AK.

The cab was empty. The shift knob and console were slick with steaming blood. Dees swiveled to his right and whispered, "He's wounded. Get in the—"

"No, Peter. No, no, no. I don't think so."

Dees looked toward the familiar voice, and saw Kingen smiling, his body hidden behind Melinda, his right arm around her throat, his left hand holding the Glock to her temple.

"Drop it. Now."

Dees lowered the AK and placed it on the ground.

Kingen kept smiling. "Kick it this way."

Dees shoved the stock with the toe of his boot. It scooted across the pavement.

Kingen shoved Melinda forward and snapped, "Sit down! Both of you! Now!"

They sat next to an Iraqi army truck that had almost rear-ended the wrecked tanker. A dark stain covered the bicep of Kingen's right arm, from the sleeve of his khaki T-shirt to his elbow. He held his right arm close to his body, steadying the Glock with a rigid, outstretched left arm.

"Painful, but not fatal," Kingen said.

Dees, hands behind him, tried to search the ground under the truck for something, anything. Nothing except a soggy cloth and metal shards. He looked at Kingen. "So, doesn't it hurt your face to keep smiling like that?"

The smile faded. "Not anymore," Kingen said through clenched teeth. "Nothing hurts anymore. Nothing that money can't fix."

"You know, we could keep quiet about this," Melinda said. "And you just take your money—"

Kingen laughed. He was smiling again. "Do you know if money can buy absolution, Ms. Genius? Tell me, do you know that?"

It was Dees's turn to laugh. "Do you want to spend it or not? You kill us, you won't get away. You'll have Uncle Sam and the Saudis and maybe even the Iraqi secret police, for all I know, looking for you. Don't tell me they won't know who killed a POW."

Kingen made a sucking sound through his teeth. Dees continued, "Oh yeah. We found the Iraqi colonel's body. Your trademark. He still had my lighter."

Kingen moved closer, standing almost directly over them. "Purely financial. And anyone looking for me should understand that. It's all just business. Oil. Chemicals. Money. And I seriously doubt anyone is too anxious to let this get out.

"Besides, history is written by the winners." He chuckled, then looked thoughtful. "I mean, Jefferson Davis might have given a speech better than the Gettysburg Address. But we'll never know, will we? We'll never know about sarin or anthrax or mustard, hm? Just like Mr. Davis's speech."

"Oh come on!" Dees said heatedly, trying to gauge the distance to the AK-47 without looking directly at it. "We've all been sick. It may get worse. We'll know, all right, if enough people come down with something from all this."

The grin seemed frozen on Kingen's face. "Synergy again, um, synergy. Take burning oil wells and anti-nerve-gas pills and stress and combat and Arabian Peninsula parasites and who knows what caused what? All working together. Synergy."

Kingen, left arm still stiff, moved closer and pushed the barrel of the Glock into Dees's left eye. "Besides," he hissed, "the government will deny it and the Saudis will deny it and your boss will most certainly deny it, and I'll be rich, and you'll be dead."

He thumbed the hammer back with a click. "So go away now."

Melinda's hand came from behind her so quickly that Dees at first couldn't see what it was she half threw, half thrust into Kingen's face.

With a muffled sputter, Kingen drew away, the pistol swinging away from Dees's face. As he pitched forward and dove for the rifle, Dees saw a human hand, viscera and tendrils trailing from the wrist, drop from Kingen's face.

Kingen, gagging and wiping his eyes, raised the pistol blindly toward where Dees had been and fired. The slug entered Dees's right boot.

"Shit!" Dees yelled. Kingen aimed the Glock toward the sound at the instant Dees reached the rifle. Rolling on his back, Dees fired, twice. The first bullet entered Kingen's throat just below the Adam's apple, severed the carotid artery, and exited. The second entered the right cheek and cut a transverse path through the main sinus cavity, severed the left optical nerve, and came out the top of his head with a soft *pop*.

As Kingen toppled backward, Dees pulled the trigger again. The firing pin clicked on thin air.

Melinda, shaking, got up and looked down at Kingen's body. He still clutched the gun, teeth bared in a half smile, half grimace.

Dees stood, and barked, "My foot."

Melinda went on staring at Kingen, seeming not to notice. Dees dropped heavily on the Montero's running board, took off his boot, and saw that he'd been shot in the little toe. The slug had grazed it enough to rip away the very tip and the toenail.

He put the boot back on tenderly, laid the empty AK inside

the Montero, and hobbled toward Kingen. "Open the rear door," he said.

"What?"

"Open the door!" Dees said. With a *whoof*, he reached under Kingen's armpits and dragged him to the Montero, meanwhile muttering "Shit, shit, shit," because of the pain in his foot.

Melinda opened the door. An aluminum case lay on the floor of the cargo area. Dees sat the body on the bumper, holding it upright with one hand while the other fumbled with the latches.

He opened the lid. Inside, cushioned by black foam rubber, was a rifle barrel, a stock, a telescopic sight, and two ammunition clips.

"For sniper work," Dees said, almost to himself. "Khafji. He missed."

Melinda sighed. "C'mon, let's go."

Dees shoved and tugged until he had Kingen crumpled up inside the cargo area. Melinda picked up the Glock and removed the clip.

"He must've had several," she said. "This one's almost full."

She sat in the Montero driver's seat, plopping the pistol on the center console. "So get in. You can't drive with that foot."

Dees hobbled into the passenger seat. As she shifted, using one headlight to pick her way through the debris, Dees said, "By the way . . ." She looked at him. "Thanks for the hand."

He expected a laugh. She merely stared at him coldly and said, "Right."

CHAPTER 19

MARCH 1, AL MUTTWA ROAD

Volga was just where they had left him, curled up in a fetal ball. He looked at them with glazed eyes when the Montero pulled up, but didn't speak.

Melinda paused, door open. "So," she said, "did the tape work?"

Dees reached into the upper left patch pocket on his photographer's vest and pulled out the microcassette recorder. The two-hour-per-side tape was full. He rewound it to the end and heard a muffled tinny voice say ". . . better than the Gettysburg Address," just before the tape ran out.

He pushed rewind again, waited a few minutes, and hit play. It was all there; muffled, some indistinct, but all of it.

"Gimme," Melinda said, holding her hand out. "Let me hear how much we have to goose it electronically to make it understandable."

"Okay. Here." He handed her the recorder. "Meantime, let me see about Volga."

"He's not going anyplace. Just rest that foot." She leaned over the console, kissed him lightly on the cheek, and slipped the Glock into the rear pocket of her jeans.

Dees sighed, contented. He pushed the passenger seat back as far as it would go and started to elevate his foot on the dashboard, hoping it would stop the throbbing.

He looked to his left and saw Melinda, illuminated by a small fire that still sputtered and smoked on the ground after all these hours. Dees didn't dwell on what might be fueling the smoky mass that occasionally burst into flames.

Melinda lifted the tape player to her ear and listened, nodding. Just as the debris pile stopped smoking and began burning again, she clicked the recorder open, popped out the tiny tape, and tossed it into the flame.

Dees's eyes grew wide. "What the hell are you doing?" he yelled, trying to get his leg and pounding foot down from the dashboard.

With two quick strides, Melinda walked to Volga, removed the pistol from her hip pocket with a fluid motion, and held it in a two-handed shooter's grip.

Volga had time to groan and cover his face with his clutched hands before the Glock cracked twice, each bullet entering his brain.

She strode to the Montero and aimed at Dees, using the same grip. "The disk," she said.

Dees's mouth sagged open. "Melinda? What the—"

"Don't whine," she said, and sneered. "The disk. You always carry it with you, cowboy."

Dees shook his head, bewildered. "Marco has it. Remember? We dropped our bags off and then I got hijacked. It's in the duffel at the Sheraton. Probably in the uplink tent."

"Keep your leg up there," she said. She hopped in the driver's seat, held the gun in her right hand, reached for his crotch with her left, and squeezed. "I'm going to search you. If I find the disk, fine. If not, fine. You die anyway."

"What the hell is going on, Melinda?"

"You are such a chump." She laughed, her hand now digging into his vest pockets. "Do you know who I am?"

He stared at her as she rooted through another pocket. "When we first spoke, do you think it was an accident? We knew Marmelstein's computer was missing with another disk inside it. We knew you had it. So when you called Phoenix looking for help, you got me on the phone."

She unfastened the Velcro of the vest's built-in backpack and reached inside. "C'mon, lean forward," she said, "or I'll shoot you now. Hmmm. Hello."

She withdrew her hand, holding a laptop diskette wrapped inside several Baggies, secured with a series of rubber bands.

She stared at him. "Loser. What a great excuse." Her voice became a mocking singsong, " 'I left it with Marco.' Pathetic. Don't move an inch, Dees. Don't even wiggle your ears."

She started the Montero with her left hand, then expertly steered it with that hand, the gun in her right leveled at Dees.

"What are you—"

"I'm going to make sure there's not much of you or Kingen left. Then I call Daddy."

He scrunched his eyebrows.

She sighed. "What a dunce. It's more of a pet name, but since he's older than me, it's actually a cute thing to call your husband. And it drives him crazy in bed."

She steered without looking at the road, slowly, keeping the pistol aimed at Dees's nose. "I might as well say hello properly. It's Melinda Adams Burke."

Dees narrowed his eyes. He whistled. "Mac? His wife?"

She smiled, steering the Montero slowly toward the edge of the road, facing the sand and mine fields. "Mystery girl genius, that's me. Look, it became apparent Kingen couldn't kill you, and Timothy just knew too much, so I arrive in Baghdad to get close to you and find out everything. Which I did."

She smiled with satisfaction.

Dees felt his face burning. "Some Daddy. He orders Scud attacks on us, on *you*. He knows all about the fallout from the ammo dumps. For chrissakes, look. Just look."

He nodded toward the scaly patches of skin on the inside of her right arm, which was still holding the pistol aimed at his head. She bit her lower lip, gently, eyes squinting, still smiling.

"Mac and I will discuss that when I get home," she said. "Surprised me, too. Either Timothy lied and did it on his own, in which case it doesn't much matter since he's dead, or Mac did it, in which case I become head of GTV sooner than expected after his demise. From suicide probably. A bullet to the head. And I get, oh, a billion and a half, more or less."

He kept staring. She nudged the stock of the empty AK out of the way with her right arm, nestling it between her seat and the console. "Now," she said, "imagine me marrying a rich redneck for love. Radcliffe. The Sorbonne. All that to be a trophy on Mac Burke's arm?"

She laughed, and Dees still thought her laugh sounded like a tinkling wind chime.

"Look," she said, "I charmed him. I intrigued him. I flattered his mammoth ego. I screwed his brains out. And I get a prenup that lists me as 'Mrs. McKinley Burke, Executive Assistant to the Chairman,' and gives me anonymity and power."

Dees shook his head. "So that doesn't make me the only chump, I guess."

Her smile faded. It was Dees's turn to crack a grin. "You get all this on paper, all right. You kill Volga. Hell, you may even kill me."

"Oh, I'll definitely kill you."

"Yeah, maybe. And you still weren't able to see that Kingen was trying to ice both of us or that sweet Daddy tried to do the same thing long-distance by missile. Love's blind, all right. How about greed?"

She chewed momentarily on her lower lip, staring at Dees.

"Yeah, Kingen. There's a wild card. I'm busy finding out what you know, and I never knew about him. Oh, I realized people were being whacked, but given Mac's contacts, I just assumed it was more of his employees, so to speak, doing the job. Never figured it was a one-man lead epidemic."

Dees absently glanced at his watch. Four-thirty. "Look," he said, "I'm going to move this foot off the dash and onto the floor if it's all the same to you."

She shrugged. He slid the throbbing foot off the dashboard and onto the floor. He pressed his back into the door, locating the latch with his left shoulder blade.

"So," he said, "you knew all about Dick and what he'd found out. And you were part of murdering him?"

She laughed, which made Dees want to punch her. She laughed again. "Aww. That make you mad? Tough shit. I knew, we knew, he was on to something, especially when some moron in the shipping room fucked up and sent him one of Mac's laptops. So, yes, I knew Marmelstein was going to be whacked, I just didn't know by who or how. But he dies and we still have a problem, since you have the laptop. So we entice you to Cairo and figure that idiot Saed could do something right for once in his life. He gets the laptop, all right, but we don't know you have a disk copy until we get you to Baghdad and I find out."

"And Saed getting killed by the guy who was supposed to kill me but didn't? And Kingen arranging all that? Looks like you weren't as much in the loop as you thought, wonder woman."

She jerked the Montero to a stop, her foot on the brake, and aimed the gun at Dees's chest, the Montero idling. "You're good in bed and you don't seem to give a shit who you piss off, which almost makes it a shame that you're dead. Yeah, I didn't know Daddy had Kingen on the payroll and that he was trying to kill you.

I didn't know that Volga and Mac got together to try and kill all of us. But I know now, so I win in the end, which is all I care about."

The spreading faint light of the sun under the horizon began to turn the carnage all around them a dirty purple, streaked with wisps of gray oil smoke.

Dees asked, "Mind if I smoke?"

"Smoke. Burn. I should care?"

Dees felt vaguely sick. Not from fear, he decided, but from having said he loved the woman with a tinkling laugh and a nine-millimeter who was ready to kill him.

He lit the cigarette. "So you're number two only to Mac?"

"Oh, much more than that. My name on the organization chart looks like another of Mac's idiosyncrasies. Total anonymity, the perfect disguise. Remember Lear? 'We will be God's spies'? *C'est moi.* I circulate quietly in the company. I report to Mac."

Dees focused on the flatbed truck behind her. The wooden barricades held in the cargo had been blasted askew, and were spread now and aimed at the sky like a pair of wooden hands raised to heaven. He shifted his gaze to her face, trying to see some trace of the Melinda from before the last few minutes. He saw it in the hint of a smile line up her right cheek. It made him feel even worse.

His voice was tired. "And you take over when Mac . . ." He let the thought hang.

She nodded slowly. "I know all he knows, and then some. In fact, more than then some."

"And if it turns out he did order that missile attack on us?"

She paused. "Then he'll be as dead as you two," she said, nodding at Kingen's crumpled body in the cargo area. She smiled, faintly. "Good-bye, Peter."

Dees jammed the burning cigarette into the inside of her

wrist. She squealed and jerked her foot off the brake, meanwhile loosening her grip on the pistol just enough for him to grab her wrist with his right hand. He tried to lean forward to force her wrist and the gun backward, but the searing pain from his foot, sudden and surprising, pushed him back in the seat.

With Melinda's foot off the brake, the Montero had begun to move forward, across the ten feet of highway separating it from the mine-laced sand.

She took advantage of his sudden sagging into the seat and fired, his hand still gripping her wrist. The roar deafened Dees in his right ear. The slug smashed into the lower right corner of the windshield, leaving a neat hole and a starburst of fractured glass.

Leaning forward under the pistol, still holding her wrist, Dees groped almost blindly with his left hand. He grabbed the barrel of the AK-47, jammed tightly against her seat, and shoved it forward.

The edge of the rifle stock caught the accelerator, and the four-wheel-drive jumped forward. Melinda rocked back in her seat, still wedging the Kalishnikov tightly between seat and console. Dees gave the barrel a final shove downward, and the engine rpm increased even more as the vehicle hit the four-inch lip separating the highway from the sand.

Dees yelled, forcing his bad foot up until he guessed it was under the door latch. He pushed upward and felt the door give. He shoved himself backward, letting go of her wrist, his legs sticking out the open door.

Dees looked up then, and saw her eyes narrow as she aimed the pistol at him. He pitched himself upward, intending to flip backward out the door and onto the sand. His torso was upright when she fired.

The force of the impact shoved him out the open door. He landed flat on his back, blood gathering on his shirt where the bullet had scored across the right pectoral muscle, entering just under his collarbone. He prayed it would stop without hitting any major blood vessel or bone.

The Montero churned forward, tossing sand behind it, engine roaring. Dees heard a sharp click, almost like a twig breaking.

Melinda, eyes wide, leaned out the window. *"Peeeterr!"* she screamed.

The scream cut through him more than the pain in his foot. He had time to see her face, mouth open, eyebrows arched in surprise, before he buried his head in his arms barely in time to avoid the explosion.

The mine detonated under the Montero's left front, flipping the red truck over to the right. It landed with a muffled crunch on its roof.

It had barely settled when two more mines exploded under the roof, shoving glass, rubber, and steel toward the pink sky. The truck turned end over end once as it arced twenty meters across the desert and slammed to earth, rear first, releasing gasoline vapor and mist in all directions and igniting a fireball.

The fire engulfed the entire vehicle. Three seconds later an explosion ripped what was left of the red four-wheel-drive apart.

Dees staggered to his feet. The orange and pale yellow flame sent gray smoke skidding into a sky shifting from purple to dirty blue. Dees thought it was odd that it all seemed rimmed in faint red. He stumbled a step backward, feeling dizzy, and heard the growl of an engine. No, several engines. He forced himself to turn around in time to see two Humvees and a Bradley, a trooper mounted at the .50 caliber gun position, appear from behind the blasted highway wreckage.

Two figures in chocolate-chip camo, one black, one white, got out of the front Humvee. They quickly moved to Dees, Odell taking him under the left arm, Hopkins under the right.

"Ow! Shit!" Dees said, not knowing whether it was the arm or the foot that caused the most pain.

Hopkins looked him up and down, then over his shoulder at the burning wreck of the Montero. "What the hell happened?"

Dees looked directly at him, said, "Must've taken a wrong turn," then passed out cold.

CHAPTER 20

FOUR YEARS LATER, JUNE 28, HAVANA

The 1954 Plymouth belched smoke as it sputtered along the Malecon. To the right, the Florida Straits smashed waves against the seawall, waves the same gray-green as the glowering clouds pushing south from Key West.

To the left of the smoking coupe, a black Lada stretch sedan with tinted windows flashed its lights twice and slid past, narrowly missing a young dark-eyed couple on a bicycle, he pedaling, she perched across the handlebars, both laughing.

"Marecón," the driver of the Plymouth muttered. He turned to the man sitting beside him. "Like they say, you get a Lada, you get *nada*."

They both laughed.

The Lada slid past a tattered billboard bearing a red silk-screened likeness of Che Guevara overlaid with SOCIALISMO O MUERTE! done in black type designed to look like military stenciling. The car passed through once-grand neighborhoods now faded into muted pastel people's housing and government offices, past fishing villages perched green and brown on the shore barely above the angry sea, into the diplomatic area near the Marina Hemingway.

The Lada stopped in front of a two-story white bungalow with a red barrel tile roof, unremarkable except for the iron picket fence that surrounded it, two satellite dishes, and a gate opened by remote control.

The tall American with cowboy-style white sideburns stepped out, and in several long strides was inside the house. He walked into a rear bedroom converted to an office. The window opened onto one of the Marina's canal-like slips and, just beyond, the tossing ocean.

He picked up a satellite telephone receiver from its cradle, punched a rubber switch until "Atlantic East" appeared glowing green on the screen, and punched fifteen digits into the keypad.

"Hello," he said. "This is Mr. Mac." A pause, then a low chuckle. "Yes, very well. Hmm? Oh, no. I'd call it more of a strategic repositioning."

He listened, nodded, laughed. "Yes, I know you can appreciate that sort of thing. Hmm? Aerosol dispersal shouldn't be a problem. We could deliver within, oh say, six days. . . . For pest control, of course."

As he looked out the window a lightning bolt miles offshore etched a clean, thin white line across the gray sky. The sound of a glass breaking behind him caused Burke to snap his head around. "José!" he yelled. "Goddammit, what the hell are you—"

He was interrupted by the muffled sound of angry voices speaking in rapid-fire Spanish.

"Can't understand a fucking word these damn Cubans say," he muttered, and turned his attention back to the phone. "Of course, of course. Can you telephone me again tomorrow, about this time? Hmmm, yes. I look forward to it."

Burke nestled the receiver back in its cradle and strode across the polished terrazzo floor toward the closed mahogany door that separated his office from the large foyer.

He jerked the door open, started to speak, and immediately

closed his mouth. José Canteras, whom he had hired away from the manager of the Hotel Nacional and who served as everything from chauffeur to handyman, sat in one of the two dark wood, high-backed chairs that flanked the open front door. Two men in green military fatigues stood on either side of him. A broken coffee cup lay at his feet, the dark liquid splattered across the tiles. He stared straight ahead, breathing through his mouth, his hands twisted together on his lap.

Three other uniformed men stood to Burke's left. Two of them carried AK-47s, their right hands cradling the barrel guards, their left index fingers wrapped around the triggers. The tips of the barrels were pointed at Burke's navel. All the men were clean-shaven except for the soldier who seemed to be in command. He stood in the doorway and stroked his mustache thoughtfully. His pistol was secured in its holster. Burke didn't see any rank insignia on his shoulders.

"*Señor* McKinley Burke?" he asked, making "Burke" sound like "Bork." A thin, lopsided smile creased his face. "Of course you are *el señor*, since I have seen your photograph. You are now under arrest. You will be coming along with us."

"Por que? Soy un gran amigo de la revolucion," Burke said. He continued smoothly in Spanish, "I do not believe your superiors will react very well when I tell them about your insolence. I demand that you telephone—"

"Basta!" the officer interrupted. The smile was gone. "You wish to speak in Spanish, very well, we shall. I will now add threatening an Interior Ministry officer to the charges. You are under arrest for illegal profiteering, for crimes against the revolution, and for committing espionage through the use of an illegal satellite telephone."

"That telephone is legal!" Burke barked, pointing back toward his office. "I have paid to have it there and have permission to use it."

"No longer," the officer said. The smile returned. "And since you have no permission, it is not legal."

"But why? I have been here for years. I am a friend of *el jefe*. I support the revolution."

The officer cocked his head to the side. "You are the man of international media, no? So why have you not kept track of what is happening in Washington?"

Burke looked puzzled. The officer sighed. "There is a vote in the *yanqui* Congress in a few days on perhaps loosening the trade embargo. You are an international criminal. Cuba respects international law. When we arrest and try and convict a criminal like you, well, some people in Washington will notice. But you are a man of the world. I do not have to explain this to you."

He nodded, and the soldiers approached Burke until their rifle barrels were less than a foot from his midsection.

The officer placed his index finger under his nose, as if in thought. "By the way," he said, "do you play tennis?"

Burke looked confused, and nodded. "Yes, when I have time."

"Good," the officer said, swinging an imaginary racket with his right hand. "Then you will have no trouble chopping sugarcane. It is the same stroke, really. Just address the cane and follow through." He laughed.

THE PRESENT, WASHINGTON, D.C.

Even by standards of a Washington summer, it was hot. The obscure subcommittee of the House National Security Committee had been meeting for days, and each day had produced a scene like this one—a hearing room only a third filled, one network TV camera, a handful of print scribes.

Subcommittee staffers had suggested to the chairman that the publicity from the hearings was minimal, so why not cut them short? D.C. was emptying out for the Fourth of July, and anybody who mattered, media and government alike, was already at the beach house in Rehoboth firing up the grill.

The chairman was almost inclined to agree. But the home folks back in Alabama had been raising hell about Gulf War Syndrome for a few years at least, spurred by a series of newspaper articles that linked possible chemical exposure to some very strange ailments among the Heart of Dixie's thousands of Gulf vets. They voted, and their kin voted, and the chairman had spent too long waiting for his party to take control so he could finally end up as chairman of something. He was willing to muddle through the sweltering heat and humidity at least one more day before he adjourned.

Dees sat calmly at the witness table, facing the chairman. He looked essentially the same as he had in the Gulf, even though he was now dressed in a neat double-breasted tan suit. To his left sat Robert Hopkins, a good twenty pounds lighter than during Desert Storm, shifting nervously in an ill-fitting gray sport coat.

Next to him sat a chubby blonde, a tiny bit of lipstick on her teeth, wearing a pale blue flowered dress. In her lap she held a gurgling toddler.

To Dees's right, Carl Odell's form-fitting LAPD summer uniform showed the effect of the body-building regimen he had started since the Gulf. Only two fist-sized patches of gray, scaly skin beneath the right cuff of his crisp short-sleeved shirt spoiled the effect.

"Mr. Dees," the chairman said, "when we left yesterday you barely had time to introduce yourself after General Olson testified and before we adjourned."

"I thank the chairman," Dees said, thinking the phrase sounded like something off the House floor feed.

The chairman nodded. "The general told us the armed forces

have no evidence of any confirmed link between the so-called Gulf War Syndrome and any chemical exposure. Indeed, they deny any exposure at all. You have produced a body of work"—the chairman indicated a six-inch stack of clipped articles, two videocassettes, and a book, all piled to his left—"that disputes that."

Only three other subcommittee members had showed up for the hearing. One of them, a hawk-nosed congresswoman from California, said, "Mr. Chairman. I believe it would be in order for Mr. Dees to restate his credentials."

She smiled sweetly and skeptically above her half-lens reading glasses. Dees folded his hands on the tabletop.

"As I told the subcommittee yesterday, I'm a freelance journalist and filmmaker. I've written articles for overseas publications from the *Times* of London to the *Capetown Star*. I've contributed articles to various magazines, from *Atlantic Monthly* and *Vanity Fair* to *Rolling Stone* and the *Foreign Affairs Quarterly*.

"I've written articles for about thirty American newspapers. I've produced and written two documentaries, of which the chairman has copies, one for the British Broadcasting Corporation, the other for *Frontline* on Public Broadcasting.

"And I've written a book, of which the committee has several copies."

"Mr. Dees," the congresswoman said, "what does the title mean? *Dead Air*?"

Dees winced inwardly. He was the one who had thought the title self-evidently clever.

"It's a bad pun. Dead air is what broadcasters call a time when there are no pictures or sound. It also refers to air poisoned by chemicals and nerve agents, and to the lack of news coverage. And to a computer file labeled 'Dead Air.' "

He looked at Odell, who flashed a thumbs-up. He turned. Hopkins winked.

"The thesis of the book," Dees began, "and of the documentaries, and the articles, is simple. Allied personnel were exposed to chemical agents in the Gulf War. Those chemicals were often supplied to Iraq by American companies. The United States government has evidence that such transactions took place, and that chemical exposure took place.

"What we do not know are the direct toxicological effects of such exposure. Cancer, birth defects, skin lesions, all could conceivably be by-products of exposure to agents such as those used in the Gulf. But I want to emphasize that there is no direct link yet, despite thousands of anecdotal reports. Someday, there may be."

He looked pointedly to his left at the toddler on the blonde's lap. A fly had been buzzing the table for some minutes and the child had been batting at it. The three congressmen present followed Dees's gaze. The toddler waved his hands, attached to his shoulders by stumps no more than five inches long.

Dees rose from the table slowly, and said, "May I?"

The chairman nodded. Dees walked to an easel holding a three-foot by five-foot map. His limp was so imperceptible that only Hopkins and Odell noticed.

He picked up a pointer. "What is not deniable is that chemical exposure took place from the beginning of the war at an ammunition dump near Wafra, here"—he jabbed the map with the pointer—"to immediately after the war, when another dump near Kamisiyah was destroyed."

Again, the pointer clicked the map. "And in between, dozens of reports of chemical attacks. If I could have a hand, please . . ."

Two subcommittee staffers removed the map, and revealed a flow chart. Black boxes were linked by red arrows.

Dees cleared his throat. "Here is one example of how this happened, and why it's been largely denied. You are all familiar with the Burke Company. And McKinley Burke. Burke's holdings include GTV, of course, and a number of other companies, including this one. A little company called Archgate. Over a period of six years . . ."

Dees's voice drifted up to the top of the ornate hearing room. A TV reporter nearby looked at his cameraman and made a cutting motion across his throat with his finger.

The cameraman switched the camera off. The grainy one-inch-diagonal, black and white image in the viewfinder blinked, and went black.

About the Author

CHARLES JACO gained worldwide fame with his reports of SCUD attacks on Saudi Arabia during the Gulf War. During a career with NBC, CNN, and CBS, Jaco has covered nine wars, a half-dozen riots, and countless earthquakes, floods, and hurricanes. He has also covered Congress, the White House, the Pentagon, and various intelligence agencies. He was declared an Enemy of the State by Manuel Noriega, and *persona non grata* by regimes in Iraq and the Sudan. He has won two Edward R. Murrow awards, six National Headliner awards, and two dozen other national and international journalism awards; two programs on which he worked have received the prestigious George Foster Peabody Award. He has written for dozens of publications, including *Rolling Stone*, the *Chicago Tribune*, *The Boston Globe*, and *The Miami Herald*. He currently hosts his own radio show on KMOX in St. Louis. This is his first novel.